HEARTLESS

STEEL DEMONS MC BOOK SIX

CRYSTAL ASH

All American Nightmare - Hinder
Notorious - Adelitas Way
Hail to the King - Avenged Sevenfold
O Death - Ashley H
Joan of Arc - In This Moment
Radioactive - Imagine Dragons
Bad Company - Five Finger Death Punch
Love Me to Death - No Resolve
(Don't Fear) The Reaper - HIM
David - Noah Gunderson
Apocalyptic - Halestorm
Blue on Black - Five Finger Death Punch
Machine Gun Blues - Social Distortion
Wanted Dead or Alive - Chris Daughtry
I Get Off - Halestorm
You Shook Me All Night Long - AC/DC
Nobody Praying for Me - Seether
Loyal to No One - Dropkick Murpheys
Crazy in Love - Daniel De Bourg
Be Free - King Dude & Chelsea Wolfe
Raise Hell - Dorothy
Coming Home - Skylar Grey

Listen on Spotify at:
crystalashbooks.com/sdmc-playlist

Trigger Warning

Chapters 23 and 24 contain an incident of assault against the main female character. It is ***not*** sexual in nature, but she is badly injured. The author recommends skipping these chapters if you are sensitive to this content.

Chapter 25 and beyond will refer to the incident in a way that the reader will be able infer what happened, without the explicit details.

Prologue

MARIPOSA

FIVE YEARS EARLIER

"Now this is a surprise." My dad grinned cheekily as he set two shot glasses on the counter.

"I have to take the opportunity while it's here," I said, parking my butt on the stool across from him.

"And here I figured my twenty-year-old daughter would have better things to do than drink with her lame old dad." He twisted the cap open on the bottle of *reposado* and started pouring carefully, shooting me a *dad look*. You know the one. "I could get in trouble for this, you know."

"What, like the militia are gonna peek through our windows, know instinctively that I'm underage, and toss us out into the street?" I rolled my eyes, but neither of us laughed. It wasn't a joke anymore, but a reality.

The latest push from our wannabe governor had been to make drinking illegal for women only. Apparently, it made us unfit to be wives. That crazy old fundie from the newly formed territory of Texahoma had been trying to absorb our county for six months. His utterly insane proclamations weren't laws for us yet, but thousands of others weren't so lucky. So far, Warsaw County's little rebellion had been able to hold the border, but that could change at any time.

Dad didn't respond to my retort, but smiled at me fondly as he sliced limes for our drinks. "So what's on your mind, *mija*?"

He always asked me that when he'd started letting me drink with him, ever since I was sixteen. This was our time to open up, to let me vent without judgment while he listened. My mom would always be a mom to me, but the ever-increasing hostility in our society made me grow up fast. Mom wanted to shield me from it all, so I could have a normal childhood. But Dad took a different approach. He started treating me like an equal and became my friend.

"I, um." I grabbed one shot glass and slowly pulled it toward me. "Carlos broke up with me last week."

"Aw, *mijita*." Dad's smile fell, his eyes warm and sympathetic. "I'm sorry that didn't work out."

"I'll be okay. I just didn't expect it to hit me like it did." My face tensed like I expected tears to come, but I knew they wouldn't. I had cried them all out already. "Like, I knew we probably weren't gonna get married or whatever, but it still fucking sucks."

"I know it does," Dad said. "It doesn't feel like it now, but you'll see it was for the best. Besides," he smirked before putting on his stern dad face, "you should be focusing on school. You don't need some boy distracting you. Your career field is going to make a real impact when you graduate."

"He told me I was *too* focused on school and didn't make time for him," I grumbled. "I confronted him about getting cozy with some girl at a party and he told me *that* shit."

"Even better," Dad huffed. "A boy like that is not worth your time."

"I know you're right, just why does it have to hurt so much? I don't *want* to miss him, but I do."

"Emotions are weird, *mijita*. Hell, people are weird." Dad took a small, thoughtful sip of his *reposado*. "I'm sure this guy cares about you. He probably just wasn't mature enough to tell you how he really felt." Dad put his glass down and suddenly released a sigh that made him look a lot older. "When people can't communicate properly for whatever reason, we sometimes end up hurting the ones we love."

Neither of us said a word, but I knew what we were both thinking about. On his second day home this week, he blew up at Mom over the tea kettle whistling. One minute he was fine, reading the paper and having his coffee. The moment that high-pitched whistle sounded, he started yelling a bunch of nonsense at her, completely unprompted. It was like some uncontrollable violent force had possessed my gentle, mild-mannered father. Mom and I were dumbfounded, and she was most definitely hurt by it.

He calmed down later and apologized, but everything had felt *off* since then. Awkward, like we were walking on eggshells. I attended a seminar on PTSD last semester, and had tried to broach the subject gently with my dad the last time he came home and started displaying symptoms. But he brushed me off, the machismo of his upbringing causing him to refuse to see it as a treatable medical condition.

Only during these heart-to-hearts with our prized tequila, did things seem normal. It was the real reason why I asked for this, for some semblance of normality.

Dad polished off his shot and reached for mine to put in the sink. I cupped my hand around the small glass and brought it closer to my chest.

"One more?"

"Nah, *mija*," he said sadly. "I gotta pack my shit and get ready to leave in the morning."

"Aw, come on, *viejito*. One more shot won't kill you."

"I *am* old," he laughed. "Can't keep drinking with my college-aged daughter no more."

"Dad…" I rolled the shot glass between my hands. "What if you just didn't go?"

His face hardened. "They'll come looking for me and I'll get thrown in jail. You know that, sweetheart."

I slid my glass angrily across the counter to him. "At least then you wouldn't be forced to fight in some bull-shit war that doesn't even matter."

"That may be true." He turned and placed the glasses in the sink. "But who's to say I'll survive prison too? And I'd never get to come home and see my girls."

I had nothing to answer that. Of course I didn't want my dad in jail. But I didn't want him out *there* either, fighting for no cause while doing irreparable damage to his mind and body.

He rounded the counter and pulled me into a tight hug, one that made me feel tiny and protected. The type of hug that a little girl burrowed into so the monsters under her bed wouldn't get her.

The monsters were out in the streets now, looting and pillaging. It didn't matter if they were in riot gear or in rags. If they were strangers or familiar faces. The Collapse had changed people. It brought out the worst in them.

"I'm so sorry, *mijita*," he sighed over the top of my head, though I wasn't sure what he was apologizing for. "Your mom and I never wanted you to live in this kind of world. But we're all in this stupid bullshit war, whether we like it or not."

I just let him hug me, let him be my dad. He couldn't save me from anything, but for right now, they couldn't take this away from us.

I didn't know it would be the last time I saw him.

ONE

MARIPOSA

PRESENT DAY

Arms, legs, chests, and backs provided solidness and warmth on all sides. I didn't even need to open my eyes to know who was who anymore.

My forehead nuzzled the burn scars on Jandro's back. I kissed them in my half-asleep state, a smile coming to my face at the memory of kissing another man's scars last night.

Jandro didn't stir, still fully in dreamland, but Reaper's arm tightened around my waist. His lips found my ear, pressing a soft kiss there before murmuring, "You awake?"

"Mmm." I flipped over to face him, taking care not to disturb Jandro. Eyes still closed, I nuzzled my head under his chin, kissing his chest while curling up and burrowing into him. "You?"

He was silent for a moment, stroking my back.

"I talked to Daren."

"Hm?" That forced my eyelids open, hands lifting up to rub the sleep and fatigue from my eyes. "When?"

"Just now, before I woke up."

I tried to listen carefully to his tone, to piece together his feelings from his voice, but it was impossible with him speaking so softly. "What did he say?"

"Shit that wasn't good." He pushed himself up from the mattress with a groan, blinking at the pre-dawn light coming in from the window. "Take a walk with me, sugar?"

"Yeah, coming."

We climbed out of bed carefully, crawling over the splayed arms and legs of Jandro and Gunner to get dressed. I pulled on my thickest jeans, wool socks, and a gray flannel shirt. Every day grew colder, and the air before the sun came out was downright chilly.

Reaper got ready in his leather jacket, jeans, boots, and cigarettes, and together we headed out the front door of the Four Corners B&B. Right after stepping off the front porch, we heard the door open slowly again and turned to see who was following.

Hades had pushed the door open with his front paw, and he and Freyja followed us out to the quiet street.

"Can't go anywhere alone," I chuckled as Reaper lit up. "So did he come to you in a dream like," I tilted my head toward the animals, "*they* said?"

"Yeah." He grabbed my hand and started walking, sucking on his clove with the opposite hand. "I was riding and it was too perfect to be real, you know? Perfect weather, full gas tank, smooth road. I stopped to look out at the edge of a canyon and he just walked up behind me."

"Did it feel like you were really talking to him?" I

snatched his cigarette for a quick drag. "Or just your brain pulling up memories of him?"

"It was really him, sugar. Well and alive." His eyes brightened on a distant focal point as we walked together. "He said he saw the whole rescue mission in Blakeworth, thanks to Freyja." He looked at the cat over his shoulder with a chuckle. "He's seen you, seen all of us. Sounds like he's into you, sugar. I knew he would be."

"I would've liked to meet him," I said, with a squeeze to his hand.

"I wouldn't," Reaper laughed. "He'd steal you away from me."

"Never." I held onto his arm with both hands, pressing my cheek against his shoulder. "What did he say that wasn't good?"

My husband's smile dissipated, green eyes hardening as he sucked on the last of his cigarette before tossing the butt away.

"I keep running it through my mind and can't even decipher it. I told you his visions were just random bits of information, right?"

"Yeah, that they didn't make any sense without context."

"Right. So he told me I needed to break down the door." A scowl crossed his face. "That 'she' would die if I didn't. Now, is this 'she' Noelle? Is it Freyja? Mrs. Potts? Gods fucking forbid, is it you?" He released my hand and lifted his arm to wrap around my shoulders. "It's driving me nuts that you might be in danger. And that I could—" he swallowed, "I could…lose you if I don't act fast enough."

I slid an arm around his waist, our footsteps on the street the only sounds as I absorbed his words. Breaking down a door could mean any number of things, depending on how literal or metaphorical Daren was.

"Did he tell you anything else?" I asked as we turned a corner.

Reaper looked over his shoulder at Hades sniffing the ground a few paces behind us. "That I had to obey the order when it came, and that it would hurt a lot, for a long time." He squeezed my shoulder, pulling me into his side. "Sugar, I have this bad fucking feeling that I'm gonna have to kill someone to protect you. Someone close to us."

I nodded with a deep breath. For the Steel Demons, killing someone could be business as usual. Or it could be one of our own, someone we trusted, and therefore catastrophic.

We had dealt with a betrayal before, with Python. Another person working against the Demons from the inside didn't seem likely, especially after making such a public spectacle of Python's death. I didn't have a single suspicion about anyone else in Reaper's club. Some people I personally liked more than others, but had no doubts about any of their loyalty. Big G was on thin ice, but he seemed eager to correct his behavior.

We could speculate and walk in circles all day. With so little information to go off of, there was just no way to narrow it down.

"Whatever happens," I looked up at him with my head on his shoulder. "I'm sure it'll be the right choice."

"Daren said something like that too," he muttered, the wheels still spinning in his head. "That it would hurt, but it would be the right thing. God, fuck." He rubbed his forehead. "This shit's giving me a headache."

My hand slid up his back to his neck, where I rubbed the tight knot of muscles. "Do you want to tell the other guys?"

"I don't know if I should," he said. "What if that changes things? He made it sound like I was the only one who *could* do it. I dunno. Fuck, I hate this." He turned to address the animals silently stalking behind us. "Any input you all have would be fucking great."

Hades lifted a leg and pissed on a fence post. Freyja paused to lick her paw.

"Perfect." Reaper turned back around with a snort, fishing for another cigarette.

I held on to his arm again as we continued our walk. "Hades said he was here to guide you and protect me. And I have all of you." My fingers laced through his. "How can anything bad happen to me when I'm loved by Demons and watched over by gods?"

"I fuckin' hope you're right." His finger rubbed affectionately over my ring. "I need something better to talk about. How'd it go with Shadow last night?"

A lightness lifted in my chest, the smile on my face instant. "Good. We talked for a bit and…kissed."

"Kissed?" Reaper coughed. "You mean that guy knows how to do something with his mouth besides suck down booze? Ow!"

"Don't be an asshole," I growled, jabbing my fist in his ribs a second time.

"Sugar, do you know who I am?" He grinned, catching my wrist before I could smack him another time. "I'm kidding, but can you blame me for being surprised?"

"He's a good kisser actually," I said smugly. "And he's…just really sweet."

"*Sweet?* Are you sure we're talking about the same person?"

"There's a whole side of him that is just so tender and gentle," I went on. "I saw moments of confidence that had nothing to do with his killing skills. He laughed and cracked jokes with me. He just held me and didn't try to take anything further than kissing. It was refreshing, honestly."

"So you want someone who will just kiss you without trying to get in your pants?" Reaper squeezed my ass and laughed when I smacked his hand away.

"Not necessarily. I mean, you know how much I love sex."

"Mm, I have some idea." Smoke curled from his grinning mouth.

"But with Shadow, I think I'd enjoy taking it slow. I could work with him to build up his confidence, and really take the time to learn what he likes. What we both like."

"Okay, but it's not like either of you are virgins. Why not just fuck and learn about each other that way?"

I gave him a pointed look. "We did that already and look what happened."

"I know, but it's different now. We're all aware of what's between you two." Reaper flicked some ash away and returned the cigarette to his mouth. "Do you love him?"

My heart crashed against my sternum at the question, my insides heating up in response. Did I?

"I care about him, a lot," was the answer that left my mouth. "But I think it's too soon to tell if it's like…what you and I have."

"Is it really?" Reaper challenged. "You've known him as long as any of us."

"Sure, but my interactions with him haven't been the same as with all of you. I'm still getting to know him beyond the whole 'silent killing machine' thing."

"Fair enough." Reaper released a sigh with an exhale of smoke. "Just keep us in the loop before you make it official, sugar."

"I will," I said with a squeeze of his hand. "I promise I will."

We turned another corner, rounding the block heading back to the B&B. The sun was just starting to come up and Jandro would likely be awake, getting coffee started or feeding the chickens.

The four of us, Hades and Freyja included, walked back in to find both of my other husbands awake and hovering over the coffee pot and breakfast pastries.

"Where'd you go, baby girl?" Gunner was still shirtless, hair up in a messy man-bun, pajama pants low on his slender hips as he pulled me in for a kiss. "I woke up to this dude spooning me instead of you."

"He loved it," Jandro cut in without missing a beat.

"He was so impressed by my cuddling skills, he said we should run away together."

"A likely story," I murmured, kissing under Gunner's chin, then sliding over to get my love from Jandro. "We just went for a walk. But it's true, your cuddles are wonderful."

"Fuck yeah they are." Jandro's arms were protective and heavy around my back. "I don't see why these guys can't appreciate it. The Sons cuddle up all the time."

"Because they also fuck each other up the ass," Reaper grumbled, helping himself to the coffee pot.

A door creaked open and my stomach began doing somersault motions. Freyja took off immediately toward the sound with soft, chirping meows. Shadow's footsteps were light, lighter than the murmuring of "Hello, kitten," as he greeted her.

My guys thankfully didn't openly stare, but turned away and busied themselves in conversation, either real or contrived, as I approached the large man holding my cat.

"Good morning, Shadow," I whispered, excited nerves wavering in my voice.

His smile was shy, his gaze downward on the ball of fur in his arms. "Good morning, Mari."

I stepped closer, hoping to convey privacy and a bit of distance from the others as I kept my voice low. "Did you sleep well?"

"Yes, I did." He lowered Freyja gently to the floor then returned upright, eyes now on me. "Did you?"

"I did, thank you." I leaned into him with a smile, my shoulder brushing his chest.

His gaze flickered over me in a thorough reading of my body language. He knew what I wanted, what I gave him permission to do last night. Now it was a question of whether or not he felt comfortable doing it in front of my guys.

My whole upper body burst into flutters when Shadow's hand came to my waist, a steadying, affectionate touch. He leaned down swiftly, neither rushed or slow, and placed a warm, brief kiss on my lips.

I smiled against his mouth, savoring what I could of him before he straightened up. The guys didn't need a full-on PDA to know how things had shifted between us. Longer kisses would be better enjoyed in private anyway.

My hand touched his on my waist, fingers lacing through his. "Are you having breakfast with us?"

"Um." His eyes lifted to meet those of my guys, who now no longer pretended to focus on anything else. "Sure, if that's all right."

"Mornin', big guy." Jandro scooted back and stood from the chair he was in. "Take my seat. I'm gonna collect some eggs."

"Thanks." Shadow moved toward the chair with more hesitation than he did when he kissed me. His eyes darted everywhere, looking for signs of how to behave.

Next to him, Reaper leaned over the maps and documents on the table with a mug of steaming coffee in hand. "Mornin'," he grunted, as though it were any other day. "Shadow, you want to come with me on a tour of the new development with the governor today?"

"Ah, sure." He found an empty mug and began pouring coffee into it. "I mean, yes, Reaper."

"It's a request, not an order." Reaper leaned back in his chair, setting his coffee mug on his knee. "You don't have to if you have something more pressing, but Vance seems keen on showing us this new area he's developing. And I think he's curious about the injured hero of Four Corners."

Shadow bristled at being called a hero, and I couldn't help from running a hand along his upper back, where Blakeworth's arrows came too close to killing him, and down his arm as I took a seat next to him.

"I'll go. I don't have anything else going on." His fingers clasped mine briefly before letting go.

"What are your plans today, sugar?" Reaper lifted his mug to his lips as his gaze settled on me.

"I was thinking of checking out the hospital." I reached for a pastry from the basket in the center of the table. "See if the head doctor has time to give me a tour, or if I can lend my services in any way."

"On that note," Gunner leaned back in his chair next to me, placing one of his feet in my lap, "how do you feel about driving there?"

"Drive?" I nearly choked on my Danish. "You mean, your bike?"

"Not *mine*, but one of the little dirt bikes." He snatched an apple from the basket and tossed it in the air with a grin. "It's about time you learn, baby girl. I'll have Jandro check them over and get you the most reliable one."

I swallowed the lump in my throat nervously. "You'll be there with me?"

"Course I will." He poked his toes into my side. "I'll be in your bitch seat. A little roll reversal, how about that?"

Reaper snorted. "Of all of us most likely to be in a bitch seat."

"You're just sour you didn't get her ass first." Gunner took a loud bite out of his apple, pointedly ignoring my glare. Holy shit, could he not drop details of our sex life out on the breakfast table? In front of Shadow, no less? We just started making out, he did not need to know who had my ass first.

"It's too fucking early for this," I groaned, shoving Gunner's foot out of my lap. "I'm getting a shower first."

He laughed and leaned over to smack a kiss on my cheek. "I'll let Jandro know what we need."

I finished wolfing down my pastry and coffee, then returned my hand to Shadow's shoulder as I stood. He was like a magnet, I just could not stop touching him. He watched me curiously, only slightly shorter than me standing even while he was sitting down.

"You guys have fun with the governor today." My touch slid up his shoulder, fingertips brushing along his neck and cheek.

"We will." His arm came around my waist in a gentle hug to his side. "Enjoy the hospital and riding lessons."

"Will do." I leaned down, only planning for a sweet, brief kiss, but all my lips wanted to do was linger on his.

Who was I kidding? All I wanted to do was crawl into his lap and shove my tongue in his mouth, to feel and explore this mountain of a man with every inch of my skin until I uncovered every mystery about him.

His arm tightened around me, soft sighs escaping him as I pressed kiss after kiss onto the mouth that had learned mine so thoroughly and quickly the night before. He returned every one, sipping lightly with just enough pressure and sensation for me to feel like I was floating.

Reaper and Gunner only looked amused when we finally separated. "Did you forget we were here?" the president chuckled.

"Not another word out of you," I warned, rounding the table to kiss him full of teeth and rough scraping of lips, just how he liked it. My fingers speared through his hair, gripping the dark strands to hold his head in place. Reaper emitted a growl of satisfaction that lit up my core like a match. "Have a good day, love," I whispered against his mouth.

"Yes fuckin' ma'am." He grinned in return. "And hey, listen." His face turned hard, eyes sharp and jaw clenched. "Be careful, sugar. You hear me?"

I stroked my husband's face, pushing his hair back and trying my best to soothe the worried lines etched into his forehead.

"I will," I promised him with another long, lingering kiss.

TWO

MARIPOSA

"Squeeze the brake lever nice and slow. Easy, easy…" Gunner's hand guided mine with steady patience on the dirt bike as we pulled up to the hospital. My stop was abrupt, but not as hard as when I took my first spin around the block and nearly lurched over the handlebars.

"Good job, baby girl!" He patted my sides. "You're getting the hang of it."

"Thanks, Gun." I swung a leg over to stand next to the dirt bike as Gunner scooted up the driver's seat. Freyja popped out of the front of my jacket, shaking her fur out and sniffing the air. "You picking me up for lunch?"

"I *can.*" He leaned over the handlebars with a playful smile. "Unless you'd rather have Tall, Dark and Scarred pick you up? Since you're in the early, getting-to-know each other stages."

A familiar fluttering lit up inside me and I couldn't

fight the smile pulling at my lips. Having Shadow like this was new and exciting, sure. I wanted to shout *yes* instantly, but remembered how sensitive Gunner could be about feeling excluded. As wonderful as a budding new relationship felt, I couldn't neglect any of them for a fresh high. Especially not him.

"No." I grabbed the sides of his cut, bringing his mouth to crash against mine. "I want you."

I tasted his smile, and melted into the arms that slid around me. "You sure?"

"Positive."

My fingers extended, tracing the sharp angles of his jaw as I savored each of his slow, sensual kisses. The world outside my golden man's arms ceased to exist for a few precious moments. Our lips barely separated when we parted, soft puffs of breath still mingling in the chilly air.

"Love you," I whispered, dragging my fingers through a stray lock of blond hair.

"Love you more," he sighed contentedly with a final kiss before reluctantly pulling away. "I'll be rendezvousing with Reap and Shadow, see if I can meet this mysterious general soon before I come back to get you."

"Okay." I untangled from him, walking backward to watch him ride off. "I'll be here."

He shot me a heart-melting smile over his shoulder as he turned the bike around, then shot down the road at speeds much higher than he allowed me to drive.

I turned to the hospital doors and walked through, hoping the cool outside air had prevented my face from getting too red. Nothing could be done about my body temperature, though. My guys were just too hot.

The hospital lobby looked clean and well-maintained. Only a few small hints gave any indication that this place had been looted a few years ago. The freshly painted wall behind the front desk covered up some kind of graffiti that was just barely visible. One more coat should be enough. Some of the waiting area furniture looked beat up, as if someone had turned the couches over or thrown chairs across the room.

I approached the front desk, which was empty. Not a soul was in sight on this floor, so I opted to go exploring. Heading for the elevators, I pressed an UP button and was surprised to see it light up. The panel above the doors counted down from five floors, then the door slid smoothly open when it reached my floor. Freyja walked into the metallic box like she rode in elevators all the time.

I hesitated for a moment, then stepped inside, still in a state of awe. It had been years since I'd seen or been inside a working elevator. Luxuries like these ceased to be maintained once the Collapse hit. Now it just had to not get stuck on the way up.

I hit the button for the second floor, stepped back, and held my breath. The door slid closed with a soft *ding* and the sound made a giggle burst from my chest. Who knew an elevator would be such a luxury?

When the doors slid open again to another lobby, this time a woman's head was visible behind the front desk.

"Hello," I called, eagerly stepping out and heading toward her.

She jumped, looking at me with startled, wide eyes. "Goodness!" She brought a hand to her chest. "No one comes through this way, I didn't expect to hear a voice."

"Didn't mean to scare you." I stopped at the edge of the desk. "I'm Mariposa. I came into town last week."

"That's right." The woman's eyes narrowed in recognition at me, but more out of curiosity than suspicion. She was middle-aged and solidly built, with streaks of gray through her carefully curled dark hair that fell to her shoulders. "You're the one who saved the governor's daughter."

"With the help of a few good men," I laughed lightly. "But I'm trained as a medic and wanted to check out the hospital. So far, it seems a bit, ah…"

"Empty?" the woman chuckled. "That's because it is. I'm Rhonda, by the way."

"Well-met, Rhonda." I shook her hand across the desk, noticing her pale blue scrubs were well-worn and carried various stains that lingered after probably hundreds of washings.

A memory hit me of some of the nurse instructors back in school. They wore their old tattered, stained scrubs with pride until they were threadbare. Every rip and stain was like a badge of honor, remnants of someone they once helped.

"If you're looking for the doctor, he's in surgery at the moment," Rhonda said, straightening up.

"Oh, no problem. I don't want to bother him—"

"Good," she smiled. "Because you won't be."

I couldn't resist the smile back. Typical head nurse, stern and quick to put people in their place, but kind once they got to know you. At least I hoped so. It felt like I was back in nursing school, and the nostalgia bloomed in my chest.

"But seeing as there's no one rushing in here with blood pouring out of various orifices," Rhonda continued, making her way around the desk toward me, "I can show you around a bit."

It wasn't until she grabbed a cane and leaned on it heavily that I realized she walked with a significant limp.

"Gunshot, border wars," she grunted out. "Don't know what they're calling it now, but it was at the old Oregon-Idaho border about five years back."

"Sorry to hear that." I picked up my pace as she walked alongside me. Even with a cane, she was fast.

"Heh, I'm not. About time I got a soldier's welcome everywhere I went," she cackled. "And all these nice young men offering me their hands and holding things for me. It's not a bad trade at all." Her sharp eyes roamed over me as we walked down the hallway, my boots and her sneakers an odd mix of sounds.

"I did about three years in the border wars too," I said. "From East Texas to Arizona, just following the battles west."

"You're in damn good shape for being a battle medic," Rhonda observed. She was right—I had no major scars or injuries to speak of from those times.

"I don't know how," I admitted. "I traded pills to get

me out of some hairy situations, but even still, I got lucky."

"Someone must've been watching out for you," Rhonda muttered.

Freyja's loud purr sputtered to life as she headbutted my ankle, walking in perfect time with my leg as she rubbed against me.

"Maybe." I smiled. "'Til I ran into a biker gang, and then *they* became those someones."

Rhonda lifted in an eyebrow, taking note of the black cat for the first time. "We don't usually let animals into the hospital, but your little critter sure is stuck to you like velcro. He better not get into anything, though."

"She," I corrected. "And you don't have to worry. Freyja sticks by me and she's great with patients. She's like a," I paused to think of the pre-Collapse term I learned in school, "like a therapy cat."

Rhonda nodded, the gesture stern, like she'd give me one chance and no more than that.

"So, is it true you're married to all of them?" she asked. "The bikers you rode in with?"

"No," I laughed. "I'm committed to three, and… I guess, in the early dating stages with a fourth."

Both eyebrows shot up and Rhonda resumed facing forward with a chuckle. "Oh, to be young and beautiful again."

She took me to a large room at the end of the hall where an actual, real CT scanner sat. My jaw dropped open and I nearly wanted to cry. Hell, I wanted to kiss that beautiful machine.

"How did you get this?" I asked in an awed whisper,

approaching the machine. "I thought there were hardly any working ones left."

"Governor Vance bought it himself and had it shipped from overseas," Rhonda declared proudly. "See? All the words are in German."

"I can't imagine what it must have cost him," I said, shaking my head. "But this is amazing! No more guessing games like out in the field."

"It's quite possibly the only one in the southwest." Rhonda fondly ran a hand over the machine. "And it's helped us save hundreds of lives, that's for sure."

"What else does the hospital have?" I turned back to her, giddiness running through me. "Ultrasound machines? X-rays? How about a lab?"

"Down, girl," Rhonda teased with a chuckle. "We have all of those, yes, but not many, and even fewer people with the skills to use them. Our poor lab tech is always run ragged. He works the longest hours out of any of us and is always behind. We're working on getting more people trained, but you know how it is. Medical professionals don't grow overnight."

"I'd love to help." Excitement continued to brim throughout me despite her *down, girl.* "My specialty was in labor and delivery, but you can put me anywhere that needs the most support. Anything I haven't learned out in the field, I can pick up quickly—"

"Ah, just the person to decide where an eager young medic should go." Rhonda tilted her head down the hallway and I followed her gaze.

A tall, slender man was coming down the hallway with long strides. He wore the iconic, long white coat of a doctor with plain jeans and a T-shirt underneath. Glasses sat on an attractive, friendly face with a medium-brown complexion. What surprised me the most was how young he looked, close to the same age as any of my guys.

"Dr. Brooks, this is Mariposa," Rhonda introduced. "Accomplished combat medic and Kyrie Vance's personal savior."

"Oh please," I laughed, shaking off my surprise at the sight of the young doctor. "It's amazing what a small knife and a huge dose of adrenaline can make you do."

"I've heard you're exceedingly modest too," Dr. Brooks teased me gently with a warm smile, accepting my outstretched hand. "It's a pleasure, Mariposa. I'm sorry we didn't get to meet at the governor's dinner party. We were swamped here."

"That's why I'm here," I offered. "Heard you could use some extra hands and Rhonda was nice enough to show me around."

The doctor nodded, his warm expression turning grave. "Rumors of a retaliation from Blakeworth are already swirling, even an all-out war. We'll need lots of combat medics, and soon. People who can move fast and treat major injuries on the fly."

"You're looking at one." I crossed my arms. "Have you been a combat medic yourself, doctor?"

"Ah, no." He blushed slightly. "I went to medical school in Canada. University of Toronto, to be exact."

"Canada?" I repeated. "Why on earth would you leave Canada for *this* place?" I had been hoping to escape to the great frozen north before running into my guys. It was a major refugee destination that few were actually able to reach.

"Governor Vance reached out to me," Dr. Brooks admitted. "I had recently graduated, just started my residency, and apparently was near the bottom of a long list of candidates he'd called."

Rhonda scoffed. "I can't imagine why anyone else would have said no."

"Right?" Dr. Brooks laughed. "A hospital job in a foreign land in the middle of civil and political unrest. Also, I wouldn't get paid for the foreseeable future, but housing, food, and all basic necessities would be taken care of."

My curiosity got the best of me. "So why did you say yes?"

The doctor straightened. "I wanted to help those who needed it most—the ones without any access to medical care."

"We also take in patients traveling from other territories," Rhonda explained. "Some cross hundreds of miles to get here. They have to be screened by the army at the borders, so we try to have medics posted there in case it's something life-threatening. But it's like Dr. Brooks said," her eyes lifted to him, "we need more people. Badly."

That sealed it for me. I wanted to work here. Their mission matched mine exactly—the same one I'd carried with me since leaving Texas.

"When can I start?" I asked.

———

MY STOMACH GROWLED as I stepped out of the hospital front doors two hours later. Dr. Brooks and Rhonda had given me an extensive tour, even allowing me to visit current patients and other staff. The time flew by and I hurried out when the tour was all done, hoping I hadn't kept Gunner waiting.

The cold was the first thing that hit me when I stepped outside, a shock to my system after walking back and forth inside for several hours.

Even the landscape looked softer, grayer than this morning. This chill on my morning walk with Reaper had been nothing compared to this. My little flannel jacket didn't stand a chance. I reached down to hold Freyja for some warmth, but she decided to be uncooperative, twisting out of my arms to stay planted on the ground. No motorcycle was waiting for me out front, so I wrapped my arms around myself as I peered down the street.

"What the…" Something was falling on my face, sticking to my eyelashes. I blinked and looked up, holding my palm out for what seemed to be an impossibility.

"It's snowing!" I laughed to no one in particular, spinning in a circle just outside the awning of the hospital entrance.

I was freezing my ass off, but didn't care. Weather patterns had become so unpredictable in recent decades and snow was rare. All my life I'd been used to droughts, freak thunderstorms, flash floods, and even the occasional hurricane in my part of Texas. But *snow!* I had few precious memories of the magical white stuff.

My laughter and spinning continued until I got dizzy, slowing down as the roar of a motorcycle steadily grew louder as it came down the street. I leaned against a parking sign, my surprise apparent as the leather clad rider approached.

"Didn't expect to see you here," I said.

REAPER

The morning sun disappeared behind a blanket of clouds, and the warmth with it, as Shadow and I rode to the City Hall building. I zipped my jacket up to my throat, grateful that I'd dressed for the cold.

"Feels like rain," I remarked as we took up a parking space in front of the building.

"I think it's snow." Shadow stretched and curled his gloved fingers, dismounting his ride.

"That'll be somethin'." I reached into my jacket pocket for smokes, then remembered it wasn't allowed inside the building. My hand dropped with a sigh. I had to start getting used to cutting back anyway.

The governor's assistant, Josh, waited for us in the lobby of the same building where we attended the dinner party last night.

"Morning, gentlemen," he greeted, hands shoved in the pockets of his pressed slacks. Even inside the building, it wasn't much warmer than outside. Heat was expensive, a precious resource, and I knew Governor

Vance was conscious of budgets. "The governor is just finishing a meeting in his office, then he'll be at your disposal."

"We're waiting for one more anyway," I said. "Gunner should be on his way back from dropping off our wife at the hospital."

Josh's eyebrow twitched at the use of *our* before he schooled his features again. "Oh, I see. Is Mariposa all right?"

"Fine, just meeting the staff and getting a tour." I inclined my head. "As we are here."

"Yes, of course." Josh clasped his hands in front of him and looked at Shadow. "Did you enjoy the governor's gift, sir?"

The man's face froze, his throat working a nervous swallow. "Um, yes. Please thank him for me. It was very much…enjoyed." He almost appeared to be sweating, despite the cold.

"I'm glad to hear it." Josh turned to a side table with a coffee press and pastry spread. "Help yourself to anything. I'll see how much more time the governor needs." His shiny shoes clacked on the marble floor as he walked away.

"You didn't mention anything about a gift from the governor," I muttered, helping myself to a small paper cup of coffee.

Shadow's eyes flicked to the spread but he didn't move to grab anything. "When I went home last night, he, um," his jaw ticked, "he sent a woman to my room."

"Yeah?" I kept my voice as expressionless as possible while filing this information away. "And did you in fact *enjoy* his gift? Before or after you put your mouth on my wife?"

"I didn't," Shadow insisted, his gaze level on mine. "Nothing happened and I sent her away. She was gone before any of you got home."

I hid my smile behind a sip of coffee. That was exactly what I'd hoped to hear. "Good man." I clapped my palm on his shoulder. "I'm not sure if you're aware of how this works, but while she has all of us, we cannot be with any others."

"I understand," Shadow murmured, turning to look blankly at the mostly-empty lobby. "I wouldn't. I don't want anyone else. And anyway—" He stopped talking abruptly, busying himself with a cup of coffee.

"Yes?" I implored.

"It's nothing, president."

"Shadow." I turned to him. "If we share a woman, we need to be able to talk about things. That's the *only* way this works. If something's on your mind regarding her, please just spit it out."

He wrapped his massive hands around the paper cup, staring down into the dark liquid. "I was going to say, I never imagined having a woman I could call mine, let alone one I could share with men I respect." He swallowed thickly, raising his eyes to me. "I'm not experienced at this, but I'll do my best, Reaper. I only want to do right by her."

The man's odd-colored eyes were starry with daydreams. He cradled his coffee as gently as if it were Mari's hand. It was all I could do to keep from snickering. Shadow was completely and utterly smitten.

And Mari was too. She tried to play it cool on our walk this morning, but I could tell how excited she felt about him. I was a bit taken aback that she didn't want to fuck him right away, but it was cute how she wanted to take things slow. Shadow was a different animal than the rest of us, that was certain.

"Hey! You all still waiting?"

Gunner's voice floated toward us from the entrance, his boots echoing off the high ceiling.

"Governor's finishing some business," I muttered.

"Politicians," Gun scoffed, moving toward the pastry table. "No one's time matters but theirs." He helped himself to a cheese Danish, folding the thing in half before shoving it all in his mouth.

"Mari get off okay?"

Gunner stared at me, the muscles in his jaw working as he chewed his pastry. "I didn't exactly have the opportunity to get her off, but yes, we made it to the hospital and she's fine."

"Ass." I slapped his puffed-out cheek, hoping to make him choke on his food.

The nerves in my stomach that had been twisting all morning remained, despite Gunner's assurance. Daren's warning filled my head like a beacon. If something happened at the hospital, would she be alright? Could I get there in time?

You're going to have to break down the door. She'll die if you don't.

Fuck, I'd be as bald as T-Bone if I kept tearing my hair out over this shit. The easiest solution was to keep Mari home and guarded at all times, but she'd never go for that. I could only do it for so long too, before even my paranoid ass started to feel uneasy about keeping her prisoner. And that was *if* the warning was even about her in the first place. But why would my brother come to me in a dream to tell me about anyone else?

Damn it, Daren. Would it kill you to give one premonition that made sense?

"Ah, sorry to keep you gentlemen waiting."

Governor Vance headed our way from his office wing with Josh in tow. While suited up and sharp as usual, the governor looked slightly disheveled from a few small details that were easy to miss. His voice was a bit hoarse and his tie was slightly askew. His face was flushed, skin dewy. But the most telling sign was the young woman storming away from his office, her blonde braid swinging angrily against her back.

"Daughter troubles, sir?" I inquired casually, although I wasn't just making conversation. I wanted him to know that small details wouldn't slip past me. As long as this politician knew he couldn't cut any deals behind my back, we could have a very productive working relationship.

"Don't get me started," he sighed, wiping his brow with a handkerchief delicately. "Sometimes I wonder if a boy would've been easier."

"We're living proof that they're not," Gunner chuckled.

"Fair enough. Right this way, gentleman." Vance and Josh turned, leading us down a corridor. "I'm eager to show you what I couldn't after dark last night."

We went out another set of doors in the back of the

building. Hades waited patiently for us at the back door, seemingly unperturbed about not being allowed inside. To our left, I spotted the patio where we had cigars after dinner. The small lake just off the patio stretched out in front of us, appearing to wrap around the back of the building. The water lapped softly at the shore, choppy and gray with the new winter-like weather.

Governor Vance led us over a quaint wooden bridge that crossed over the narrowest part of the lake. On the other side was a large expanse of land in various stages of development, from the completed house on the water he showed us last night, to work crews still pouring foundations and sawing lumber.

He led us down the freshly-paved perimeter roads first, waving to crews setting up the frames of houses. We stopped to talk to one of the master builders who showed us floor plans of the structures going up. Most of the homes were spacious, big enough for families. Another set of floor plans showed a condo project, smaller spaces for single people and couples without children.

If nothing else, the governor was making sure to cover all his bases. We ventured inward, toward the center of the development where the roads were still dirt and gravel. He pointed out areas where he planned for businesses and schools to go up, and a central square for gatherings and celebrations. According to his vision, this whole area across the lake would become its own city. The territory of Four Corners stretched out far beyond the main city, but was mostly uninhabited desert and ruins. With so many people flocking here, it was a constant race to rebuild fast enough.

"This is going to be a playground for children." Vance swept his arm over a crew of men welding metal pieces together for some climbing structure. "And here, a community garden. Something for the women to do, eh?" He chuckled to himself, the only one to laugh.

"Or the stay-at-home dads," Gunner returned. "That's the life path I'm ready for."

"Mari *might* let you do that," I mused. "If you get any better at cooking than Jandro."

"Shit, I'm fucked. I can barely use a toaster."

"Rich bitch."

"Whatever, broke bitch."

We laughed together while Shadow kept silent. I wondered how he felt about the whole child-rearing thing, or if he gave it any thought at all. The guy probably had zero positive association with childhood or parental figures. All the better that there would be four of us, should Mari decide to bring him into the fold. And if we could all learn to be as patient as she was, maybe we could show him how good raising a family could be.

"You see?" Vance beamed at us ribbing each other. "Your whole club can find home in this community. Your officers could be a neighborhood watch, of sorts, working with the army to keep the territory safe."

"It's got a lot of potential," I admitted, looking around at the half-constructed buildings. "And it's a beautiful dream to have."

"I'm sensing hesitation," the governor pressed gently. "What are your concerns, president?"

"The fact that you're bordered from the north, south, and east by enemies," Gunner answered for me. "At least one of which has a personal interest in attacking you."

"That," I agreed. "It's wonderful what you're doing here, Governor, but we can't help but feel like you're building a future on a very shaky present. Blake and Tash's territories need to be dealt with first, before we make any plans of putting down roots."

"Oh, I don't disagree at all, Reaper. General Bray will be here any moment to discuss plans for securing the borders—"

"Secure borders aren't enough." I shook my head. "We had secure borders at Sheol. They got in anyway with drones and bombs. We need to go on the offensive, governor."

Gunner nodded through everything I said. Shadow stood by with his own silent support while Vance and Josh exchanged nervous glances.

"While I certainly understand your feelings, Reaper, Four Corners is a territory of refuge. Our army is built on principles of protection, of defense first and foremost. I'm hesitant to send soldiers to almost-certain deaths when the vast majority of them came here to ensure safety for their families."

"We want the exact same thing, sir." Gunner clasped his hands in front of him. "I wasn't kidding about the stay-at-home dad thing. I want to live in a world where my wife can do work she loves and I spend my retirement doting on my kids. But none of that is possible if we just sit and wait while Tash and Blake wreak destruction all around us. We have to fight, bleed, and sacrifice for that peaceful life."

"General Bray would agree with you," Vance sighed. "He can tell you himself when he gets here how frustrated he is at my inaction. The army is sharp and well-trained under him, he's just waiting for my command. I know I've had a privileged life compared to you men, but I don't take the responsibility of my citizens' lives lightly. If Bray says we must go to war and you do as well, I am prepared to make that call, but only if there's no other way."

"Is he supposed to get here soon?" Gunner tilted his face up, making note of the sun directly overhead as it peaked through the clouds. "Mari wanted me to pick her up for lunch soon."

"Yes, yes. Anytime now." Josh looked at his watch.

"He has some new recruits he might be spending some extra time with," Vance mused. "A father figure to all the runaways, that one. He demands a lot from his soldiers, but has a soft heart underneath."

"Shit." Gunner rocked back on his heels, looking around in all directions. "She wanted me to come get her, but I don't wanna miss this meeting."

"Shadow," I angled my head toward the large, silent man. "Why don't you pick her up?"

"Me?" His eyes widened. "But if she asked for Gunner—"

"Yeah, go, man." Gunner slapped his arm. "You're her shiny new toy."

Shadow looked between us both as if wondering if this was a test, or a trick. "Are you sure?"

"Positive." Gunner gave him a playful shove. "She didn't want to hurt my feelings, but it was really you she wanted anyway. Go."

"Unless you're just *dying* to listen in on military strategy," I chuckled, pulling out a cigarette.

"Ah, okay. I'll...I'll pick her up from the hospital."

"Don't look so excited," Gunner ribbed. "Get goin'. We'll fill you in on who to assassinate later."

Without another word Shadow turned, walking quickly across the small bridge. I daresay the guy had a spring in his step. The anxiety in my stomach eased just a little. Gunner was a great shot and more than capable of protecting Mari, but Shadow would make a swift kill before the enemy even knew he was there. Our woman was in good hands with him.

"He's, uh," Josh cleared his throat politely. "A bit of an odd one, isn't he?"

"You get used to it," I said, lighting up and taking a deep drag. "He's had it rough but he's good, loyal. And the most efficient killer the Steel Demons has ever had."

"Ah. Good, good." Josh smiled politely but paled a little, swiftly looking away. "Oh, there's General Bray now," he said, sounding relieved.

Gunner and I turned in the direction he looked, spotting the man decked out in a camouflage uniform marching toward us. I squinted through my smoke, feeling an eerie sense of familiarity in the general's posture and the way he walked.

I've seen this man before, I realized. More than that. I *knew* this man, but from where?

"Gun." I leaned toward him, lowering my voice. "Does he look familiar to you?"

He gave a slight shake of his head. "No, Reap. Can't say he does."

"I know him," I growled under my breath. "But fuck if I can remember how."

"Do I need to draw?" His hand was already drifting toward one of his guns.

"Not yet." The general's face was shaded under the brim of his hat, but the width of his shoulders, the mouth set in a firm line--they were all features that poked at long-buried memories.

"General." Vance outstretched his hand. "So good of you to join us. This is Reaper, president of the Steel Demons MC, and his captain of the guard, Gunner."

"It's a pleasure, gentleme—"

General Bray turned to me, his hand outstretched in greeting and his face now clear to me. But it was his voice that finally clicked all the pieces into place.

Both of us froze in disbelief as we stared at each other. His beard was gone, but that was definitely *his* mouth. The brown eyes and bridge of his nose were exactly the same, if a bit more tan than before. He took off his hat with a shaking hand, his dark brown hair speckled with far more gray than I remembered.

He spoke first, a barely audible whisper. "Rory?"

Somehow, I found my voice in the wrangled knot that my throat became.

"Dad?"

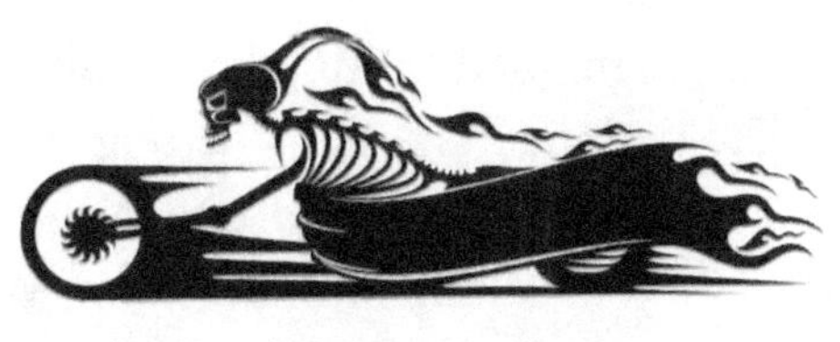

SHADOW

I could see Mariposa from up the road, twirling around in front of the hospital, arms out like wings and her mouth open with laughter. A light dusting of snow had just started falling, quickly melting and turning to mush when it hit the ground. But she kicked and danced underneath it like a girl from a Christmas movie.

She slowed her twirling as I approached, leaning heavily on a metal pole outside the hospital. "Didn't expect to see you here." Her cheeks were flushed from her spinning but she hugged her arms close, her flannel shirt doing little against the cold.

"Gunner asked me to come," I said. "He and Reaper were waiting on the general."

Mari smiled, looking down at her shoes as she rubbed her arms faster. "That Gunner. I should have known."

"Are you cold?" I shrugged off my cut before she could answer, then unzipped my hoodie and peeled it off my arms. "Here, wear this." I held my sweatshirt out to her.

She stared at my arm extended out to her, and then to my face. "Are you sure?"

My throat tightened with the familiar fear of wondering if I'd done something wrong. I'd seen old ladies wear their men's shirts and hoodies all the time. Mari wasn't *mine* yet, as far as I understood. Was I being too presumptuous in offering my clothing?

But even if I was, who gave a fuck if I had a jacket and she was cold?

"I'm sure. Take it before you freeze."

"What about you?"

My breath stuttered for a moment at the stark reminder that she cared enough about me to ask. "I'll be fine. Cold doesn't bother me."

She finally accepted the sweater from me and fed her arms through the sleeves. I looked away for a moment to pull my cut back on over my T-shirt. When I glanced at her again, it was all I could do to keep from laughing.

"What's that look for?" she demanded.

"Nothing."

"*Shadow.*"

"Really, it's nothing! I just didn't realize it would be so big on you."

She was swimming in the fabric. Her head floated above the hood at the top like she was treading water, and her legs stuck out of the bottom like skinny trunks on a tree. In the middle, her body was lost in the black circus tent of my hoodie. It was a comical sight, but not in the least bit unattractive. I wanted to pull her to me and warm her up better than any article of clothing could.

"Come on." I scooted back as far as I could and patted the seat in front of me. "Do you know what you want for lunch?"

Mari approached the side of my bike and threw a leg over, settling in front of me until her ass brushed against my crotch. Fuck me. She'd be warmer in front, but maybe for my own sanity I should have told her to sit behind me.

"Can we explore the town for a place to eat?" Her head touched the center of my chest and she looked straight up to talk to me. "We haven't seen all it has to offer yet, and I want to support the locals."

"Sure." I dropped a kiss to her forehead before I could overthink it.

She turned to look over her shoulder in response, lips landing softly on my mouth. I halted my gasp as I returned her kiss, my body still reacting with shock to her affection. It lessened every time though, giving way to that warm, melted feeling that took over whenever she touched me.

The kiss ended slowly, her soft mouth dragging over my beard as she resumed facing forward. Freyja had jumped into her lap and was now cocooning inside my hoodie. "Anything you in the mood for?" she asked, her voice slightly breathy.

You. Always you.

"I dunno." I returned my grip to the handlebars, caging her between my arms. "Just not soup."

"Aww." She leaned her head back on my chest and looked up at me again. "Are you associating soup with being sick now?"

"Probably." I turned us out of the hospital lot and headed down the main road leading through the center of town. "It just doesn't sound appealing."

"No soup, then," she agreed, planting her hands on my fuel tank. "But something hot and hearty would be good in this weather."

The ride was slow, with no particular destination in mind as we checked out the bustling center of Four Corners. It had stopped snowing already and road crews were already raking the slushy snow-and-mud mix off the sidewalks.

"Oh, shepherd's pie!" Mari pointed at a sandwich board outside of a squat brick building. "How does that sound?"

"What is that? I've never had it," I admitted.

"Oh, it's amazing!" She was already wriggling in my seat, eager to get off. *Ugh, don't think about getting off.* "It's a savory pie with a meat filling and mashed potatoes on top. It's *so* good, Shadow. You'll love it."

"Sounds good. I'll try it."

I maneuvered the bike close to the building and looked for a place to park. There didn't seem to be a rhyme or reason to vehicle parking yet, so we found an alley on the next block where a few scooters and motorbikes sat and decided to take our chances. Crime was supposed to be low within Four Corners, due to the governor's strict entry requirements. My Harley would be tempting to a thief, but also too big to steal without alerting me in the next building.

Freyja jumped out from under my hoodie and Mari's hand slipped into mine once we got off the bike. I did my best to walk normally while my heart went crazy. She appeared to have no second thoughts about being affectionate with me in public.

Like I was one of her men.

That thought was almost as staggering as her being affectionate with me at all.

"I like your hoodie," she said, bringing the fabric over her nose. "It smells like you."

I looked at her, surprised again. "That's a good thing?"

"Yes," she laughed. "I might steal it, so it feels like I'm wrapped up in you when you're not around."

"You can have it, then." I took my gloves off and stuck them in my cut pocket so I could feel her hand better as I held it. "But what if I want to steal something of yours?"

She gave me a playful look. "You already have my cat."

"That's true," I chuckled, looking ahead to where Freyja waited for us at the end of the alley. "She's lovely, but a poor imitation of you."

"I could say the same for your hoodie."

No words came to me in response to that, so I just rubbed my thumb along the back of her hand. She returned the gesture, squeezing around my fingers lightly.

We turned the corner and walked into the restaurant

where the shepherd's pie was advertised. It was a simple, rectangular building with a ceiling almost too low for my head. The tables and chairs were obviously scavenged from other places, spread out with few matching pieces in the dining area. The original counter had been ripped out, but there was a window in the far wall looking into the kitchen. A hand-drawn sign was taped next to the window that read 'Order Here'.

There was plenty of room to sit, with only a few tables occupied. Customers paid little attention to us, keeping their conversations low over their soups and sandwiches. Two chefs cooked over stoves in the kitchen, the closest one looking up and nodding at us as we stepped inside.

"Just holler when you're ready," the chef yelled before turning back to his stove.

He was a stout guy, red-faced with strawberry blond hair. The collar of his chef's jacket was turned up, which was curious, considering the sweltering heat from the stoves. He wiped sweat from his brow before grabbing the handle of a frying pan to sauté his dish. The movement showed a peek of a tattoo on his neck—two straight lines intersecting at the ends—before he readjusted his collar to hide it.

"I hope I have enough to trade for food." Mari dug through her pants pockets. "I always carry a few pills on me but it's not always—"

"Don't worry about it," I said with a light touch to her elbow. "I'll get us lunch."

"Are you sure? I don't mind—"

"I got it, really. Why don't you find us a place to sit?"

"'Kay." She nearly had to jump to kiss my cheek before meandering through the eclectic collection of tables.

I went up to the window, catching the eye of the red-faced chef. He paused his chopping to grab a notepad and a pen.

"What can I get ya?" He tilted his head, making a clear effort to hide his neck tattoo.

"Two shepherd's pies," I said. "Please," I added.

He scribbled it down. "Any sides? Drinks?"

Mari didn't ask for anything else, but I ordered teas for us both.

"Mmkay." The chef looked at me pointedly. "How you payin'?"

I steeled myself with a breath. This could go horribly wrong, but I couldn't continue to be fearful of human interaction. It was always a risk, but lately it felt just terrifying rather than suicidal.

"You looking to get that covered up?" I asked in a low voice.

The chef's eyes widened, his hand immediately clapping to his neck. "What?"

"That neck tattoo you're hiding. You want it covered so you don't have to keep wearing a jacket in a sweltering hot kitchen?"

His hand lowered slowly, but he still looked uneasy. "So, what, you know a guy?"

"You're looking at him," I said. "I'm a tattoo artist. I'll cover that up for you, and do any other work you'd like."

"You will, huh?" He looked me over, taking in my

cut and patches. "You with them bikers that just rode in?"

"That's us, yeah," I said. "We're not here for trouble. Just looking for a home like everyone else."

"Stickin' around then?"

"For the time being, yes."

"All right." He rubbed his jaw, nodding agreeably. "Yeah, okay. I'll trade ya grub for ink."

"Good. I'm at the B&B in the northwest part of town. Come by when you're ready and ask for Shadow."

"Right on, man." He ripped my order off of the notepad and stabbed it onto a receipt spindle. "I'll grab your shepherd's pies. They just came out of the oven."

"Thanks."

I scanned the dining room as I waited, spotting Mari at a table next to a window looking out onto the street. A woman with two small children walked by on the sidewalk, and Mari waved to the little girl holding her mother's hand.

"Two shepherd's pies." The mismatched ceramic bowls clattered on the serving window. "I'll bring your teas out in a sec. And hey, man…"

"Yeah?" I grabbed our food, mouth already watering at the sight of the savory filling and lightly browned mashed potatoes.

"This thing?" The chef pulled down his collar to show me the full tattoo. "I was a dumbfuck when I was young, okay? I don't subscribe to any of that shit—"

"You don't have to explain it to me," I told him. "I'm the last person to judge on poor decisions."

He nodded once more, thumping the counter with his hand. "Enjoy your meal, man."

I headed for the table where Mari waited and set our food down in front of her.

"Thank you for lunch," she said sweetly, sliding a napkin and utensils toward me.

"Thank you for telling me about shepherd's pie." I dug in with a fork, watching the steam rise from the piping hot filling.

"If you don't mind me asking..." Mari licked a small piece of mashed potato from her fork. "What did you trade for the meal?"

"Tattoos," I said, sneaking a glance toward the kitchen, then lowered my voice. "The chef has a swastika on his neck. I'm going to cover it up for him."

"Oh." Mari's brows lifted in surprise. "I didn't see that."

"He's hiding it under his jacket. I offered the cover-up on a hunch, glad he took it."

Mari took another bite of her food thoughtfully. "I haven't seen any tattoo shops here yet. You'd probably make a killing if you opened one. You'd have no competition."

"Maybe." I turned it over in my head as I chewed my food. Tattooing and drawing all day would be a dream career for me. My only hesitation was in having to deal with people I didn't know. That part still made me uneasy. But I did gain a possible new client by offering my services to a complete stranger, and that hadn't been so bad.

Mari and I talked lightly until we were scraping the

bottoms of our bowls. Fuck, shepherd's pie was good. Maybe I could talk Jandro into making it if we ever settled permanently.

Once finished, we returned our dishes to the serving counter. On the other side, the chef and his partner chopped potatoes, I assumed for more pie.

"Thank you, it was delicious!" Mari called through the window.

"Thanks for comin' in," the chef called. "And I'll be seeing you soon, man!"

"Looking forward to it." Taking Mari's hand, we headed back out onto the street, the now-emerging sun making us squint. Freyja waited patiently for us just outside the front door, apparently having made friends with some doves.

"Can we walk off this food?" Mari rubbed her belly with one hand. "Or do you have to head back?"

"No, I don't need to be anywhere." I was actually relieved that she didn't want to get back on the bike right away. Any opportunity to spend more time with her, I jumped at.

Fingers laced between us, we started a leisurely pace down the sidewalk. Freyja followed after us at her own pace, her doves in tow. The next block over was some kind of shopping district. Some shopkeepers worked out of established buildings, while others set up folding tables and canopies.

Mari released my hand to look through a rack of clothing, while I mused over an airbrush artist's display. The artwork wasn't *bad*, just no finess yet. Probably a young artist.

"Alright, mate." Greeting me with a thick foreign accent, the kid nodded at me from his folding chair, dark sunglasses over his eyes and a fat blunt in his hand.

"How's it goin'," I mumbled noncommittally. "You do good work here. Keep it up."

"Cheers, mate."

I wandered over to the next table where Mari looked over jewelry and chatted with the vendor, an attractive older woman with green eyes and streaks of gray in her reddish-brown hair.

"I love that one." Mari pointed to a stone pendant encased in a silver setting. "It matches my ring."

"Oh, so it does!" The jeweler fixed her gaze on Mari's ring, the one Reaper gave her. "Um, may I? Do you mind?"

"Of course not." Mari stretched her hand out for the other woman to inspect.

The woman seemed to go pale as she carefully looked over the stone and setting. "May I ask where you got this?"

"It was a gift from my husband." Mari beamed, wiggling her fingers.

"I see." The jeweler turned to me, a tense smile on her face. "What a thoughtful gift. You must love seeing it on her finger."

"Oh no, I didn't—I'm not, um—"

Shit. My eyes slid over to Mari, who didn't seem at all distressed by the misunderstanding. Her hand wrapped around my arm, fingers resting on my bicep.

"We're together, but he's not the one who gave me the ring. It's part of my husband's culture you see, for a woman to have multiple partners. Everyone involved is aware and consenting."

"I see," the woman repeated, looking no less pale and nervous than a moment ago. "If it's not too personal, can I ask your husband's name?" Her voice wavered slightly.

"It's Reaper," Mari answered. "He's the president of the biker club that came into town a few days ago.

"Well, he has excellent taste." The jeweler brought her hands together, clasping and wringing them. "I wish you all much happiness."

"Thank you so much." Mari smiled politely as we continued walking. Once out of earshot, she leaned her head on my shoulder. "Was that a little weird?"

"I was just about to ask you that."

"Something was definitely off there." She stroked her thumb over her ring, toying with the colorful stone as it caught the sunlight.

FIVE

REAPER

"**D**ad?"

I blinked several times, certain that the man standing in front of me couldn't be real. Or alive, for that matter.

"Holy shit." He rubbed his face, staring back at me intently. "Is it really you, Rory?"

"Fuck," I breathed in disbelief. "No one's called me that since—well, my old lady does to give me shit, but—"

"You have a wife?" he asked in an awed whisper. "And you…you lead a motorcycle club?" Only then did he take in my patches, my cut, and Gunner standing next to me wearing the same uniform.

"I, uh, fuck. I guess I should make introductions." I ran a hand through my hair, purposely tugging at my scalp to make sure I wasn't dreaming. "This is Gunner, my sergeant at arms. Gun, this is…my old man."

"My birth name is Finn. Finn Daley." Dad gave a

sheepish laugh and awkward wave. "But for the last five years or so, I've gone by Finn Bray. Long story, but I also went by Carter for a little while to escape being detected."

"Carter?" I barked, my anticipation jumping at the mention of my other father's name. "Is he around?"

I regretted the question as soon as it came out. Dad's smile faltered and he gave a small shake of his head. Of course not. He wouldn't be using my second father's name if he were alive and well. But I couldn't stop the questions once they began.

"What about Mom?" I demanded. "Is she okay? What…fuck! What the hell happened?"

Gunner cut in with a friendly squeeze of my shoulder. "We should probably give you some time alone. Right, governor?"

"Oh, yes. Of course." Vance and Josh seemed content to watch the spectacle from the sidelines, but had enough sense to start heading toward the bridge. "Take the rest of the day off, General. Give Alisa my love."

My chest relaxed just slightly. So my mother *was* okay, and still with him.

"I'll join you fellas!" Gunner slid up to Vance's left side, sandwiching the governor between him and Josh.

Good man, I thought. That was Gunner, always rubbing elbows with the powerful people we needed on our side.

Turning back to my dad, we both blew out a long breath and laughed nervously.

"Fuck," we said in unison, and laughed again.

"Holy shit, son. You look good. Little rough, but good." He inspected me from head to toe. "You're a *man*. God, you were what, nineteen the last time I saw you?"

"Something like that." I squinted like he was an optical illusion about to disappear at any moment. "It's been a long fuckin' time."

"How are your siblings?" he asked, crossing his arms. "Still with you?"

"Noelle's good. She's with me," I said, taking a moment to gather myself before dropping the bad news. "Daren…we lost him just over a year ago."

"Oh no." His face fell. "Fuck, that poor kid. Ugh, how?"

"Um, he got sick. A virus, we think." Surprisingly, I didn't feel the need to self-flagellate over his death. At some point over the last few months, I'd been able to release some of the guilt. Plus, I'd just seen him and knew he was at peace.

"Your mom's gonna be devastated." Dad's brow pinched, his eyes lowering with a pained gaze. Daren wasn't his by blood, but none of that mattered to us growing up.

"Were you with him?" he asked. He kept a stoic face but I could see how hard it was for him not to choke up. "How did it happen? When did you get a dog?" He looked down at Hades, nuzzling his hand. "And fuck me, son, where have you been all this time?"

"Got a few minutes?" I angled my head toward the

riverbank and pulled out a fresh cigarette. "Why don't we take a walk?"

My father regained his composure and nodded, then promptly shook his head when I offered him a smoke. "Those things will put you in an early grave, son. You don't get to be my age, and running past young punks, when your lungs are all tarred up."

"I never planned on living long anyway," I muttered. "But I'm cutting back. I got a woman now, and we'd like to have kids in a couple years."

"You, a husband!" he laughed, slapping me on the shoulder. "And a dad-to-be, my goodness. Tell me about her! What's her name? Does she have other men?"

"Hang on, old man," I laughed, stunned at how easily we fell into our old banter despite not seeing each other for over ten years. "Let me start at the beginning."

———

"HOLY SHIT, ROR." My dad scraped his cigarette butt on the ground. He finally took one after I told him about nearly getting blown up at the Sandia outpost. "That's a hell of a few years. And Mari, damn." He shoved me playfully, lines deepening around his eyes as he grinned. "She must be a hell of a woman to deal with a punk-ass like you."

"She is." I pulled out two more cigarettes and held one out to him. "The other guys are good for her. I'm just trying my best."

"You all gotta come over. Lis and I miss having a

busy house, and we need to meet our daughter-in-law." Dad took the smoke and went to light up, then hesitated. "But maybe a little bit after I tell her about Daren. She'll need some time, you know."

"Yeah," I said. "Noelle and I have already had a year to grieve. She's got a man too, you know."

"Oh, what's he like?"

"Eh, you'll meet him soon."

I could picture Larkan now, his back ramrod straight as he shook my father's hand and called him 'sir'. He'd be the type of guy to compliment my mother's cooking and do the dishes for her. My parents would love him, and as much as I hated to admit it, he was pissing me off a lot less. He protected Mari on that mission to Blakeworth, and returned her to me without so much as a scratch. The kid deserved a patch, and my respect, for that alone.

"He's her only one? She always did prefer that."

"Yes, and before you ask any more questions..." I pointed at him, cigarette between my fingers. "You've kept me waiting long enough, old man. Your turn to tell me where you've been all these years."

"Alright, alright." He took a deep drag, holding it in his chest for a moment before releasing it out.

"Some militia came to the commune one night," he began. "They were all in black, no insignia, unmarked vans, that whole business we heard whispers of, but never thought it was true. They came in with rifles and riot gear, started pounding on doors and yelling for people to get in the vans."

"Fuck," I said. My cigarette was already halfway gone.

"Noelle was asleep. Carter stuck her in the cellar and told her not to move or make a sound until you came for her. But other than that, no one had time to react. We were outnumbered and they were taking *everyone*, kids and old folks too. No one wanted to provoke these sons of bitches."

"Where'd they take you?"

"Their base, a bunch of old bunkers in Nevada. These guys called themselves the Original Patriots, saying they were trying to restore the country to its former glory, can you believe it? Kidnapping a bunch of families just trying to live peacefully and they call themselves patriots?"

"What did they want with all of you?" I finished my smoke and stuck another one in my mouth, already way past my usual daily amount, but also past the point of caring.

"Different tasks, depending on what they needed to run their camp. Soldiers, cooks, cleaners. They used children to run messages back and forth. We had to do everything we were told, on penalty of death. Some patriots, huh? And they wanted all the multi-husband families separated. It was to repent for our 'sinful ways'," he air-quoted.

"So what'd you end up doing?"

"They deemed Carter and I too old to be soldiers, so we were assigned to be mechanics. On opposites sides of the compound of course, once they figured out we were part of the same household. Your mom was in laundry and cooking for the first two years or so. That was hell. Carter and I barely saw her, and we weren't allowed to talk to her either. Then, uh," Dad paused, looking out over the river as he ran a hand through his salt-and-pepper hair, "Carter got hurt."

"How?" I demanded, anger already boiling in me for what my second father must have suffered.

"Piece of machinery fell on him," Dad sighed. "Broke his leg in three places. I didn't know until days after. When your mom found out, she somehow got hold of a welding torch and made him a cane so he could get around a bit. But his leg was fucked and the poor guy was in so much pain."

"Was there no medic?" I snarled. "Did no one even try to heal him?"

"Only the chosen ones, the Patriots, got medical attention," Dad said bitterly. "We had to repent for some indefinite amount of time before we could have that privilege."

"Fuck." I dragged on my cigarette only to find I had finished that one too. "How long were you there for?"

"Seven years." His voice was heavy with sadness. "We lost Carter after five. His leg got infected and he just kept getting worse. Your mom tried to sneak over to see him whenever she could, but he put a stop to that. He didn't want to risk her getting caught and punished. Last time I saw him, he was feverish, weak. Leg smelled like death." Dad sighed. "He was just gone the next morning. Bed stripped clean."

"You never saw his body?"

"They had a mass grave out in the desert for those

that passed. Most likely they dumped him out there, but we'd be shot on sight if we tried to go find him."

"Fuck," I groaned, the desire to smoke completely gone. My stomach turned with nausea instead. "Guess I'm pouring my first whiskey out for Carter tonight."

None of my fathers had been weak men. Finn, my bio-dad, served twenty-two years in the Air Force and retired as a Major. Nolan, Daren's dad, had worked in farming his whole life and was built like a brick house. Cancer had taken him too young, withering him away to nothing within a year when Daren was twelve and I was fourteen. But it was Carter, Noelle's father, who stood like a mountain even when the other two had met their limit.

Never in my life had I heard Carter moan about being in pain. My dads were all roughly the same age, and I remembered Nolan and Finn bitching about aching joints and sore backs when I was a preteen. Carter would just snort and tell them to stop being pussies. They always ran in the early mornings and worked out together, with Carter always pushing himself the hardest.

I looked to Hades, sitting regally on the lawn next to us with his paws stretched out in front of him. His ear flicked in my direction, head tilting to acknowledge the question in my mind.

Carter Daley is at rest, the omniscient voice echoed through me. A brief summation, but one that comforted the agitated churning in my stomach.

"I always thought he'd last the longest, of all of us."

Dad nodded, echoing my thoughts while giving no indication that he heard the voice.

"How'd you and Mom make it to Four Corners then?" I asked

"The bunker hideout got attacked by another militia," he laughed drily. "These fucking Patriots thought the Collapse was God calling them to take over, but oh no. It never occurred to them there'd be bigger fish out there. So they were getting their asses handed to them and demanded all hands on deck. Guess they wanted to go out in a blaze of glory. So I grabbed a rifle and made it look like I was headed to the front lines. Instead, I grabbed your mom, stole a motorbike, and floored it in the opposite direction."

"*You* on a motorbike?" I laughed. "Shit, Dad. Want a cut and a patch? You've earned it."

"Hell nah. I ride like a grandpa now that I'm not running for my life."

"So then what happened?" I asked. "You just headed east 'til you ran out of gas?"

"Yeah, pretty much. Ran out of gas maybe fifteen miles or so outside of the border. We kept walking until we saw armed guards and almost ended up running the other direction. But our feet were bleeding, we were starving, dehydrated. Figured we'd either get shot or die out in the desert anyway, so we decided to take our chances."

"And how'd you end up as a general?"

"Well, after a few weeks of recuperating in the hospital, Vance came to see us. Four Corners was a lot smaller then, so the governor liked to personally meet all the refugees. We told him our stories and it turned out he was an Airman too, back in the day. Didn't stay in as long as me, but he knew where I was coming from. Said he needed a leader for his army. Not to fight and conquer like everyone else, but to keep people safe. I told him I was done fighting other people's wars, but I could whip some brats into shape. Five years later, and here we are."

"How do you feel about a war that's likely to still come?" I asked. "Especially with the territory being so prosperous, and now with taking Vance's daughter back from Blakeworth. Tash and that bastard up north have to have eyes on us."

"Oh, we're ready for it, " Dad said with a soft growl. "We're not looking for war, but those seven years opened my eyes, son. People with just an ounce of power are doing terrible things out there, and the less fortunate are suffering for it. We were damn lucky to make it to Four Corners, but not everyone is. How many people do you think collapsed out there in the desert, running from the exact same thing we were?"

"Hundreds," I mused. "Maybe even thousands."

"Exactly. So yeah, I'll take up arms for those who couldn't. And everyone else is just trying to live free in a safe place for their families." His face softened, lips pulling into a smile. "So you're trying to make me a grandpa, huh?"

"Afterward," I said. "When we win, and I can sleep at night without all this shit running through my head."

"I hear you, son." He clapped me on the shoulder, looking out over the lake, which was starting to sparkle from the sun peeking out from the clouds. "We'll get there. Maybe not in my lifetime, but hopefully in yours."

"Better be in yours," I huffed. "Who am I gonna pass my spawn off to when I want to fuck my old lady into next week?"

"Then you have to be ready, Rory," Dad said softly. "Ready to fight like you never have before."

SIX

MARIPOSA

"Do you mind dropping me off at the bar up the street? The one that's been renting out rooms on the top floor?" I leaned back against Shadow, tilting my face up to look at him. "I haven't seen Tessa in a few days and I'd like to visit."

"Sure." He kept his eyes on the road, but released one of the handlebars to caress my back as he gently accelerated forward.

Every touch from him turned me to jelly. It was more than just chemistry and the newness of being together. Everything felt more meaningful, knowing how averse to touch he had been when we first met. He placed those fingers along my spine or threaded through my hand because he *wanted* that contact, not because it was expected of him. Knowing it was all intentional and thought out by him made me soak up every piece and hold on to every sensation.

When he pulled up to the bar, I never wanted the

warmth of his chest to leave my back, nor his arms to come away from being extended on either side of me.

"Huh, looks like the Sons are here," Shadow noted, nodding at the bikes parked out front. "That's Grudge's ride. Pretty sure the other two are T-Bone and Dyno's."

"Oh, you should stay too then." I stretched up and long behind me to wrap my hands around the back of his neck. "Hang out with the guys while I visit Tess. We can go back home together, if you're up for it."

I expected him to refuse, knowing he had his limits when it came to social interaction. Eating lunch in a restaurant and window-shopping for a half-hour on a busy street would have been enough for one day, I figured.

Shadow stroked my sides, planting a kiss on me with a soft hum as I stared at him upside down. "Maybe I'll stay for a drink or two," he mused.

"You will?" I squeaked.

"Yeah, why not?" He swung a leg off the bike and lifted me out of the seat with a firm hold on my waist. It took a monumental effort not to swoon.

"Come to the upstairs room and knock if you get sick of them." I squeezed his forearm as we walked up the front porch together.

"I should be fine." He pulled the door open and stepped aside to let me through. "Grudge will tell the other two off if they get annoying."

"Well hey there, little lady—Shadow!"

Seated on worn leather couches and armchairs around a coffee table, all three Sons of Odin turned to face the door, mouths pulling into grins at the sight of the two of us together.

"So this has finally happened, huh?" T-Bone gestured between us. "Thought I saw sparks flying between you two on our little Blakeworth getaway."

"Don't you three have jobs or something?" I teased, rubbing my hand over T-Bone's shaved head.

"Hey, it's hard work being on official business from the governor," Dyno piped up. "We require lots of R&R."

"Uh-huh. Hi, Grudge!" I leaned over the back of the couch to hug the silent man around his neck. He hummed a greeting in return and smiled up at me, squeezing affectionately around my arms.

"How are you, brother?" Shadow eased into the seat next to him, accepting the empty glass and pour of whiskey the other man offered.

"Having a drink with us, Mari?" T-Bone lifted the whiskey bottle up to me.

"Later, maybe. I wanted to see Tessa and the baby for a bit."

Dyno cleared his throat. "You might want to, uh," he curled his hand into a fist and made a knocking motion as he clicked his tongue, "knock before you go in there."

T-Bone snorted, trying to hide a laugh behind his drink, his face going red. My eyes narrowed. What had they seen that they weren't supposed to?

"I delivered her baby, Dy," I laughed it off with a wave of my hand. "There's nothing I haven't seen."

Dyno slouched into the couch cushions, hiding a grin behind his whiskey tumbler. "Suit yourself."

I ignored him, turning to run a hand along the back of Shadow's shoulders before heading to the room upstairs. "I shouldn't be long, but come find me if you need me."

"Take your time." He tilted his head up for a kiss and I happily planted a long, slow one on him in front of our audience.

T-Bone immediately started with the wolf howls, and Dyno was quick to join in with barks, howls, and aggressive hip thrusts.

"Just kidding, man. Don't kick my ass." T-Bone smirked as Shadow and I separated. I didn't hear Shadow's reply, but the two jokers burst into peals of laughter that filled up the bar, Dyno nearly sliding off the couch to the floor.

Giggling at their antics, I made my way to the stairs tucked off in the corner of the bar. Freyja ran ahead of me and jumped up the rickety steps to wait for me on the landing. Despite what I told Dyno, I did knock when I reached Tessa's door. Even while sharing a single room with three other people, I still knew the need for privacy. A room to myself was starting to sound downright heavenly.

"Who is it?" Tessa called from the other side, sounding nervous.

"Santa Claus," I snickered. "It's me, Mari."

"Oh! Uh, just hang on a second."

I waited patiently by the door, trying not to eavesdrop as I heard multiple footsteps on the other side. Voices murmured through the wood, not just Tessa's, but another woman's. My mind remained curiously blank until the door pulled open slowly, and it was Andrea, Dallas's widow, on the other side.

"Oh, hey." My voice carried a tone of surprise before I could control it. "Uh, I could come back later?"

"No, no, it's okay." Andrea blushed, palming her neck nervously. "I was just stopping by, and on my way out."

"Okay." I watched her hurriedly gather up her things, large bags full of several changes of clothes and toiletries, as though she had stayed over much longer than she let on. Like she had spent the night, or several nights by the looks of it. "You don't have to leave—"

"No, it's okay! I should get the kids anyway." She hurried out the door, sending a flustered smile over her shoulder at Tessa, sitting up in the unmade bed. "See ya, Tess."

"Bye, Drea." Tessa looked like she wanted to hide under the covers and never come out.

"Hey." I approached the end of the bed cautiously. "Everything okay?"

She raised her hands and flopped them back down over the comforter. "It's exactly what it looks like. You can just come out and say it, Mari."

"Say what?"

"You know." She looked at me with her chin tucked low. "That Drea and I are two women sharing a room. And a bed."

I lifted one shoulder in a shrug. "That's not for me to speak on. But we can talk about it, if you want." I tentatively sat on the far corner of the mattress.

Tess looked hesitant, fingers curled over the

bedspread. "Promise you won't tell anyone? Not any of your men, even Reaper. And definitely not my ex-husband."

"Nothing you tell me will leave this room." I moved to sit in front of her, reaching for her hands. "So, what's going on?"

"So I wasn't completely honest with you and Reaper," Tessa picked at the comforter on her lap, "when I talked about separating."

"What do you mean?"

"This didn't just happen out of nowhere. Andrea and I have a…a connection that Big G doesn't like. We have for years."

I nodded calmly. "A romantic connection, I take it?"

"Yeah, I…had feelings for her before, a long time ago, that are kind of rekindling now." She swallowed nervously. "There was, uh, an incident a couple years back."

"A, uh," I cleared my throat, "sexual incident?"

"Not *exactly*, and we didn't cheat on our guys or anything. They were there. It's just, fuck." She slapped her palms to her cheeks too late, they were already reddening. "I'm just digging myself into a hole here."

"Why don't you tell me what happened?" I scooted further up the bed and took her hands, rolling my thumbs over the back of her palms in an attempt to soothe her. "You're my friend, Tess. I won't judge."

"Really?" She looked skeptical.

"Hon, I sleep with, and am basically married to, *three* guys. I'm the last person that should be judging you."

"But...Andrea and I are women. People have been killed for that."

I nodded my head toward the door I had just come through. "I'd like to see someone try. There's at least three men downstairs who would cut through anyone trying to harm you for loving another woman." *Four, if you include mine sitting with them.*

The worry eased slightly in Tessa's brow, a small smile coming to her lips. "The Sons are good allies. They're staying in rooms here too, and have essentially appointed themselves as our bodyguards. They eat with us downstairs, come with us on errands. It has helped to alleviate the gawking and dirty looks."

"See?" I told her. "I can't even imagine what they've had to face. It's sweet of them to want to protect you from that."

"It's amazing," Tessa mused. "They're so openly affectionate with each other. They don't care who sees, they just are who they are."

"They love each other," I said. "And the fact that they're all men doesn't matter, they're fucking adorable together. No one deserves to be killed over that." I squeezed her hand again. "Had you dated women before Big G?"

"I had a girlfriend in high school," she admitted, her worried frown returning. "I loved her, but her family was set on moving away when the Collapse got real bad. We thought it would be safer to break up. People used to yell horrible slurs at us, and anyway," she sighed, wiping quickly at her eyes, "I liked guys too and wanted to start a family. I thought Big G was the person I needed."

"What happened to make him so upset about Andrea?" I asked gently.

Tessa blew out a long breath. "So, there was a party one night, a couple years back in Sheol. Dallas, Andrea, G, and I all went back to their place afterwards. We got the kids set up for a sleepover upstairs while us adults continued drinking downstairs." Her throat worked nervously. "At some point, Andrea kissed me. It was a super quick peck on the lips, practically nothing. We were drunk and being silly. But Dallas was into it and encouraged us to kiss some more."

"And Big G?" I pressed.

"That's what pisses me off so much. He acted like he was into it too." She brought a hand to her chest. "I remember feeling so elated and relieved. Like yes, my husband *does* accept and love me, even though I'm also attracted to women. It felt like a huge weight off my chest."

Anger heated inside me on her behalf. "But that turned out not to be the case?"

She shook her head. "Two-faced bastard. I must have asked him like ten times if he was seriously okay with it. Even then, we kept things pretty tame. Andrea and I made out for a little while, then she and Dallas went off to fuck. As soon as G and I were alone, he did a complete fucking 180."

"Jesus." My chest ached for her. "What a betrayal. I'm so sorry, Tess."

"He berated me, accused me of all these awful things, called me names." Her voice cracked. "It was exacerbated because he was drunk, of course. Not that

that fucking excuses it. I trusted him, and it hurt so bad. So yeah, he's always pitched a fit any time she and I happened to be alone. Nothing happened since that night, but he didn't care. Not even the death of her husband was a good enough reason for me to spend time with her, even just as friends."

"I'm sorry, sweetie." I reached over and rubbed her arm. "If Andrea makes you happy, you're much better off with her."

Her face lit up for the first time since telling me her story. "Thank you for being supportive, Mari. It's still tough, you know. She loved Dallas so much, and she's never been with a woman before. We're taking it slow, but it's nice. We're able to comfort each other. Take turns watching each other's kids. It feels so good, being with someone who listens and just *understands* me. Even if it's just a temporary thing, we'll always be there for each other in one way or another."

"That's how it should be," I said with a light squeeze of her hands. "I'm glad you're happy, honey."

"Well shit, I'm glad you are too. You're absolutely glowing!" She leaned over and poked me in the belly. "Got anyone cookin' in there yet?"

"Nah." I slid a hand over where she poked me, just under my navel. "Not for a little while longer."

"Your men must be on their best behavior then, for you to look so blissed out. That, or you got laid just before coming here. In which case, I *highly* resent you knocking when you did."

"Sorry about my awful timing, but it's not that either," I laughed. "I've been seeing someone new."

"Another one? Jesus, woman. There are whores getting less dick than you!"

"We haven't slept together yet," I clarified. "But it feels like that high school kind of relationship, you know? Lots of kissing and hand-holding. Innocent and sweet. It's actually really nice."

Tessa looked confused. "Okay, is Reaper letting you date a barely-legal Four Corners native? Because that sounds like absolutely no one in the SDMC."

I grinned coyly at her. "It's Shadow."

Her mouth fell open, eyelashes fluttering rapidly. *"Shadow?"*

"Mm-hm."

"The big scarred, scary guy who always looks pissed off and doesn't talk to anyone?"

"He's never been scary to me," I said, feeling a little defensive with her assessment. "And he does talk when he feels comfortable enough to do so."

"Wow, guess I've been out of the loop." She climbed out of bed to tend to Vivi who had started to fuss in her bassinet. "How long's this been going on? I thought he hated women."

"Well, we first kissed last night after the governor's party. But before that we'd been slowly getting used to being in each other's company. For months, really."

Tessa settled back into bed to nurse the baby. "Well, he's got to be something special to make you look so doped up with happiness."

"He is." My dreamy smile returned. "He's so sweet in ways I never expected. And to see him come out of his shell, expressing himself and socializing with ease—it's amazing."

"If he's *that* perfect, then his dick is small," Tessa joked. "Or something else is wrong with him. With men, there's always something."

He definitely isn't small. I could recall our first time together with far less guilt now. As for what was 'wrong' with him, it didn't feel right to discuss any of his trauma or his coping mechanisms with her. Especially not as his medic, nor while he was actively trying to better himself every day.

"How are things going with Big G?" I asked. "Is he staying civil?"

"Yeah, now that he knows he's on thin ice with Reaper," Tessa scoffed. "He's damn near father of the year now. Picks up the boys right on time and drops them right off."

"Hopefully he keeps that up, and not just because he has to."

"Yeah." She shifted her grip on the hungry baby. "He still doesn't know anything about Andrea and me, so I'm worried about all his cooperation going out the window if he finds out."

"I understand that, but if you keep seeing each other, it'll have to come out eventually."

"I know that. Believe me, I do." Vivi unlatched and Tess brought her up to her shoulder, patting her back. "One thing at a time though. I'd like to just enjoy being happy for once."

"I don't blame you." I smiled at the sight of her with

her daughter, a small twinge of envy running through me. *One day. Not yet.* "Once you've found what makes you happy, you have to hold on to it with everything you've got."

SEVEN

MARIPOSA

"What do these do?" I picked up one of the metallic contraptions on the table and turned it over in my hand.

"That's a fuel injector," Jandro told me with a smirk. "It injects fuel."

"Don't be a smart ass." I went to swat him but he dodged out of my reach.

Glaring at him across the work table, I set down the fuel injector and spread my feet, poised like a cat.

"Oh, you coming to get me?" He copied my stance, bending his knees and bringing his chest forward like a football player. "Come on, pretty medic."

I faked to one side, then darted around the table in the opposite direction, but he saw me coming. And Jandro knew I was no match for him. I tackled him with a roar and he just laughed, catching me under my thighs as he pressed kisses to my neck.

The feeling of his mouth was electric, as were his strong hands gripping so close to my ass without a second thought. Going slowly with Shadow *was* nice, but there was nothing like the confidence and ease from the men who were already mine.

I locked my ankles behind Jandro's back, squeezing my thighs around his waist as I found his luscious mouth.

"Mm, you can tackle me any time for this," he chuckled, fingers digging into the fabric of my jeans.

"Don't use this as a reason to be more of a smart ass with me." I pulled at his lips lightly with my teeth.

"No promises," he murmured, turning us and parking my ass on the table strewn with bike parts. "Fuck, I want you," he added, spreading my legs around him as he pressed flush to me. "I want you to myself."

"We're alone, aren't we?"

I released his lips to kiss my way to his earlobe, sucking on it until he moaned, then moving on to the warm skin of his neck.

Shadow and I had returned home from the bar an hour earlier, kissed, and went our separate ways. Gunner and Reaper were still gone, and Mrs. Potts, the B&B owner, left us alone for the most part. She remained swift and unseen when it came to cleaning our rooms or refilling coffee and pastries in the common room. Although getting it on out here in the yard probably wasn't the wisest idea, I never got the sense she was spying on us.

"Ugh, no," Jandro sighed, pulling away. "We're not."

"In the room, then." I tugged his cut to return him closer, kissing his throat and under his jaw.

"I see Reap coming down the hill," he said. "Riding

fast. I bet you anything he's about to tell us something urgent."

"Fuck, what now?" I groaned, leaning my forehead against his chest. Not that I didn't want to see Reaper. Having him and Jandro in bed would be intimate and cozy too. But he was already worried about me from Daren's message, and I hoped his meeting with the general didn't tell him anything to exacerbate that fear.

Moments later, Reaper's bike roared its way up to the B&B entrance and he quickly waved at us over the fence before cutting the engine.

"Good, you two are together. Stay there, I'm coming over."

"Does he seem happy to you?" I asked Jandro.

"Damn near ecstatic," he replied with a confused frown.

Sure enough, Reaper was beaming as he came out to the backyard with us. He also reeked of clove cigarettes, like he went through an entire pack since breakfast.

"You're not gonna believe this." He was downright giddy, practically giggling with excitement. "My parents are alive. Vance's general is my fucking *dad*."

"Wait...what?" Jandro blurted out after a beat of silence. "Your parents are alive? And they're *here*? All of them?"

Reaper shook his head. "Just Mom and Finn, my bio-dad."

"Carter?" Jandro asked hesitantly.

The glow of Reaper's happiness faded just slightly.

"No, they lost him a few years back. I still have to break the news to Noelle."

"Damn, no one's made it this far without some losses." Jandro rubbed a hand over his head. "But dude! Finn and your mom, that's amazing! And he's a fucking general?"

"I know," Reaper laughed. "It's fuckin' wild." He turned to me, a smile lighting up his gorgeous face that I couldn't help but echo. "My parents are alive, sugar. You'll get to meet my family."

"I'm so happy for you!" I held my arms out to him. "And relieved that they're okay. I know how heavily that weighed on you, my love."

A pang cut through my chest. I'd give anything to know if my parents were alive and well, much less in the same town as me. But there was no way I'd diminish Reaper's joy. He deserved to have his family back, something that was so rare after the Collapse tore thousands of families apart. Even more, he could finally be absolved of the guilt he carried.

Reaper pulled me into a tight embrace, his heart hammering against mine. "It sucks about Carter, but fuck, it feels like that weight's been lifted now. A little bit, at least."

"How'd your mom handle seeing you?" Jandro grinned. "I bet she's still hot."

"Fuck off." Reaper shoved his shoulder, but it was lighthearted with no real strength behind it. "I actually haven't seen her yet. Dad and I spent a long time talking, catching up. He wanted to break the news to her about Daren privately, before a whole bunch of us come to see her."

"Oh yeah," Jandro nodded. "That's probably a good idea."

"But yeah, when she's ready, she'll want to see your dumbass for reasons unknown." Reaper shoved him playfully again. "She'll want to meet Mari, of course. Dad's already obsessed with you, sugar." He dropped a kiss to my forehead. "They'll need to see Noelle, who will drag Larkan along, I'm sure. Then eventually, they're going to want to meet all of your men."

"Yikes, that's going to be a crowd," I muttered.

"It's how we do things, sugar." Reaper rubbed the back of my neck. "Big gatherings with lots of hustle and bustle, just like the club parties. You'll be fine. You know almost everyone already."

"You know, come to think of it, I, um." I rubbed my forehead, remembering my lunch date with Shadow earlier that day. "It might be possible that I've met your mom already."

"What?" he gasped. "When? Where?"

"Downtown today, after Shadow and I got lunch. I stopped at a jeweler's table because her pieces reminded me so much of my ring." Reaper's hand wrapped around mine, shaking slightly as he twisted the band. "She seemed very interested in my ring and where I got it from."

"I'll be damned," he whispered.

"Was she hot?" Jandro asked. "You know, for a lady about Mom-age?"

I rolled my eyes. "Yes, Jandro, she was attractive.

And—" My gaze returned to Reaper's, the exact same green eyes of the woman I met staring back at me. "Oh yeah, she was definitely your mom."

"Holy shit." Reaper dipped his head back and laughed. "I can't believe this is really fuckin' happening."

"Believe it." I wrapped my arms around his neck. "You deserve this, to have your family back together. No one deserves it more than you."

His grin was wicked as his hands surrounded my waist, fingers caressing my belly. "My family's not complete until I put a little one inside you, sugar."

Jandro pressed into my side, his hand on my back just above Reaper's. "Our kids are going to have living grandparents that actually see them and spoil them. Do you know how rare that is now?"

"You two better stop talking like that." I quickly kissed Jandro, then planted one on Reaper. "I just got back from seeing Tessa, and I do *not* need babies on the brain right now."

"Let's make some." Reaper's voice was already husky, his hand sliding up my ribs to frame the underside of my breast. "Me and Jandro can put twins inside you right now."

"That's...not how it works."

"Oh well, whatever." Jandro's lips grazed the shell of my ear. "I know you can't right now, *Mariposita*, but we can practice."

"Why do I even let you two fuck me?" I laughed, leaning my head back so they could both attack my neck from different angles.

"We have nice cocks." Reaper chuckled, nipping at the column of my throat.

"Aw thanks, Reap," Jandro cooed.

"Sure thing, buddy."

"Nice cocks aside, you two are ridiculous." I planted my hands on the table behind me, relishing in their mouths and hands on my body, shifting from affectionate to passionate.

"You want to do this out here, sugar?" Reaper's hand skimmed over my breast, lightly squeezing before his touch moved on to my shoulder. "Out in the open?" His tone made it clear he had no qualms with that notion.

"I don't care where, but you need a shower first."

His eyebrow lifted. "Excuse me?"

"You stink of those cloves. How many did you smoke?"

"A lot," he admitted. "Dad and I shared my pack while we talked."

"In the shower sounds good to me." Jandro pressed a kiss to the side of my face before dragging his lips to my ear. "We can take turns with your sweet little ass that way."

Reaper made a purr of agreement while I let out a soft gasp. "All three of us in there? Will we fit?"

"We're about to find out." In one quick motion, Reaper hoisted me over his shoulder and started carrying me inside like a damn caveman.

The shower *was* spacious, since we had the biggest bedroom in the B&B. It even had a waterfall shower head with decent water pressure. But none of us had tried to cram in more than one at a time before.

"Kick your leg out for me, sugar," Reaper instructed with a slap to my ass.

I flailed my foot out behind me, hitting the wooden door of our room with a loud thunk to Jandro's howling laughter.

"You got a free hand, dude. Why make her kick it like a donkey?"

"Just wanted to see her do it." Reaper set me down with a laugh and started stripping out of his clothes. The smoke smell was already dissipating, clinging more to his shirt than his skin.

I was slower to undress, not wanting to miss a single moment of them pulling off shirts, tearing apart belt buckles, and exposing swaths of ink, scars, and delicious masculine flesh.

"It's rude to stare, Mariposita." Jandro grinned as he stepped out of his pants and boxers, his thick torso making the tattoos on his ribs expand with every breath.

"I'm a rude girl, what can I say?" I continued to unabashedly drink in the warm tan of his skin, the muscles in his legs, and the broadness of his chest and arms that I loved to wrap myself around.

"Get fucking naked right now," Reaper growled, coming at me from the side with his cock already halfway erect.

"Make me." The challenge was on my lips without thought, my palm wrapping around and stroking his stiffening length.

"Oh, you are a rude girl," Reaper purred like he was pleased, caressing along my neck and shoulder. "You know where rude girls belong?"

He shoved me to my knees before I could come back with another smart remark, pressing his hips into my face. I took him in my mouth just like he wanted, the thrill of his dominance surging in my body.

"Ohh, fuck yeah," he hissed, fingers diving into my hair. "Jandro, come get her clothes off."

I had already gotten started with undoing my pants and taking Shadow's hoodie off. Jandro's hands were indulgent and sensual as he finished the job, running over my body as he kissed my neck and shoulders. I felt him up blindly as I sucked Reaper, my palm finding his lips, chest, then the hard wall of his stomach before finding Jandro's cock.

"Suck him too, sugar." Reaper withdrew from my mouth, turning my head toward his best friend.

Jandro had been kneeling at my level and returned to standing, letting out a deep, satisfied hum as I wrapped my lips around him. "Such a good rude girl," he said with a loving stroke to my cheek.

I would have smiled if my mouth wasn't stuffed. This felt just like how things were in the beginning—the simple contrast of Reaper's rough love with Jandro's tender sweetness. Not that I didn't love Gunner or the slower pace with Shadow, but these two were my rocks. The foundation on which my love for four different, incredible men grew.

I slurped around Jandro's thick head until I needed to breathe, then returned to take Reaper down my throat.

"Ugh, Jesus," he groaned, head tilting back. "Too fucking good."

"So are we nixing the shower? Mm, fuck!" Jandro gasped more curses as I drew him into my mouth again, tongue licking the sensitive underside.

"Nah, let's move there." Both men supported my arms to help me to my feet. "See how well we *fit*," Reaper added with a swat to my ass.

I darted into the bathroom first, leaving them to fight over who came after me first through the doorway. I turned the shower handle and stuck my hand under the spray when an arm wrapped around my waist, pulling me against a solid chest.

"I miss our baths, sugar," Reaper murmured, nipping at the shell of my ear.

"Me too," I sighed, arching against him.

"One day." His mouth made a burning trail from my ear to my shoulder. "We'll have a tub big enough for all of us." He jerked his head to indicate Jandro behind him. "Even this asshole."

"Excuse you, this asshole doesn't stink like a smoke factory, and would like to get in to suds up our woman. Move."

Jandro slid past us into the shower and ripped me out of Reaper's arms to join him under the spray.

"Ah! It's not hot yet!" The water wasn't cold either, but tepid enough to raise goosebumps on my skin as I hugged myself.

"I know." Jandro tugged my arms away and skimmed his mouth over my chest. "It makes your nips nice and tight."

He laved over one with his tongue, soothing the cold, tense peak with the heat of his mouth. Reaper stepped in and closed the shower door behind him, replacing the water running over my back with his hands.

"Wash me, sugar," he said in a seductive whisper before chuckling, "since you think I stink so much."

I turned around slowly, sandwiched firmly between the two of them. We had some extra room, but not much. Reaper's eyes never left mine as I grabbed a loofah and a soap bar from the shelf carved in the shower wall. He was standing directly under the shower-head, so I had to reach around him to lather up the loofah.

Jandro pulled me back toward the far shower wall with a hand on my hip, and Reaper followed, stepping out from under the water.

His gaze was so hungry, so full of fire as I squeezed the loofah over his shoulder first, lathering down his arm before going back up and across his chest. The soap ran down his body in white rivulets, outlining the hard lines of muscles before getting washed away. Jandro used another loofah to wash my back, scrubbing with luxurious pressure from the back of my neck to my ass. Reaper's lips parted as Jandro came around to the front of my chest, squeezing lather over my breasts as he ran his sponge back and forth in a slow zig-zag motion.

I had just reached Reaper's hips, circling the loofah around the base of his cock, which now jutted out, fully engorged, when he tugged me impatiently back under the water.

"You trying to make me fuckin' explode, woman?" He held my jaw and dove down with a harsh kiss, the taste of him cooled by the water running over us. Barely giving me a moment to breathe, he spun me around. "Wash Jandro now."

I leaned in to kiss my other man first, bracing my hands on his chest as I sought out those pillowy soft lips. He indulged me, his mouth as gentle and hot as the water falling over my skin. Lost in kissing him, I squeezed the loofah over his back, massaging it over his burn scars to the sexy moans rumbling from his chest.

His touch returned to my breasts, kneading and rolling while another hand pressed between my legs. I gasped into Jandro's mouth while pressing back onto Reaper's hand, hips wiggling in search of friction.

"Fuck, so wet," Reaper grunted, gliding through my folds. He brought his touch higher behind me, the firm pressure of his thumb circling my back entrance.

"Yes!" I pleaded, arching back further towards him. "Yes, I want you both."

"Climb on, *Mariposita*." Jandro bent his knees deeply and lowered, sliding his hands around to my ass.

I wrapped my legs around his waist, my arms around his shoulders, holding on tight as he straightened up.

"Reap, grab my cock and stick it in her."

"Fuck you, grab it yourself."

Jandro laughed, adjusting his grip on me. "Had to give it a shot."

I clung to him tighter as I felt his wide head nudge my sex, seeking entrance.

"Ohh, yes," we groaned together as he sank in, his hands returning to my ass.

The angle was steep, the friction delicious. I was able

to bounce on him with some assistance from his hands. My clit crashed into his body with each downstroke on his cock, and I knew my first orgasm wasn't far off.

Jandro's large hands pulled my cheeks apart as he drove me up and down, giving Reaper plenty to play with behind me.

One hand rested on my back while the other toyed with my ass. He inserted one finger and kept it still, letting me ride it while my pussy rode Jandro.

"More," I begged, stealing a glance at him over my shoulder. "I want your cock in my ass."

Reaper chuckled, his eyes fixated on watching my ass bounce. "Rude girl doesn't even say please." He inserted a second finger and spread them apart, making me gasp and whimper at the stretch.

"Too much?" Jandro nipped a kiss at my jaw, reminding me to communicate my needs.

"No...no, but I'm gonna come soon."

"Come first." Reaper sucked at my nape, rocking his fingers in and out of my hole. "And say please. Then maybe you'll get my cock in your tight little ass."

Jandro lifted me higher to fall harder, the impact sharp and my body already so full. My thighs squeezed his waist, fingers digging into his shoulders as my whole body tightened and shook with my oncoming release.

Reaper's fingers stilled in my ass, sensing me tensing up as he reached around to pull on my nipples.

"Relax and come for us," he commanded, breath hot in my ear. "You're our wife. We've got you."

The pleasure was almost unbearable, tightening like a fist in my body as I reached back with one arm to wrap around the back of his head. Our mouth crashed together in a hard, clumsy kiss.

"I love you." It came out a choked whimper, my breaths ragged with my pleasure so close to cresting.

"Fuck, I love you." Reaper supported my upper back with his chest, fingers still working in and out of my ass as his other arm banded around my chest.

Jandro crashed into me hard once, twice, three more times before my pleasure burst free. My men supported me as I shook and convulsed between them, drawing out my orgasm with kisses and affectionate words.

"Please," I whispered to Reaper, when the peak softened into a dull roar. "Please fuck my ass."

"Let's be real. You never have to say please, sugar." His voice was warm, hands gentle as he secured both of my arms around Jandro's neck. "You know I'm yours. Everything you want from me is yours."

Jandro held my thighs, Reaper spread my cheeks apart and nudged his head against my hole. He pressed in slowly, allowing me to adjust and breathe through every inch.

I rested my forehead on Jandro's, hanging onto him limply as Reaper filled me from behind.

"I love you." I scratched my blunt nails over his head, pulling more kisses from that luscious mouth.

"I know you do," he smirked, bouncing me on both of their cocks and making me cry out.

"Easy, Dro!" Reaper barked.

"It's okay, it's good," I moaned, throwing my head back as I dug into Jandro's shoulders. "Oh God, *so* good..."

Reaper's hands went to my waist, directing the movement carefully while Jandro held me strong, with no signs of fatigue. The way they both surged in and out of me was decadent, so intensely intimate as their bodies pressed and slicked against my skin.

"I love you too, *Mariposita*," Jandro moaned, bouncing me more while sucking a tender kiss on my collarbone. "Fuck, I love you so much it scares the shit out of me sometimes."

"Don't be sca—oh, fuck. Oh God, don't stop!"

Reaper moaned a low curse into my ear, driving harder into me as my muscles tightened around him. My next orgasm came without warning, clasping so hard around both of my lovers that they both cried out after me.

"Holy fuck! I gotta put you down for a sec, babe."

Jandro carefully lowered me to the shower floor, both men slipping out of me as I braced an arm against the wall. Reaper panted behind me, his hand on my hip while Jandro sucked in deep breaths, his cock still erect and pulsing.

"You good?" I shot a smirk at him.

"Yeah, just got close there," He grinned. "I didn't want to come before I got a chance in that ass."

"You up for that, sugar?" Reaper squeezed my waist with a wicked smile.

"I guess I can handle a little switcheroo," I grinned back.

"Let's switch up that water temp," Jandro panted. "I might pass out if it gets any hotter in here and I do *not* want to be in your ass if that happens."

We adjusted the temperature, soaped up all the necessary parts and rinsed off again before Reaper spun me to face him and grabbed my ass with a growl.

"Ride me, cowgirl."

I wrapped around his shoulders and jumped, landing safely in his firm grip as I locked my legs around his back. He sucked my lip in a bruising kiss, swallowing my moan as his freshly washed cock slid into me. I heard the wet sliding sounds of Jandro stroking himself behind me, and wiggled on Reaper in invitation.

"Aw, Jesus," Reaper hissed. "No wonder he almost popped off like a teenager."

"You say that like you're surprised," I teased, using my toes on the wall behind him for a bit of leverage as I rose off his length, then sank back down.

"I'm always amazed by how good you feel," he said. "And this ass is just mm!" His fingers curled into my flesh. "Top fuckin' shelf."

Jandro's soft lips touched my shoulder, the wet skin of his chest caressing my back. "You ready for me, Mariposita?"

"*Por favor,*" I begged, turning my head to kiss him.

His kiss was fast, his gaze lowering to focus on where he was about to press inside me. Slick with water and lube, his head rested at my entrance and began to press through.

"Ah!" I cried at the light sting as he pushed past the first inch. He was thicker than Reaper, but not quite as long.

"Take it easy!" Reaper chastised.

"I am, man. I'm not going any further."

"I'm good, really." I already felt so full and desperate to move, eager to feel both of my men through me again. "Bounce me, please."

Reaper raised and lowered me on him slowly, his arm muscles tight and flexed as he carefully controlled how far I went down. Jandro kept still, only caressing my waist and kissing my back while I adjusted to him.

"More," I pleaded, leaning my head back when the stinging gave way to a delightful stretch. "Please, Jandro. More."

He thrust forward, filling me with another thick inch that had me gasping.

"Sugar?" Reaper prompted, ever watchful of my limits.

"Yes, good, fuck, yeah…"

My grip on his shoulders loosened with my delirious, pleasure-babbling, leaning back on the hard support of Jandro's chest. The gorgeous man in my ass kissed me, tongue licking tenderly into my mouth as his hands swept forward over my breasts.

Reaper's grip remained steadfast on my hips, holding strong as he crashed into my pussy. The guys worked in tandem now, filling and emptying me with rough grunts and wet slaps of flesh. While every thrust was punishing, every caress was caring. They supported me between them, taking and defiling my body while answering every plea for more.

My next orgasm swept them up with me, tipping me over the edge with how they swelled and then spilled into me. Our shouts of release were distorted by the water running over us, and then only harsh breaths as we untangled and leaned our exhausted bodies against the shower wall.

Reaper stood at my back, his forehead heavy against the back of my head like he might fall asleep standing up. Jandro and I faced each other, our pants mingling as our hooded gazes met.

"Sorry we didn't get to be alone," I whispered. "Next time."

He shook his head, his grin spreading. "I know we will, but there aren't many things that can top this, *Mariposita.*"

With a quick nudge to Reaper, we all washed off for a third and final time before leaving the now-cold shower.

EIGHT

GUNNER

Governor Vance's meeting room in the City Hall building was humble compared to the grand ones I sat in at McAlister Academy, my old military college. While people like my uncle got fat and rich from their first taste of power while their citizens starved, the Four Corners governor was living lean in comparison.

Aside from when his daughter went missing, Vance wasn't suffering, but he wasn't draped in riches either. I met many politicians who were good at pretending to be humble, to be in touch with ordinary people's needs and made lofty promises to be different from all the slimy puppets before them. I often hoped that they would surprise me and actually be sincere for once. But after they got done shaking hands and delivering emotional speeches, it was always the same story in private.

Even before Horus, I had a knack for seeing things most people missed. I saw leaders lying through their teeth. I heard conversations behind closed doors that contradicted everything they said in public. Reaper was one of the few leaders consistently the same person both in public and private, which was why I chose to follow him.

Governor Vance, I started to realize, might have been another one of those rare breeds. Without the suit he wore, he would have been just another guy across the room laughing at one of Jandro's ridiculous stories.

I learned a few interesting pieces of information straight from the horse's mouth while Reaper was catching up with his dad. Like me, Vance was born into a powerful family. Bred and groomed to be a politician from a young age, thirst for power didn't come naturally to him. He was a helper, and reminded me of Mari in that sense. In his university years, his spare time was spent on projects to provide for the lowest income members of his community.

"You did better than me," I had snickered over a glass of bourbon in his office. "I did well in school, but I also partied. Hard."

"I heard the Youngbloods were known for their debaucherous ways," he chuckled.

I spread my hands in a shrug. "My reputation precedes me."

Vance ended up meeting his wife, Kyrie's mother, at one of these community projects. It was a classic opposites-attract love story. She ran herself ragged working three jobs to support her disabled parents, and had come to a food bank for assistance. He was the son of a US Senator, at the same location to volunteer, and also to keep up a positive image for his family.

"I wasn't a go-getter at that age," he said leaning

against his desk. "I was shy, nerdy." He nodded at me. "Guys like you probably would have put my head in the toilet."

"Probably," I agreed.

"But when I saw Val, I just," his eyes went misty, "I *had* to talk to her. Trust me, Gunner, I was not the type of guy to just strike up a conversation with a girl I'd never met before. I was terrified."

"Yeah, can't relate."

"But I pulled it together, introduced myself, and well," he smiled wistfully, "the rest is history, as they say."

"I'm sorry you lost her," I told him sincerely. "The thought of losing Mari, just…fuck, I can't even handle the thought."

"Thank you. Yes, I'm sorry too. Kyrie barely remembers her. And it's painful because I see so much of her mother in her. They're so much alike and our daughter has no idea." He sighed and lifted up his glass. "To our women, eh?"

That conversation told me more about Governor Vance than what he ever said in words. I watched his mannerisms—where he looked and the tone of his voice as he spoke of his daughter and late wife.

When corruption was so easy, and with no system in place to hold him accountable, I was hard-pressed to believe that a governor would ever truly act in his people's best interest. But every doubt I had since first meeting Vance slowly began to erase. He was of a different generation than us, and differing opinions would cause some friction, sure. But he was sincerely good, and that kind of person was a rare find.

I still got that timid vibe from him now that he spoke of in his office, and suspected it to be the reason why he still hadn't taken military action on Blakeworth for kidnapping his daughter. While he was taught to be a leader, it still didn't come to him innately. Luckily for him, he did the next best thing—surround himself with capable people who could advise him.

Governor Vance was hesitant to use violence, but that didn't make him a weak leader. In his interactions with Josh, General Bray, and men of his cabinet from the dinner party, he allowed none of them to steamroll over him. The man had a backbone without a thirst for blood—a rare but highly useful combination.

The more I thought about it, the more I wondered if Horus and the other gods steered us here, to give us the best chance to win against Tash.

As the last person to our meeting arrived, a gangly teenage boy in army camouflage at least two sizes too big for him, we all began to settle around the table.

"Everyone, I'd like you to meet Eduardo." General Bray clapped a hand on the teen's shoulder. "He's a newer recruit, a refugee from the Blakeworth territory. He hopes to be a general one day, so I've taken him on as a mentee. He'll be shadowing me for a while to get a sense of what I do from day-to-day."

My eyes darted around the table as everyone took their seats. Was no one else concerned about a brand-new recruit hearing sensitive information at this meeting? Only Shadow met my eyes before flicking back to the young man sitting next to Reaper's father. But Shadow was suspicious of everyone he didn't know, which didn't mean he shared my concerns. In any case, he chose not to speak up, so I filed my own thoughts away.

"Welcome, Eduardo. Thank you for coming, everyone. Have a seat, please." Vance took his place at the head of the table while everyone got settled.

It was quite the crew of faces. Me, Reaper, Jandro, and Shadow lined one side of the table. The Sons of Odin lined the other. General Bray, his recruit, and a lieutenant sat across from Governor Vance and Josh.

"You're all here because I believe you're key players in Four Corners' defense," Vance began, his palms together on the table. "Every one of you has different abilities, different strengths. I want to utilize every advantage we have to keep the territory safe and our enemies at bay. An army general is not necessarily better than a biker's sergeant-at-arms when it comes to combat."

T-Bone's jaw ticked, clearly put off by that statement for some reason as he pulled his lip between his teeth.

"Blakeworth, and evidently General Tash, have no problem using underhanded techniques for their personal gain," Vance continued. "They've taken someone from all of you, and I'm letting you know that I too, am not above using dirty tactics, as long as it's for the right reasons."

I allowed a small smile. The governor was wise to let

us and the Sons in on this meeting. Biker gangs lived and breathed dirty tactics.

"With that, gentlemen, I'll turn it over to you." Vance spread his hands. "Many of you have told me I need to go on the offensive and I listened. Now is the time to start forming a plan of attack."

"If I may, sir." General Bray was the first to speak up, as expected. All eyes turned to the man who looked like Reaper's twin aged by about twenty years. "We're getting more and more refugees from neighboring territories by the day. Blakeworth and New Ireland have much bigger populations than us, but their numbers *are* decreasing. Many of the younger men are enlisting with the army if they're in good health, but that's maybe thirty percent of our refugees. Thinking long-term, we'll need to expand our border to make room for the population."

"Any expansion toward Blakeworth or New Ireland, they'll see as an attack," I pointed out.

"Right. So we need to take care of the problem first. In the meantime, I think we should set up field hospitals just outside our borders, roughly five or ten miles or so. People are dropping dead out there, so we'll save lives and boost our numbers for the long-term."

"Do we have enough medics for field hospitals?" Josh pinched his forehead as he scribbled down notes on a legal pad.

"I'm not sure, but Dr. Brooks and his staff are training them as fast as they can."

"Mari says they have about a half dozen trained

combat medics ready, not including herself," Reaper added.

"For an army of roughly a thousand? That's stretching 'em thin," I remarked.

"Not for the army," General Bray corrected. "Not at first. This is just to provide aid to the refugees. And show our neighboring territories that their refugees will get the care they need from us."

"I don't like the idea of field hospitals out there in the open," Dyno piped up. "Who's to say Blake or Tash won't give the order to just blow 'em up?"

"Because *they* will have the option of using them too," Bray said. "The medics and their tents won't have any flags or insignia that show loyalty to Four Corners. It will be there for medical services to anyone who needs it."

"What's this gotta do with an attack plan?" Jandro asked. "I get that you're thinking of growing the army and helping those in need, but what's the first strike? Is it gonna be us, or are we gonna wait for them?"

"We need to send scouts," I said. "The best scouts you have, General, that have the lowest probability of getting captured. Tash has had this advantage on us because we've been blind. We don't know his numbers, what kind of artillery he's packing, nothing. The very first thing we need is information. Then we can plan an attack."

"I agree with that," General Bray nodded at me, and damn if my ego wasn't stroked a little. He was basically my father-in-law, and since my own dad was a colossal piece of shit, that validation from Bray felt good.

"I'm sure you and I can offer some assistance with that, captain." T-Bone nodded at me from across the table.

I smiled openly. Our birds had become inseparable in recent weeks. Even just Horus would be a huge advantage to the scouts with his eyesight, but with him and the raven Munin working together, we could use even fewer humans on the ground and thus put fewer lives at risk.

"We'll talk later, sergeant," I agreed, then swept my gaze between Bray and Vance. "I assume you have topographical maps? Maybe aerial photographs of this region? We'll need a lay of the land before sending people in."

Josh and Bray's lieutenant retrieved maps and laid them out on the table. We poured over them for the next two hours, mainly the Four Corners natives explaining the geography to us who were unfamiliar. By the end of the meeting, my brain was thoroughly muddled and I craved a stiff drink. The work wasn't over, though. T-Bone and I would have to discuss where to fly our birds to oversee the scouts. I borrowed a map and told the Sons I'd meet with them back at the bar where they were holed up.

"Hey, thanks for being here. Gunner, is it?" I turned to find Reaper's dad, General Bray, holding his hand out with a friendly smile.

"Yeah. Uh, thanks for having me." I shook his hand. "Sir." I cringed at my awkward delivery, stuck somewhere between familiar and formal.

He was a general, deserving of respect. My school

background demanded that I salute him, but no one around here seemed to bother with formalities. In any case, I had never been an enlisted soldier, despite my education. I lived outside the law now, and in that sense, not even a general was above me. And the fact that he was my president's father added another layer of complexity that I wasn't sure how to handle.

The general just continued to smile as he returned the pressure of my handshake before withdrawing his hand. "You bring up important points and I like the way you think. Looking forward to the next meeting, captain."

"Same here, sir. Thank you."

With a curt nod, he filed out of the room, his lieutenant and new recruit stepping out after him. The teenage kid stared at me with big, empty eyes and I narrowed mine in return. Something was off about him. I'd have to remember to check him out through Horus at some point.

"Hey, Gun." Reaper clapped a hand down on my shoulder, the two of us the last ones in the room. "I gotta tell you something, and I don't want you to be upset."

"What?" I sighed. "The Sons are waiting on me."

My president seemed nervous, a rare look for him. "We're having breakfast at my parents' house tomorrow, so they can meet Mari and, you know, get together as a family and shit."

"Cool, I won't hit the booze too hard tonight," I said absently. "Just let me know when we're riding out."

"Um, that's the thing." Reaper sucked in a breath.

"We don't want to overwhelm my mom with too many people because she's grieving Daren. Don't want to put too much pressure on her as a hostess, you know?"

"Oh, that's cool. I get it. So what, it's just you, Mari, and Noelle then? With the rest of the introductions to be made later?"

"Well." He looked more and more uncomfortable with each passing moment. "Jandro is coming too, because my folks knew him from back then. He's like another son, you see. And Noelle is dead-set on bringing Larkan, even though I tried my damndest to talk her out of it."

The pieces finally clicked into place. "So *I'm* the only one excluded?"

"No, Shadow's not coming either. And we're not excluding you, it's just—"

"Shadrow isn't even Mari's," I cut in, my annoyance itching.

Reaper rolled his eyes. "We all know he's going to be, so might as well treat him like he is."

"Does your dad even know you share her with me?"

"Yes," Reaper insisted. "You *are* part of my family, Gunner. He wants to get to know you. It's just a lot of people at once, okay? I promise you that's the only reason."

"Okay, so when? When can it be just us three and Mari with them?"

Reaper spread his hands out and raised his shoulders in a shrug. "I dunno. How does next week sound?"

"Works great." I still sounded bitter but didn't care. Shit like this was why I didn't want to get involved with this group thing in the first place. Not that I regretted sharing Mari, I actually loved it. But it fucking sucked I had to be the odd one out because of logistical reasons.

"For what it's worth," Reaper fished out his cigarettes and offered me one as we left the building together, "Mari's pissed on your behalf."

"Is she now?" Despite myself, I smiled into my first drag.

"She says you have more of a right to be there than Lark, which is absolutely true. But try telling fuckin' Noelle that."

"Fuckin' families, man." I straddled my bike and made her roar to life, wishing I was going home to my woman instead of talking more battle tactics with dudes.

"I hear ya," Reaper sympathized, sitting astride his own bike as he zipped his jacket up to his chin. "In some ways, you're lucky you don't talk to yours anymore."

"Yeah. I'll see ya later." I pulled out of the lot and rumbled down the road.

He wasn't wrong about that. Leaving the Young-blood life was the best decision I ever made, next to choosing Mari. The Steel Demons had been the only real family I ever had.

I had fended for myself for years and didn't need parents as an adult. Mine had been utterly useless at parenting when I was a child, anyway.

While Reaper's upbringing was far from perfect, he did have the kind of family I always envied. His parents seemed to have a love like my grandparents did, like what I hoped Mari and I had. Something that would withstand the years, growing stronger, deeper over time, rather than fading away.

So it stung, feeling cut out, despite Reaper assuring me that it wasn't the case.

I had to hold on to what mattered—that Mari loved me. She was my wife too, and nothing changed that.

NINE

MARIPOSA

Gunner came to bed late that night, long after Jandro and Reaper started snoring. When I asked about where he was, Reaper muttered something about discussing strategy with the Sons of Odin.

I didn't think much of it. My own day had been a long one at the hospital, demonstrating field medic techniques to trainees. Reaper, Jandro, Shadow, and I all had dinner together, and while it was nice to see Shadow feeling naturally included among my men, Gunner's presence was noticeably absent.

My guys didn't seem worried, so I tried not to dwell on it. But after Shadow and I kissed goodnight, and we went to our separate rooms, the bed somehow felt extra empty with only three people in it.

I couldn't sleep a wink, but a sigh of relief left me as I heard Gunner's motorcycle pull up outside. He entered the bedroom with the sounds of someone who was drunk enough to be clumsy, but not stumbling and sloppy.

Thankfully he had enough coordination to undress and slip into the open spot in bed quietly. I rolled over immediately, nuzzling into his skin that was still cool from the night air.

"Where have you been?" I whispered, dragging lazy kisses over his chest and throat.

"Baby girl," he sighed, wrapping around me. "I love you."

"I love you too." My hands slid around to his back, rubbing up and down to warm him.

"Were you really pissed about me not coming to breakfast tomorrow?" He mumbled the words out, lips moving on my forehead.

I sighed deeply, resting my head on his shoulder. "Yes, love. I wish you could be there. Reap's still trying to talk Noelle into bringing Larkan another time."

Gunner let out a soft noise, sounding relieved as he squeezed me tighter. "I knew you would never shut me out."

"Never, love." I kissed him more insistently, finding his lips in the darkness. "I want all of my men with me. But it's not my house or my rules." My fingers stroked the locks of hair falling down his back. "I'm actually really nervous. And I know you being there would make me feel better."

"I love being with you." His voice grew sleepier and more mumbly every time he spoke. "You make me feel like I matter. I must've told T-Bone that like twenty times, but he kept pouring me shots so it wasn't my fault."

I grinned, unable to hold back my chuckle at his

confession. "You do matter, love. So much." I pressed a kiss to his Adam's apple. "You keep me safe." A kiss under his chin. "You make my fears disappear." A kiss to his lips. "You make me the strongest version of myself."

He didn't reply, but his chest rose and fell with the steady, even breaths of sleep. Smiling, I turned in his arms and settled on my side.

"THERE YOU ARE, looking all dolled-up and sexy."

I smiled at Gunner's reflection in the vanity mirror, leaning against the door jam with his forearm raised above his head.

"Is it too sexy for the in-laws?" I pulled at the neckline of my dress, hoping it wasn't so low that it was inappropriate.

"Nah." Gunner took a few steps into the room, blue eyes following the lines of my backside. "Not anywhere close."

"And how long have you been spying on me?" I closed my compact and started putting my makeup away.

"Long enough. I like watching you get all made up." He moved the hair draped against my upper back, caressing my neck as he dropped a kiss to my head. "Not that you need it."

"I'm just nervous," I admitted, reaching back for his hand. "Scared shitless, if I'm going to be completely honest."

"For shit's sake, why?" He ran both hands over my

neck and shoulders now, massaging the nerves right out of my muscles. "They'll love you, baby girl. As much as we do."

"It's been years since I've met the parents of a guy I'm with, and it's never been as serious as my *husband's* parents. Holy shit, they're already my in-laws!"

"Relax." Gunner's lips rested in my hair, his hands sweeping luxuriously over my shoulders and upper back.

"I wish you were coming," I sighed, melting under his touch.

"Mm." He pressed another kiss into my hair. "You've got this in the bag, you don't need me. Reap's already talked you up a ton to his dad. I bet they're excited to meet their daughter-in-law."

"That scares me even more," I groaned. "What if I don't live up to the hype?"

"It's not hype, it's truth." His hands came over the front of my shoulders, smoothing down my chest and tracing the edges of my dress. "What do I gotta do to make you believe me, huh?"

His touch dipped inside my neckline, a warm palm finding my breast and pulling a gasp from my mouth. "Gunner…"

"What do I gotta do?" he groaned, lowering his mouth to my ear as his other hand wandered down the side of my hip, pulling the fabric up my thighs. "To make you see how perfect you are for all of us?"

"Gun." I turned my head, catching his hungry mouth as it searched for a kiss. There went my lipstick. "Love, I'd love to, but we'll be late."

"Will you?" he challenged, nipping at my lips. "Or will you just be on time instead of early?"

"Reap and Jandro are waiting—"

"Let them wait." He squeezed my nipple between his thumb and forefinger, the other hand diving between my legs to spread them apart. "You're my wife too."

That statement shouldn't have the effect on me that it did, a rising swell of heat and pride that had me grinning and arching against the chair back, angling my head for another kiss. I knew it already, but to hear it from him with such a possessive growl was something else entirely.

Gunner's tongue dove in, claiming my mouth in his little victory as his hand released my breast to settle on the front of my throat. "Stand up," he ordered.

I rose from the chair, bracing my hands against the vanity while he moved the chair out of the way, then slammed the full length of his body against my backside.

"Gun!" I gasped at the heat of his erection pressing against my ass. My breath was short with his hand on my neck, my pulse firing up with anticipation.

"Fuck, you're the sexiest little thing," he groaned, hiking my dress up to my waist. "How do you expect me to control myself around you?" He spanked and groped my ass, grinding his cock against me.

"When did you get so dirty?" I looked at him over my shoulder, catching a rough kiss as he groped my breasts under my dress again.

"Dunno," he laughed, dragging his teeth along my upper back. "When I was fucking your pretty little ass, maybe. You turned me to the dark side."

"As bad as your timing is, I like it." I pressed back against him, rubbing against his jeans in hopes he'd get out of them soon.

"Oh yeah? Let's see."

His grip returned to my neck, holding me firmly while his other hand dipped inside my panties. I squirmed and whined, the heel of his palm grinding against my clit while the rest of his hand stroked and teased between my thighs.

"That's my dirty baby girl." He removed his hand and delivered a wet slap to my ass. "Nice and soaked for me."

"Please, Gunner." I reached back, fumbling for his zipper, only to have both arms held behind my back.

"You want this?" His thrust pressed my thighs against the vanity, rough denim rubbing my ass while his hungry eyes stared at me in the mirror.

"Gun—"

"Or should I make you wait?" He sucked at my earlobe, teeth nipping at me. "Leave you craving me while you're smiling all pretty for your in-laws, huh?"

"Now," I squeaked, wriggling in his hold to grind my ass against his length. "Please, I want you now."

"Fuck yeah. That's my girl." He left a wet kiss on my neck, pulling lightly at my skin. "I'm gonna let you go, but keep your hands where they are."

I nodded, my teeth sinking into my lip as the heat of his hand left my wrists. The sound of his zipper pulling down made me bite harder, a whimper escaping me as his cock fell out and landed on my ass with a soft slap.

"I was gonna bind your hands together with my belt,

but *damn*." Hard flesh skimmed over my ass as Gunner leaned back and admired the view. "I like seeing you hold together all nice and obedient for me."

"I can't stay like this the whole time you fuck me," I protested.

"Ah, there's my girl." His hand came around to hold my jaw. "There's her fire. Just do the best you can for me, huh?"

He pulled back, letting his length fall down the globes of my ass until it nestled between my legs. Then he pulled my panties aside, thick cock meeting my tender sex.

"Ride me," he instructed. "Rub yourself on me."

"Gun, I need you inside me."

"Not yet, babe. Just ride that pussy over me first."

I tilted my hips and leaned back, gliding my wetness and sensitive flesh along the top of his shaft. Going forward, I could almost get his head inside me without touching, but not quite. My hand made a slight motion down, just a reflex, and Gunner's strong grip immediately came around my wrists.

"Nope. None of that baby girl," he chastised with a soft laugh. "You do as I say, or I do it for you."

Holding me in place, he did exactly that, gliding his cock back and forth against my sex without penetrating. Wetness coated my thighs and each roll of his head against my clit was unbearable without that thickness inside me.

"Huh," he mused, all calm and collected while I writhed in his grip. "I think you like it better when I do it. Guess I should leave the punishment stuff to Reaper."

"This *is* punishment," I whined.

My worst fear in that moment was him actually making good on his threat to make me wait, to send me off all frustrated and wanting to Reaper's parents.

"Think your dear husband will punish you for making him late?" Gunner taunted, hips driving against my ass. "You think everyone at the breakfast table will be able to smell how wet you are?"

"Gunner, *please!*" I lifted onto my tiptoes, squeezed my thighs, angled my hips— everything I could to fill the empty ache with my limited movement, but he was having none of it. His head met the threshold of my entrance, but he pulled back before I could sink onto him.

"Bad girl," he cooed, sounding too pleased to be truly reprimanding me. "You really want to be defiled before your nice, wholesome meal with your in-laws, huh?"

"I just want *you.*" I leaned my head back on his shoulder, aiming my lips for his neck and cheek. Maybe switching up tactics would get him to stop messing with me and put that thing where it belonged. "Please, love." His pulse thrummed under my mouth and I peppered more kisses along the length of his neck. "I want to be thinking of you while I'm with them. I want to be sore, spent. I want to feel *you* inside my body hours after you're done fucking me."

The shift from bratty to seductive worked. Gunner groaned, hips stuttering as he released my wrists to dig his fingers into my waist. He ended up bunching my dress in his fist as he *finally* aligned himself with my entrance. Using my dress like reins, he pulled me back as he surged forward.

"Fuck!"

The force of him entering me sent me jolting, palms slapping down on the vanity. I looked in the mirror to see him staring down at where we conjoined, lip pulling between his teeth, my dress balled up in his hand at my lower back. He lifted his gaze, meeting my eyes in the mirror as he pulled out, then sank back in.

"Yesss, Gunner," I hissed, pressing back with his pulls of my dress.

"Fuck, this is the best fucking view," he growled, palming the side of my ass with his free hand.

His thrusts were short, hips barely moving compared to the long pulls of me back and forth on his cock. I was raised on my tiptoes, holding the edge of the vanity counter for support as I rocked along his length.

"So fucking good," he murmured, eyes flicking up to the mirror and down to me riding his length. "My girl is so fucking pretty."

I found myself pressing back harder, eager for his satisfaction and praise as he filled me. Each stroke of him inside me chased a need just outside of my reach. Desperate whimpers left my lips as the smacks of my ass on his hips grew louder, faster.

"Oh yeah, that's it," he said in a choked growl. His hand slackened around my dress until the fabric drifted freely. He shoved it up my back to keep his view, before his grip hooked around my waist.

"Oh, fuck!"

I held on to the vanity for dear life, fighting to catch a breath as he pounded me. The force of his cock stretched and hit new depths inside me, pleasure shooting like lightning up my spine as my legs turned to liquid.

I collapsed forward, chest on the counter and Gunner's heavy hand splayed in the center of my back when I tried to lift up again.

"That's it, baby girl," he panted, swatting my ass once without missing a beat of his punishing thrusts. "Just bend over and take it."

"Oh God, don't stop," I moaned, letting the vanity support my upper body while he crashed into me relentlessly from behind. This new, dirty side of Gunner was refreshing, shocking, and utterly hot. Knowing my sweet, golden man had a rough side had me wet since the moment he came up behind me.

He always put me first and sought to please me above all else. Not even when he fucked my ass did he let himself get carried away. Every step of the way, he was considerate and careful. Now he was using my body, staking his claim on me. Being selfish. And I loved every rough moment of it.

"Gun," I whimpered, the slaps of flesh nearly drowning out my voice. "I'm gonna come soon."

"Fuck, I'm right there with you, baby." He crashed into me harder, faster, the pleasure white-hot and blinding. "Come on my cock, my sweet little wife."

The way he fucked me drove me to the edge, but his words were the tipping point. I convulsed from head to toe, thrashing to release the pleasure he'd been stoking in me since his first dirty word.

Gunner's hands slapped to the vanity on either side of me with a heavy groan, stroking through the aftershocks as he spilled warmth inside me.

He withdrew from me too soon, sliding my panties back into place and straightening my dress back down over my legs. Ever the gentleman, he pulled me up gently from the counter, straightening the top of my dress and smoothing out my hair with a cheeky grin.

"You good?" he asked with a wicked gleam in his eye.

"Uh, yeah. I think so." My legs were still wobbly, but I could walk without making a total fool of myself.

The grin remained plastered on his face as he threaded his fingers through mine and led me out of the room and to the lobby of the B&B. Jandro and Reaper looked up from the armchairs where they waited.

"You ready?" Reaper grunted.

"Yeah." I was still trying to catch my breath.

Gunner turned to me and placed a slow, smoldering kiss on my cheek. "Have a good morning with the in-laws, baby girl."

MARIPOSA

Reaper's green gaze burned into me as I stepped off the front porch, my legs just as steady as a newborn deer despite my effort to keep cool.

"Goddamn Gunner," my husband swore as he threw a leg over his bike. "Get on. We're gonna be late."

Jandro just snickered, shaking his head as he eased his ride back onto the street.

My mouth wanted to form the word *sorry* on impulse, but I had no true desire to say it. I wasn't sorry in the least. If anything, I was grateful. Gunner had thoroughly fucked the nerves right out of me, leaving me with a relaxed buzz and laid back confidence.

I shuddered at the vibration of Reaper's bike underneath me, my flesh still tender and sensitive.

"Swear to fuck, sugar, if you come on my seat on the way over there…"

"What?" I pressed when he trailed off, squeezing around his waist.

"I'll have to pull over and fuck you on the side of the road, that's what."

"And ruin my dress right before I meet your parents? You wouldn't dare."

"Try me."

"Hey!" Jandro waved his arms. "Are we goin' or what?"

Reaper pulled up alongside him, and I fought the urge to grind into the vibrations and bumps in the road. Tempting as his threat was, I really didn't need to look like we stopped for a roadside quickie. At least Gunner had left me looking mostly presentable.

"Where's Noelle and Larkan?" I yelled in my husband's ear.

"She left early to help them set up," he answered. "Finally came to her senses and left her boy toy behind."

"Well, that's good." Hopefully that would make Gunner feel a little less left out. In the same breath, I slapped Reaper's arm. "When are you gonna patch him in so they can be official? The Blakeworth mission was over a week ago."

He gave me a sideways glance over his shoulder. "That's a conversation for another day, sugar."

I dropped it, keeping silent until we pulled up to a charming ranch-style home. It didn't look brand-new, so must have been one of the few structures left undamaged after the Collapse.

Reaper parked next to Noelle's dirt bike in the driveway, and Jandro next to him. "Need help with those?" I asked, climbing out of Reaper's seat to lean over Jandro's saddlebags.

"Nope." His tone was cheerful as he removed many layers of blankets and padding to reach the gift we brought. "Safe as can be. I got it, babe."

Reaper took my hand, positioning me in the middle as we approached the front door. "Don't be nervous," he said with a brush of his lips to my temple.

I wasn't, until he said that.

He raised his fist to knock and I pulled in a breath, trying to channel Gunner's easy confidence and the strength he saw in me.

Noelle opened the door, a drink resembling a bloody Mary already in her hand. "Finally you all made it. I thought my breakfast was gonna be a liquid diet."

"Nice to see you've been useful," Reaper teased as he led us inside.

"You're *hilarious*, brother." Noelle closed the door after us and waved us through. "They're in the den, we've got a fire going. Looking cute, Mari! Guess the cold's not gettin' to you, huh?"

I only had a leather jacket on over my dress and bare legs. Gunner had left me so flushed and satisfied, I didn't even notice the cold.

"Guess not," I said sheepishly, following her down the hall.

We came to a room filled with cozy warmth, the air thick with aromatic spices. Low couches and armchairs were filled with blankets and pillows. A coffee bar looked especially inviting next to a roaring fire with a cast-iron kettle set inside the flames. Rising from their seats were a beautiful couple in their fifties, one of which was the woman from the jeweler's table downtown.

"Oh my…Rory!" She practically flew at Reaper, and would have slid to the floor had he not swept her up in a tight hug.

"It's me, Ma," he said in an awed whisper. "I'm really here."

She released him slowly, hands skimming over his clothes and face in disbelief before turning to the man at his side. "And is this Jandro? My little *Jandrito*?"

"Hey, Mama Lis," he grinned, wrapping her in a loose hug. "You're still as beautiful as I remember."

While Reaper's mother fawned over the two men, his father turned to me. His face was strikingly similar to his son's, except for brown eyes instead of green, and the white hair that dominated the few remaining dark strands. Finn Daley was also powerfully built, clearly in fantastic shape for a man his age. I guess he had to be, after a long career in the Air Force and now as a general.

"It's a pleasure to finally meet you, Mariposa," he said kindly with a warm smile. Right away I noticed he smiled more easily than his son, with no hint of Reaper's signature scowl.

"Call me Mari, please," I returned. "And the pleasure is mine. Thank you for inviting me to your home."

Reaper's mother turned to me at that point. "Hello again." She smiled sweetly, only her green eyes showing traces of sadness as she reached out for my hands. "So I was right, your husband does have excellent taste."

"In jewelry, at least," I laughed humbly. "I'm so glad to meet you properly, Alisa."

"You're welcome to call me Lis, sweetheart." Her

warmth felt genuine, filling the ache I felt over missing my own mother.

"You have a beautiful home, Lis," I said. "And you raised amazing people. Reap—uh, Rory and Noelle have been wonderful to me."

"Well, I certainly can't take credit for the last decade," she laughed, the sound a little forced. "But my goodness, I can't tell you how happy I am to see two of my children alive and well, and even in love!"

"What are the odds?" I smiled back, the pang of longing returning in my chest for a moment before I shoved it down.

"Finn, honey?" Lis looked at her husband. "Will you pour some coffee for Mari and the boys?"

"Mari, yes. The *boys* can get their own," he smirked, turning to the coffee bar. "How do you take yours, Mari?"

"Black, thank you."

"A woman after my own heart," he said, pouring from the French press into a clean cup.

Lis swatted his arm. "Oh stop flirting, she's married."

"So am I." He smacked a kiss on his wife's cheek before handing over my cup.

"Thank you. Habits of being a combat medic die hard," I said, cradling the drink in my hands.

"The Air Force was similar, I imagine. Always had to guzzle the caffeine, then get up and go." Finn squeezed the sides of Lis' waist, gently steering her toward the hallway. "Should we head to the table? I'm starvin', hon."

"Yes, but I'll need your help plating up the food." She kissed him quickly over her shoulder and let him guide her down the hallway.

Their affection was heartwarming, especially after knowing what they'd been through, and how long they had been together.

"We brought eggs," Jandro said, following them into the kitchen with Reaper, Noelle, and I trailing after. "Freshly laid from my girls."

Lis opened the carton he handed to her and gasped softly. "Ooh, these are beautiful." She ran her hands over the assorted colors of shells. "Thank you, Jandro. I didn't take you for a farmer."

"Me neither, but I guess a lot of unexpected stuff happened over the years." His fingers twirled around mine, bringing my palm up to his lips for a brief kiss.

I smiled at him before shooting a glance at Reaper, who was simply beaming at us. While I knew logically his parents had no issues with me having other men, I still didn't want to be inappropriate. Should I pay more attention to Reaper on principle? Or did the fact that they considered Jandro another son nullify that?

"Sit, everyone. Please," Finn said. "Make yourselves at home."

"Can I help with anything?" I asked, remembering my manners.

"Absolutely not." Lis smiled at me from the counter as she chopped fragrant cilantro.

"Mari, do you prefer savory or sweet crepes?" Finn hovered over the small stove with a dish towel over his shoulder, carefully pouring batter into a pan.

"Savory, please."

"Excellent choice," he smiled.

I nursed my coffee at the table while our hosts prepared breakfast. Reaper and Jandro accepted bloody Marys from Noelle, who evidently was quite the mixologist. She and her mother both had cheery expressions on, but there was no mistaking how tired they looked. Lis had just learned of her youngest son Daren's death, and Noelle, her father Carter's.

The mood was light and easygoing while the family talked, so I chose not to bring up condolences. When Noelle sat next to me, I rubbed and squeezed her hand in sympathy. She met my eyes and mouthed, "Thank you." Her lips wobbled only a little before taking another sip of her drink.

"So, Mari." Finn washed his hands and dried them on a dish towel. "How did you have the misfortune of meeting my son?" He shoved Reaper's head playfully, earning a grunt and a narrow-eyed glare.

I bit back my laugh with a smile. His playfulness reminded me more of Jandro than his birth son.

"We had stopped by the same service center in Old Phoenix," I said. "I, uh, provided some medical services there. When my work was done, I didn't have any specific destination in mind. So when his club was leaving, I went with them."

It wasn't a *complete* lie, just an omission of the killing and kidnapping details. Reaper seemed amused by my version of events, sending a lopsided smile my way.

"We heard about the Steel Demons all the way up in Nevada," Finn said as he began setting plates in front of us. "I always knew my boy loved his motorcycles, but never thought he'd become this mythical vigilante figure."

"Admit it. You're proud." Reaper smirked.

His father sat down, holding his thumb and forefinger close to each other in front of his face. "Just a tiny bit."

"So Mari, if you don't mind me asking," Lis said once everyone was seated with a plate of food. "How strange did you feel about taking multiple husbands? Or was it not strange at all?"

Reaper's hand came to rest on my knee under the table, squeezing encouragingly. "It took some getting used to," I answered. "But Re—uh, Rory, was really patient with me and talked me through it. I think what surprised me most was how normal and *right* it felt."

"That's what I hear the most from others." She smiled across the table at me before sliding a glance to her daughter next to me. "Nellie never really saw the perks, and still doesn't, from what I hear."

Noelle huffed, swallowing down her crepe with a slurp of her drink. "Larkan's still just a prospect," she glared daggers at her brother, "and it already scares me to death, all the crazy shit they make him do. I can't imagine being in Mari's position and worrying about *four* of these dicks. I'll drop dead from a heart attack tomorrow."

"Regardless, I'm glad you're happy, dear. I'm excited to meet him." Lis' gaze returned to me. "And the rest of yours, Mari? How long have you been with that man from the market?"

"Oh, Shadow and I are still newly seeing each other," I said, a light fluttering traveling up my body at the reminder of him. "We're taking things a bit slowly, getting to know each other."

"Jandro found him." Reaper cocked his head at his best friend on the other side of him. "The guy was in much worse shape back then. He's a different person now."

"Yeah." Jandro finished chewing his food and wiped his mouth with a napkin. "I did a little bit, got him into the club and all that, but it was Mari that made him come out of his shell by leaps and bounds."

Reaper's parents listened with fascination to the story of Shadow, the heavily censored one that Jandro knew anyway. He didn't betray any personal details like his nightmares or offer speculation on his scars. Everything he said was warm and respectful, as if talking about any other absent friend who'd overcome hardships. Reaper nodded with agreement at certain points in the story and added in his own anecdotes. I was proud and moved by my men, loving their camaraderie and complete lack of jealousy.

"He sounds lucky to have found all of you," Finn observed. "I met a lot of traumatized guys in the Air Force, and the camp where we were held." He looked at his wife, reaching for her hand. "It would be weeks, sometimes months where we couldn't see each other in that place, but I held on knowing Lis was nearby. I feel for everyone who had to suffer alone."

"That kid you brought to the meeting yesterday," Reaper piped up. "He must have a hell of a story. I didn't expect you to bring a new recruit to discuss tactics."

"Eduardo." His father nodded. "Yeah he's a runaway from Blakeworth. Said his family was going to be publicly executed for stealing winter coats, can you believe it? Their police force came to collect the family members, and they shoved him out the back door and told him to run. He got out of the city and was able to hide on a produce truck heading south. Four Corners was a speck in the distance when he hopped off, but he made a break for it and couldn't have ended up in a better place."

"Execution for stealing coats?" Lis repeated, aghast. "I bet they already have a foot of snow up there. Are they really so cruel to people in need?"

"Probably worse than you're imagining," I said. "The people in power up there are awful. Anyone considered lower class is just treated so horribly. I saw it firsthand."

"Ah yes, the daring rescue mission." Finn smiled at me. "You'll have Governor Vance in your debt forever now. The poor man was going nuts at the thought of losing Kyrie. That was the one time he begged me to invade, but the mere whiff of a neighboring army would send Blakeworth into full retaliation mode. I'm glad it was successful as a covert mission."

"Can you blame him though?" Lis asked. "That's his *only* child. If I had known about Daren—" Tears immediately filled her eyes, a shaking hand flying to her mouth. "I'm sorry, I—"

Finn scooted his chair directly next to hers, wrapped

a muscular arm around his wife's shoulders and pressed kisses into her temple. "It's okay, hon. My fault for bringing it up." He rubbed soothingly up and down her arms as she cried softly into his shoulder. "We all miss him."

Reaper lowered his gaze to the table, leaning into me slightly as I rubbed his back. "I wish I'd been able to meet him," I offered softly to the grieving family. "And your other husbands too, Lis. I wish I could've…"

Been there to prevent their deaths, were the words I chose not to speak. I could have given Daren the correct antiviral. I could have set Carter's leg and given him antibiotics. Because their deaths were preventable with the right medical care, it was more than tragic. It was criminal that people lost family members to issues that were so easily treatable.

Reaper's fingers clasped around mine,and he brushed a kiss along my forehead much like his father was doing to his mother. "I know you would've saved them, sugar. And I love you for it. Just knowing that gives me so much peace."

"Still." I leaned my forehead on his cheek. "I hate that you lost them. Hate that your family's been hurt so much."

"There's nothing we can do." Lis sniffed and wiped her eyes, leaning away from her husband as she regained composure. "But continue living, honoring and remembering them."

"Cheers to that." Noelle too had shed a few silent tears and wiped her eyes as she raised her glass.

"To Carter, Daren, and Nolan, who we lost too soon

to cancer," Finn toasted with his coffee cup. "But at least he passed before seeing how crazy and shitty this world turned out to be."

Lis nodded in agreement, then we all toasted and took a drink silently for their dead loved ones. I thought briefly of my parents again, but dismissed the idea of toasting to them too.

Who knew if my mom and dad had ever reunited, but if they'd died, I had a sneaking suspicion that I would know. The cat always at my side made no mention of seeing them, and until she told me herself, I would continue to hope.

MARIPOSA

Breakfast at Reaper's parents' continued with lightheartedness and good cheer. We ended up staying well past lunchtime, the conversations going on and on until my cheeks hurt from smiling so much. It wasn't an unpleasant time, but I didn't realize until we got back on the bikes how drained I was. The moment we pulled up to the B&B, I hopped off and headed for the backyard.

"Where you off to, sugar?" Reaper called after me.

"I'm just going to hang out with the chickens for a bit." But really, anyone who'd give me a bit of space and not ask a million questions would do. Chickens just seemed like the perfect creatures for the job.

"Okay, but don't leave the B&B," Reaper said. "Not without one of us."

"I know," I huffed with more annoyance than I intended. Maybe it was him being overprotective that was getting under my skin more than anything else. Ever since his dream from Daren, it felt like I could never be alone anymore.

While I escaped the chatter of the B&B, heading for the patio furniture near the coop, Freyja darted off in the opposite direction of the yard.

Shadow must be out here. He could usually be found working out when he didn't have anything else going on. The guys had cobbled together quite the collection of old weights, tires, and various other equipment to exercise with.

It took all of five minutes of sitting and watching chickens peck the ground for me to decide that Shadow was the one person I didn't want space from. As much as I tried to avoid staring, I could still see him across the yard, doing his best to work out with Freyja winding herself around his ankles.

But did he want space from *me*? He was remarkably easy going whenever we were together, affectionate and warm without being overbearing. If I didn't know any better, I never would have believed he'd never been in a relationship before. He took everything in stride, even when I left him to spend time with my other men. And now it was me wondering if I should go over and see him, or if that would be too much.

Fuck it. My cat has no shame, why should I?

Getting up from my chair, I meandered that way slowly, trying to look casual and not like I was intent on invading Shadow's personal space. Which was exactly what I *wanted* to do, especially right then as he laid back and bench pressed a rusted barbell with concrete plates.

I am too thirsty for my own good. Just his breaths and

grunts of effort heated me from inside out. The hard edges of his body, muscles coiling and stretching with his presses, pulled my gaze until I could no longer pretend to casually wander. It was almost a shame no woman had ever truly appreciated that body.

No one except me.

"Watch out, kitten. Coming up."

With a soft chirp, Freyja walked from her seat on Shadow's stomach to his thigh. She balanced on his leg as he rolled upright.

"Hey." Looking up to find me there, he braced one arm on his knee, panting slightly as he pet Freyja with the other hand. "Thought you might be near if the cat was."

"She's usually a good indication of that," I said.

Shadow had tied his hair back in a messy bun that was either hit-or-miss in terms of how good it looked on men. Unfortunately for my thirst, I'd never seen it look better than on him or Gunner. A few strands came loose, falling over his face as he looked down to pet Freyja.

"Here, kitten. You can have my bench." He picked her up gingerly as he stood, then placed her back down where he'd been reclined before, grabbing his T-shirt.

"You don't have to stop on my account." A feeble protest as I watched beautiful lines of scars disappear under black fabric.

"I was just finishing up," he mumbled, gaze turned away as he rolled the shirt down his torso. "How was breakfast?"

"It was good. Just...a lot."

"A lot?" He moved closer to me, straightening his shirt over his body.

"Yeah, a bit emotionally heavy as we took time to remember Daren and Reaper's other father. After that, it was a lot of...smiling and answering questions about my life. Being polite and engaging and sweet, so I can impress these people I've never met before." I let out a sheepish laugh, bringing a palm to my face. "I don't know if I'm making any sense, but I haven't had to do that in a long time and it was exhausting."

"I think I know what you mean." Shadow moved closer to me, close enough to touch but his arms stayed frustratingly at his sides. "I felt like that at the governor's dinner. It was why I dipped out early. Socializing feels like a performance sometimes and it's draining."

"Yes, that's exactly it." I turned to him, wanting to slide my arms around his tapered waist and rest my head on that solid chest. "Reaper's parents are lovely, and I enjoyed meeting them. It was just a big morning and I need to unwind from it all."

Shadow tilted his head slightly, like he was pondering something. "Do you want me to leave you alone?"

"No." I shook my head unashamedly. "I don't."

His face brightened as he reached for me, a tentative touch on my waist that I happily leaned into until his whole palm rested on my side. My hand came to his wrist, stroking lightly up his scarred forearm. His small smile was warm, eyes downcast and shy.

"Do you want to go for a ride?" He leaned down,

lips brushing my forehead. "I promise I won't talk much."

I looked up grinning, swimming in the elation of how light and easy things were between us.

"I'd love that," I said, reaching up on tiptoes for a kiss. "And you can talk to me however little or much you like. I never feel exhausted from you."

His mouth pressed indulgently to mine, sensual even as he pulled away, lips hovering. "Same here," he purred. The hand on my waist squeezed gently. "Let me grab a quick shower first."

I will if you let me come in there with you.

Rather than say that, I bit my tongue and reluctantly stepped out of his touch. "Okay, I'll change into riding gear."

As we made for our separate rooms, I wondered how many cold showers I'd need to stop becoming a drooling, panting mess around him.

No less than a hundred, to be sure.

———

I DIDN'T ASK Shadow where he was taking us, nor did he opt to tell me. I wanted to be surprised by the place he chose, without any expectations. This time I sat behind him as we rode out of the city, hugging around his chest as Four Corners' construction projects gave way to wilderness.

The environment out here couldn't seem to decide if it wanted to be desert or forest. Copses of evergreen trees contrasted against bright red and orange sedimentary rock. We were in that in-between area between the Southwest and what was once middle America. I was too young to really know what different parts of the United States were like, back when things were better. All I'd ever known was a culture conflict and ever-increasing tension.

The majestic mountains of Colorado and breath-taking coastline of the Pacific Northwest sounded like bygone fairy tales, as did the party beaches in Florida and rich history of the eastern seaboard.

For better or worse, we were making new history. One that I hoped places like Four Corners would remain a stronghold of, a place to tell the story of Reaper's parents and countless others who escaped unthinkable situations.

Like Shadow.

I rested my cheek on his back patch, squeezing tighter around him while my other hand idly stroked his chest. He still hadn't told me the full extent of what happened to him, the source of the scars lingering on his body and his mind. The biggest clues I got were how he regressed when I tried to cut the arrows from his back after our Blakeworth mission. It broke my heart seeing him so afraid, and knowing some people out there got away with treating him so cruelly.

Curious as I was, I'd never put my own desire for that knowledge above his comfort with me. The most effective way to treat an injury started with knowing what caused it in the first place. If that knowledge wasn't available, I had to do the best I could with what I did know.

Shadow thrived with openness and acceptance. He sought affection and care when he felt safe and not afraid of being judged or punished. I might not have known all the details of his trauma, but I knew enough to foster his healing. I knew not to hold blades near him, and that kissing and touching him in public made him feel more confident. He hadn't tried to hide his scarred eye once since we had our lunch date.

"We're here," he said over the roar of his engine with a light squeeze of my hand.

He pulled to a stop under a large oak tree, dappled sunlight speckling over a grassy knoll just beyond it. Some wild lilies lined the clearing, bright orange speckled flowers like small lamps against the lush, dark greens.

"Oh, Shadow, this is beautiful!" I climbed off of the bike before he had a chance to lift me off. "How did you find this place?"

"Just riding during some free time the other day." He shrugged. "It's quiet. A nice place to be alone."

My whole body lit up at his thoughtfulness. A smile split my face as I reached up to kiss him. "You knew exactly what I needed. Thank you for bringing me here."

"I, um..." He trailed off to kiss me some more, planting sweet pecks on my lips as we shuffled our way to a sunny area.

"You what?" I held on to his forearm, placing a kiss on his shoulder while we found a dry patch of grass to sit.

"I was going to say..." He paused as we sank down

together to the ground, eyes shyly cast away. "That I wouldn't share this place with anyone else."

I love you.

The words rang out like a bell in my head and formed a heaviness in my throat. Holy shit, I did. I was in love with Shadow, from every beautiful scar on his skin to the pure goodness in his heart. But my lips remained stubbornly, if even fearfully, sealed. I had to take this at his pace, to not overwhelm him with experiences and feelings that were still new to him.

"You're sweet," I chose to tell him instead, sitting across his legs so I could rest my head on his shoulder.

"You've told me that a few times," he murmured, placing a hand on my knees while the other slid across my back.

Because I'm too chicken shit to tell you I love you.

"Because it's true."

I brought a hand to his cheek, caressing his bearded jaw and cheekbone while staring at his full lips. Fuck, did he have a scar there too?

My thumb ran over the puckered tissue on his bottom lip as he closed the ever-shrinking distance between our mouths. Thick arms pulled me closer, wrapping me in safety as our kisses grew deeper. Lips and tongues pressed insistently, losing their finesse and growing clumsy with desire.

I love you. I want you so bad, my head screamed as Shadow moaned softly into my mouth, his fingers curling into the fabric of my shirt. *Please, make love to me out here. It's beautiful, it's perfect. You're perfect.*

But his hands and kisses never strayed. It occurred to

me that he might not know how to escalate, given that his experience was limited to transactional sex and making out with me. When we slowed for a breath, I opted to try something new.

I dragged my lips across his cheek, pausing to kiss his scar before pushing his hair back and continuing to his neck.

"Oh! Fuck, that's..."

Shadow's reaction was instant and more satisfying than I could have predicted. Smiling against his pulse, I kissed his neck again, making a small trail from the corner of his jaw to his shoulder as he squirmed.

"That," he groaned again, shuddering under my lips. "Why does that feel so good?"

Fuck, he was so cute. I could not stop grinning against his skin.

"The neck is an erogenous zone for many people," I explained.

"What does that mean?"

"It means," I said, pulling back, "it's a non-sexual body part that you derive sexual pleasure from." I ran a light touch along the side I'd just been kissing. "The blood flow here makes the area especially sensitive."

"I see," he mused, the idea already forming behind his eyes as he pushed my hair behind my shoulder. "Is it an erogenous zone for you?"

"It is." I bit the inside of my cheek to keep my grin in check.

He leaned in slowly, with a few small moments of hesitation, as if waiting for me to stop him. Like that would ever happen. I tilted my head back, baring my neck like those girls in old TV shows asking for vampire bites.

Shadow's lips landed on my neck with a tickling softness, making light presses with a closed mouth like when I first showed him how to kiss.

"Yes, like that," I encouraged him, leaning in. "That feels nice."

His kisses grew bolder, quickly finding how easy it was to suck at a person's neck.

"Hold on, not too hard," I laughed, pulling away. "You don't want to leave hickies."

"Oh no? What are those?" His eyes were bright and curious, staring at my neck like he couldn't wait to take another bite out of me.

What the hell? I wanted him and was feeling bold. Nearly a week of seeing each other and we just got to the necking stage, so I wasn't likely to see his dick anytime soon. Still, I might be able to claim him another way.

I grabbed the front of his shirt in my fist, pulling it down to expose the top of his chest. His gaze remained curious and lightly amused as I pressed my lips just below the hollow of his throat.

"Ah." He let out a small noise of surprise as I sucked hard at his flesh.

"That," I said, pulling back to admire my work, "is a hickey."

He pulled the edge of his shirt down to look at the dark red mark I left on his skin, then stared at me with wide eyes.

"That hurt a little."

"Oh, I'm sorry." I frowned. I should have realized he might not want a bruise on his chest. "It'll fade, and probably faster with some ice—"

"No, it's okay. But I mean it hurt, Mari. I *felt* it."

It took me a moment, then my mouth fell open at the comprehension of what he was saying. "You felt pain?"

"Yes! It felt...sharp. A little hot, although that could have just been your mouth—" His lips clamped shut, a blush rising up his neck.

"And..." I studied his face, trying to get a read on his emotional state. "Are you okay, now that you've felt that?"

"Yeah, just surprised really. I haven't physically felt anything like that in so long. Only during my nightmares, but...it's different." His expression turned playful, a smile twitching on his lips. "Do you think you could do that again?"

"Give you another hickey?" I laughed. "For scientific purposes?"

"Yes." His voice lowered with a light caress to my hip. "Purely for scientific reasons."

"Anything in the name of science." I pecked his lips once before mouthing my way under his chin, taking indulgent nibbles and leaving a trail of kisses down his neck until I reached the space between his collarbones.

"Do it harder," he urged, holding his T-shirt out of the way for me. "Try to make it hurt me."

I giggled at the innuendo in his request before I latched on just below the first mark I made. This time I held his flesh in my teeth, pulling with my lips and lashing with my tongue until my own mouth started to hurt.

"Wow," I remarked, pulling away. "That might be one for the record books."

It was roughly the size of a golf ball, a mottled, dark reddish-purple monstrosity surrounded by more red skin.

"I don't understand it." Shadow released his T-shirt and rubbed at the spot. "It hurt but...it also felt good." He shot me a worried glance. "What does that mean?"

"Maybe your brain has never associated pain with pleasure before." I folded my legs and returned to leaning against his shoulder. "So you've blocked it off when you know the intention is to cause you harm, but the pathway associating it with something pleasurable hasn't been explored until now." I shrugged. "Again, not a neurologist. Just a theory."

"But is that normal?" he asked. "To...enjoy pain?"

"Yes, completely normal." I kissed his cheek, my hand searching for his to hold and reassure him. "It's different for everyone. Some people like a little pain, others a lot. Some not at all."

Shadow's thumbs rubbed back and forth pensively over my hands and wrists. "I think I might like a little. Only from you. And I—" He stopped himself, pausing to think about his words some more. "Even if you liked it, I don't think I could ever bring myself to hurt you."

Why I hadn't melted into a liquid state by then was completely unknown to me. This sweet, beautiful man was just too much.

"I do like a little bit of pain too, sometimes." I

propped my chin on his shoulder. "But not all the time. And when I do want it, I can usually get it from Reaper." I stroked Shadow's rough cheek, nudging my mouth toward his. "I like what you and I have."

"I do too." He sighed contentedly, lips skimming over mine.

"And I love—" *you* "—that you can talk to me about what you like. That's important."

His arms came around me, heavy and strong as he pulled me into his chest. "What I like most is just being with you."

My whole damn body couldn't stop fluttering. How could a man with zero relationship experience know the exact words to make me fall so hard?

I knew from Shadow there was no pretense, no flattery or attempt to be charming. He was just telling me what he honestly felt. And it was me, the one with now *four* partners, who didn't have the courage to spit out my true feelings.

Kissing seemed to get the point across well enough, so I let my eyes fall shut and just tasted him. The man knew how to feel out a kiss, and matched my slow, lazy pace, just savoring and tasting.

"Do we ever have to leave?" I whispered, lips pulsing and bruised.

"Eventually," he hummed. "But not right now."

The sunlight had become harsh, almost uncomfortably warm. Being pressed up against a hot man might have had something to do with it too.

"Give me a second. I need to cool off," I told Shadow, scooting away to take off my leather jacket.

"It did get hot," he observed, tugging at the neckline of his shirt.

"This weather is nuts. It was snowing just the other day." I scooted toward a shadier patch of grass and stretched my legs out, crossing them at the ankles while I leaned back on my elbows. My T-shirt had ridden up, exposing a few inches of midriff, but not to the point where I cared. I was sweating there anyway.

"That, um." Shadow was making an adorable attempt to not stare at my body. "That shirt looks familiar."

"I stole it from Jandro, I think." I pulled the fabric straight to get a clear view of the design, now faded and cracked with age. "Looks like an early version of the club logo."

"It is." Shadow sounded pleased. "I screen-printed those shirts years ago. I remember now."

"Oh yeah? I love this shirt. It's my second favorite, next to your hoodie."

Shadow smiled, a rare full one that lit up his whole face. He opened his mouth, then promptly shut it, the smile gone.

"What?"

"Nothing." He averted his gaze.

"You looked like you were gonna say something."

"I was going to ask you a question, but never mind."

"Now you've got me curious." I rolled to my side, propping my head up on my hand. "What is it?"

"Seriously, nothing. Just something dumb that popped into my head."

"*Shadowww*," I whined, letting my head flop down to the grass. "I want to know. Please?"

"I, um." He sighed and raked a hand back through his hair, looking everywhere but at me. "I was going to ask if I could...draw you."

My mouth fell open. "*Draw* me?"

"Yeah, but—"

"Shadow, I would love that!"

Finally, he looked at me again. "You would?"

"Yes, are you kidding? I can't imagine anything more flattering." I grinned hard. "My tattoo artist boyfriend *drawing* me? I'd love nothing more. Did you bring supplies?"

"I always keep a sketch pad and some pencils on my bike," he said. "You really want me to?"

"Yes, if you do." I rolled to my stomach, kicking my feet up. "I can be flash art in your future tattoo shop."

"I don't know about that," he growled, rising to his feet. "A drawing of you on a wall for everyone to see? I'd rather keep you to myself."

I giggled to myself while he got what he needed from his bike. While he was one of the most stoic and easygoing of my men, I liked that small bite of possessiveness too.

"How do you want me to pose?" I asked when he settled back on the grass with the sketch pad on his knee.

"I think, like you were before," he said, his gaze on me now studying and inquisitive. "Lying back on your elbows, ankles crossed. Yes, like that. Can you stay there for a few minutes?"

"No problem," I grinned, glancing down at my still-uncovered belly. "Want me to fix the shirt?"

"No, leave it." He glanced up from his paper with a smirk, the pencil in hand already sweeping across the page.

"Where do you want me to look?"

"Keep looking at me like that."

I was hoping he'd say that. He was fascinating to watch. His gaze was technical, focused, but everything about this was extremely intimate.

Sometimes his eyes would meet mine before returning to his page. Other times he glanced at my body, his hand making long, sweeping movements. Sometimes he made small, fast marks, never erasing anything. I could only imagine how he was capturing me and itched to see it when he was done.

This drawing would be a rare glimpse from Shadow's perspective, I realized. The tattoos he did were a reflection of his clients, but this drawing would be a reflection of *him*. I wanted so badly to know how he saw me.

Neither of us spoke. I didn't dare break the magic of watching him work, and it was over far too quickly.

"It's rough, but I think it's done," he said, straightening up. "I'll clean it up when we get back."

"Can I see?" I was already scooting toward him on the grass, spinning to sit next to him for a peek. "Oh, Shadow!" I gasped.

He drew me in a pin-up style, not quite cartoony, but not entirely lifelike either. The face was definitely me, the nose and lips exactly like mine, eyes large and looking straight at the observer with a coy smile. He redesigned the T-shirt into a crop top, intentionally showing off some belly with killer waist and hip proportions that I wished were real. Legs stretched out long and shapely, hugged by form-fitting jeans with rips in the knees, just like my real ones.

"She's so cute!" I squeaked. "And sexy. She belongs in a magazine."

"*She* is you," he said with a soft laugh on my cheek. "Do you like it?"

"I love it. If this is rough, I can't imagine what cleaning it up will look like."

"It's just me being a perfectionist," he said. "It'll look even better when I add shading and stuff."

My hands wrapped around his bicep, hugging his massive arm. "Aren't you glad I made you tell me?"

"Yes," he chuckled, lips finding mine again. "I am."

TWELVE

JANDRO

The chickens were making their way into the coop for the night when I heard the rumble of Shadow's bike returning with my *Mariposita*.

I rubbed a hand over my head, chicken logistics blurring in my brain. We had a total of nine as of yesterday. This morning I found three more freshly hatched chicks under a mother hen. Damn Foghorn was getting busy.

With the colder weather up here, I'd have to look into some heat lamps that wouldn't hurt the birds or catch the whole coop on fire. If the eggs kept hatching faster than I could collect them, I might even have to make a brooder and bring the smallest ones inside when winter got really cold.

Who the hell was I? Vice president of a biker gang and a chicken farmer? If someone told me a year ago this was what I'd be doing, I would have laughed my ass off.

The bike engine cut off, then Mari and Shadow's

footsteps walked through the B&B. Their voices were low, meant only for each other. I listened for the direction of Mari's footsteps as Shadow went to his room, wondering if she still wanted space or would join me outside.

Moments later the rickety back door opened, and my smiling woman crossed the patio to me.

"Someone looks happy." I patted my thigh in an invitation for her to sit.

She parked that cute ass on my leg and wrapped her arms around my shoulders, kissing me deep and hungry, like she missed me.

"Where are the others?" she asked in a soft whisper.

"Out drinkin'." I laced my hands over her hip. "Honestly, I was a little over-socialized from this morning too. Don't blame you for having a little getaway."

"Really?" Her forehead dropped to mine. "I'm not neglecting you?"

"Not for a moment." I took a nibble of her plump lower lip. "Although I would like to take over your next riding lesson."

"Deal," she grinned. "You can show me how to take a bike apart and put it back together too."

"That'll take a bit longer than learning how to ride but," I swatted her hip, "I'm happy to show you what's in my toolbox."

"Don't make this sound like a weird porno," she laughed, slapping my chest.

"Why not? It's the perfect setting for it." The

thought of her covered in grease and digging into an engine with me *did* turn me on like nothing else.

"Only in your mind," she teased, fingers swirling with delicious pressure into my neck.

"Fine. I think I'm partial to shower sex anyway." I slid my hands up her back, rubbing into areas I knew would be sore from the ride. "So what were you and Shadow-man up to?"

"Not much, really. Just a ride out to a private place to sit and talk."

She was nervous. Fidgeting. Clearly holding something back.

"Yeah?" I pressed. "That's all?"

Her fingers worked idly at the edges of my cut. I felt her heartbeat speed up through my palm on her back, but stayed patient in waiting for her answer.

"I love him, Jandro."

The relief whooshed out of me in a long breath that became a laugh. "Well, I was expecting much worse. Did you tell him?"

"No." Her eyebrows knitted together, her bottom lip pulling between her teeth. "I don't want to overwhelm him with…you know, intense feelings while he's still getting used to this."

"He's not overwhelmed by you," I said. "Fuck, I'd bet Foghorn's sperm that he's in love with you too."

"But he's never felt like that before, right? What if it freaks him out?"

"He can be a big boy and get through it like the rest of us. Remember, he's got us to lean on too."

She relaxed with that assurance, leaning heavily

against me. "Please be there for him. I know you all have your manly pride or whatever, but I want him to know he has someone besides me."

"He always has me, although he doesn't need me like he used to. My boy's grown up." I scratched my head with a laugh. "Fuck, we've all been so busy running around, I just realized we haven't really talked much in the last few days."

"Talk to him," she urged. "Spend tomorrow with him."

"And what if I have plans?"

"I think you can skip cuddling the chickens and yelling at Foghorn for one day."

"I do *not* cuddle them! It's called checking for parasites, I'll have you know."

"If you say so, *guapito*." Her smile brushed my cheek. "You're the best, you know that?"

"Eh, I figure I can place in the top four." I stood up with a groan, keeping her legs wrapped around me. "You want to wait for the others or turn in now?"

"Let's go in." She kissed me deeply, palms cupping my neck. "Can we eat dinner in bed?"

"Hm, Reaper's not gonna like that." I nudged the side door open with my foot as I proceeded to carry her inside.

"Good thing he's not here." Her lips quirked. "We finally got our alone time."

"Perfect," I sighed against her mouth, carrying her through the doorway of our room. "So that means I get dinner *and* dessert all to myself."

———

IT DIDN'T TAKE MUCH CONVINCING to get Shadow to hang out the next day. I invited him to come with me and Larkan to the garage we were borrowing to do our maintenance and repairs. He accepted with his usual grunt, the only change was his insistence to kiss Mari goodbye before she left for the hospital. The big dude joined our lineup in seeing her off like he'd always belonged.

Reaper was taking her today, shooting down her pleas to drive with surly growls that turned down her beautiful smile.

"Just let her, Reap. She needs to learn," I urged.

"Nah, later," he grunted, easing the bike onto the road. "Too much traffic through the city in the morning."

"I did fine with Gunner the other day," she protested.

"Do I look like fucking Gunner? I said no."

"You and me then, *Mariposita*," I reminded her. "We'll do a lesson when you have a free afternoon."

She nodded, setting her chin on the back of Reaper's shoulder with a pout as they rode away. I watched them until they turned the corner, trying to figure out this weird sensation in my gut. Reaper was overprotective on a good day but he seemed over the top with it lately, even for him..

I shook it off, figuring it had to do with war planning and having more at stake now, knowing that his family was here. Clapping Shadow on the shoulder, I headed for our steeds. "You ready, dude?"

"Yeah." He followed me, tying his hair back to keep the wind out of it.

That was new. Every passing day, he seemed to hide his face less and less.

Larkan came up a minute after us, after struggling to release himself from Noelle clinging to him on the front porch. We pulled up to the garage ten minutes later, parking in front of the spare bay that Dave, the owner, let us work out of.

Our prospect was in a surly mood from the get-go, barely saying a word to me while throwing tools around carelessly and grumbling to himself as he worked. Shadow was being a much better helper than him just by replacing a few tires.

"Quit throwing your tantrum like a bitch and spit it out already," I told Larkan from where I lay on a creeper.

"If I do, you'll tell Reaper, so no thanks, I'm good." He proceeded to crank loudly with his socket wrench in a way that would surely strip the bolt.

"Hey, stop." I rolled out from under the bike I was working on and sat up. "What's this about? Your patch?"

"Yeah, my fuckin' patch!" he huffed, throwing the tool on the ground. "I risked my life to protect his old lady, and what do I get? Jack fuckin' shit."

"You'll get your damn patch, man," I sighed. "I hear your frustration, but we have more important shit to deal with right now, like preparing for war."

"I know, but—" He ran a grease-covered hand through his hair, leaving black streaks at his temples. "I wanna marry Noelle before shit gets bad. Set her up in case something happens to me, you know?"

"She'll be fine with or without you," I said. "As the president's sister, she does have some power even if she's not an officer."

"It's not just that, though. Like, I also just want to do it while we still can."

"I hear you, man. I do." I wiped my hands on a rag. "I'll talk to him. See what I can do."

Larkan's jaw dropped and I entertained the thought of shoving the rag into his mouth. "You will?"

"Yeah, but don't expect much. Mariposa has the most sway over him, and I know she's been advocating for you. In all likelihood, he genuinely has too much on his plate to think about club shit right now."

"Hey, a bug in his ear is more than what I could ask for." He picked up his socket wrench, a new ease in his movements as he got back to work. "Thanks, Jandro."

"Yeah, well Shadow and I owe you for that mission too."

Larkan laughed lightly. "Man, if you could be patched in twice, Shadow sure as fuck deserves that. I still cringe thinking about when they got you with those harpoons, dude."

"I didn't feel it," Shadow answered nonchalantly as he carried two tires to stack against the wall.

"Not even when you got sick?"

"Oh, I felt all of that." Shadow's hand drifted over

his stomach as if recalling the nausea and feverish symptoms. "Mariposa made it not so bad, though."

I ducked my head to hide my grin, turning to grab another tool. I didn't even need eyes to see that Shadow was completely in love with her. It was pretty fucking cute how they were both utterly terrified of telling the other how they felt.

"Here's what I want to know." Larkan flipped a wrench in midair. "How'd they fucking hit you? Whenever you come up in conversation, someone always mentions how you're untouchable in a fight."

"They were long-range weapons." Shadow shrugged like the answer was obvious. "It's true, I'm untouchable in close combat. But a sniper can hit me from a distance if I'm dealing with something else up close."

I paused in my work to listen. This was probably the most I'd ever heard him talk to someone he wasn't close to.

"How'd you get to be so good at the close combat stuff?" Larkan asked, his curiosity about the big guy thoroughly piqued.

Shadow bristled, a sign that the real answer was uncomfortable for him. But he humored the prospect anyway. "Having to watch out for myself in prison. I also trained myself to listen for people approaching when I was young."

"You gotta teach me some of that one day." With that, Larkan refocused on his work, the conversation finished in his mind.

Shadow apparently wasn't done yet.

The big dude finished stacking tires and approached

the prospect with his hands spread out to his sides. And that look on his face…was he *smiling*?

"Grab a wrench and come at me," he offered. "Here. I'll turn around."

He spun to face the other direction, Larkan glancing at me with a cocked eyebrow. I shrugged and beckoned him to proceed, knowing Shadow would be clued in immediately if he heard any sound.

Deciding to go along with it, the prospect picked up a small wrench to act as a dagger. He stalked up behind Shadow like a cat, careful to not make any noise. But the scarred assassin saw him coming like he had eyes in the back of his head.

Larkan thrust the weapon forward, aiming for a kidney. It was the smart move, rather than swinging high for his head and leaving his body exposed. But it was also exactly what Shadow expected him to do.

At the last possible moment, Shadow pivoted, turning his body in the same direction as Larkan's jab. The prospect's momentum sent him stumbling forward into nothing, giving ample room for Shadow to grab the back of his cut and wrap the other arm around his throat.

"Do a short jab if you're gonna hit me there." Shadow patted his back and released him. "Keep your arm bent and close to your body, so if I hear you coming, you can still get me in the gut or between the ribs." He turned his back to Larkan a second time. "Try again."

"Shank him like an inmate," I hollered. "Short, fast jabs."

The two of them danced around in mock combat for another half hour, leaving me to work alone while I watched and heckled. Not that I minded. Seeing Shadow step up to mentor the prospect blasted beyond my expectations, even after seeing all the strides he'd made in the past weeks.

When the day came to a close and we rode out to the bar, I wondered how many drinks he'd need to loosen his tongue about Mari, or if he'd come right out and spill his guts to me.

"So how are things going?" I asked when we got settled in, me with a beer and him with whiskey.

His brow creased, already suspicious at my digging. "Fine, I guess. Why?"

"Sure, dude," I laughed after taking a long swallow. "You spend the whole afternoon on a romantic getaway and things are just *fine, you guess?*"

Shadow's face relaxed, that smile starting to appear that looked odd on his face at first, but actually suited him. "In that regard, things are good. I think." He pulled down a hefty mouthful of his drink. "They'd probably be even better if I could stop overthinking shit and just relax."

"Believe it or not, that's normal," I said. "I guarantee you, every time a person has started seeing someone they're crazy about, they go nuts with the overthinking."

"You too?" he asked.

"Me, Reaper, *and* Gunner. Fuck, I bet even the Sons felt like that way back in the beginning. They weren't always the cuddly shits they are now. Trust me, dude. It gets easier."

Shadow huffed out a soft laugh. "When I'm not stressing about what to say, or whether or not I should touch her, it *is* easy." He shifted in his barstool, like he was seeking out a touch that wasn't there. "I can be myself and she...*likes* that."

"That's when you know you've got a good thing." I drained the rest of my beer, swatting him on the arm with a grin. "I'm happy for you, man. I had my concerns at first, seeing as she's mine too and all. But I should've known you'd be just fine. You got nothin' to worry about."

I signaled for another drink, sitting back while the bartender poured it for me. My suspicions were confirmed that I'd have nothing to report to Mari. Shadow was just as crazy-nervous-excited about her as she was about him. And that was up to them to navigate. The other guys and I would be here to support them, but it wasn't our job to meddle. Mari and Shadow had to establish their own relationship first, and then we could work him into the bigger group dynamic when he was ready.

At my side, the big guy was clearly deep in his head again, folding and spreading his hands on the bar in front of his drink.

"What now?" I asked him after a few moments of watching.

He sighed, shoving his empty glass away and shaking his head no when the bartender offered him another.

"I don't want to fuck this up, Jandro."

"Well, you can't possibly fuck it up worse than Reaper or Gunner already have," I chuckled. "And she's still with them, 'cause she's a damn angel."

"I should have listened to you before," he went on, rubbing at a spot on his chest.

"Care to be more specific?"

"You know, when…" His face darkened with the flush creeping up his neck. "Back when you were trying to tell me about how to please a woman."

"Oh, that. Yeah, that's up there in the top five, no top *three*, things you should've paid more attention to in Jandro's Life University."

He laughed, an increasingly common sound from him. "One of those life lessons I never thought I'd actually use. But when we were together yesterday—" He stopped abruptly until I nodded at him to continue. "I think she wanted to go further, and I do too, I just…my mind went blank on how to go about it."

"Holy shit, Shadow." I propped my elbow on the bar, rubbing my forehead as I tried to contain my laughter from echoing throughout the whole building.

"What?"

"Nothing, you're just a cute kid in a big, scary dude's body. In any case, you're in luck." I composed myself and let my hand fall to the bartop. "Mari knows you're inexperienced. She's also a big girl who knows how to use her words." I gave him a pointed look. "Talk to her. Invite her to tell you what she wants. Tell her what you want, and let her decide if she's up for it or not. Don't get stuck in your head, dude. She'll want to please you too."

"She already does," he sighed, his gaze drifting as he focused on some memory. "She doesn't even need to do anything."

"Alright, that's it. I'm drawing the line there." I slammed my second beer down and drew a line across my throat, signaling to the bartender that we were done.

Shadow stared at me, puzzled. "What?"

"Too fucking cute. I can't handle that shit." I punched him in the shoulder, making sure he saw my grin as we rose up from the barstools and headed out front to our bikes.

THIRTEEN

REAPER

"Oh really, now? You've protected my son and daughter-in-law, have you?"

Hades stretched out across my dad's lap, nudging his head into his hand for more petting. Dad laughed, looking very un-general-like sitting on the floor with his legs stretched out in front of him and rubbing my dog's belly. Already eager to be a doting grandpa, he pulled some strings with the building security to let Hades into the City Hall building.

"Yes, you did. That's what a good boy does," he continued as if they were having a conversation. What I would give to see the look on his face if Hades really did answer him.

But the ancient god seemed to lay dormant, only the goofy, drooling mutt with us now. Dad and I were in the City Hall conference room again, waiting for the governor to show up so we could brief him on the scouting missions we set into place.

"Will Vance have a heart attack if he sees his general

sitting on the floor?" I remarked from where I leaned over the maps spread out on the table.

"Nah, I've crawled around with his treasurer's grandson before. Can't do it too often though. These old knees quit before I do." Hades rolled off his lap and shook his fur out while Dad climbed to his feet with a groan, grabbing a chair for support.

"How's Mom doin'?" I asked absently, scanning the maps for the routes we established.

"She's alright. You know, hangin' in." He came up next to me and slugged my arm. "You oughta come over more and see her yourself. Noelle's been there a couple times in the last week, but your mom misses her son." Dad gave me a pointed stare. "You're the only boy she's got left."

"Yeah, I know," I sighed. "It's just…" My sentence trailed off, no words coming to me in a believable way. I didn't want to leave Mari out of my sight for even a moment because of what Daren had told me in that dream.

As days passed with nothing happening, my anxiety over it worsened rather than getting better. I felt like I'd been holding my breath for a week and a half, and the moment I let it out, disaster would strike. It was affecting my daily interactions with her and others. I knew I was snapping more, even more short-fused than I usually was. Every time I left her at the hospital or at home with the other guys, I wondered if it would be the last time I saw her. I stared at every door I passed by like a maniac, wondering if it was *that* door, the one I had to break down.

I felt like I was losing it, breaking down every word of Daren's warning in my head hundreds of times. Looking at the faces of the people I surrounded myself with and wondering if they would be the one I had to kill.

"I can understand never wanting to leave that gorgeous wife of yours," Dad chuckled sympathetically. "But she has other men. She'll understand you spending time with family you haven't seen in over a decade."

His voice just got lost in the chatter in my head. I didn't know what to listen to, what was real and what I should ignore. And of course, every time I asked Hades or Freyja to throw me a bone, they stayed completely silent.

Whatever was about to play out, the gods had no interest in interfering. And normally that would have been fine. I did well enough before they came around. But it was the urgency, the understated panic in Daren's voice saying, *she'll die if you don't,* that scared me more than anything. I'd sacrifice anything—a limb, my sight, my sanity, even my life, for the peace of mind of knowing that Mari would be okay.

When faced with a difficult decision, I always had some inkling of what to do. Sometimes I had to ride to clear my head, or just observe in silence what my instincts were trying to tell me. But the correct action was always there, always made clear once I stripped away all the distractions.

This time? I just felt like a compass needle spinning madly, pulled equally in all directions.

Governor Vance entered the room then, trailed by

Josh, bringing my shattered focus back to the meeting at hand. Hades rolled to his belly, stubby tail wagging and puppy eyes on point at the two men who just entered.

"Oh my—shit." Josh startled at the sight of him. "I always forget how big your dog is, Reaper."

"He's friendly," I said with an incline of my head. "You can pet him."

"Maybe later." He gave Hades a wide berth, circling around to the opposite end of the table.

"Come on now, Josh. You're making the poor beast sad." Vance put on a brave face, but I could see his nervousness as he bent down to lightly stroke Hades' head. He got a more vigorous tail-wagging and lick of his fingers for his effort.

"He knows who his allies are." I smirked.

"Smart," Vance praised, scratching him more boldly before glancing up at me. "Is it true he runs alongside your bike for hundreds of miles?"

"Dobermans are athletic dogs. They have good endurance," I answered casually before returning my focus to the maps. "Shall we get started?"

"Please." Vance took his seat next to Josh, folding his hands while he waited for me to begin.

"We've decided on three main points that would provide enough cover for scouts around General Tash's territory." I pointed to the markers on the map. "Because there's a lot of flat ground between here and there, we are recommending sending them through these valleys and canyons. It'll add time to the mission but will prevent them from being seen. T-Bone and Gunner will send their trained birds to assist as well.

"What exactly do these birds do?" Josh peered over his glasses, his hand paused in his note-taking.

"They've been trained to give certain signals if they see certain movements or groupings of people," I said coolly. "We'll teach all the signals to the scouts."

"And what about Blakeworth?" Vance's eyes narrowed at the territory a few hundred miles north.

"It'll be easier to get into, because their focus is on flashing how rich they are, not military tactics." My dad took over, stepping up next to me. "They'll be more alert since Kyrie's rescue, but our scouts heading there can use the same strategy as the Sons did. It'll be as simple as dressing like one of their elite and faking documents."

"You're sure that'll work a second time?" Vance sounded skeptical.

"They'll be checking at every entry-point into the city, but they're an extremely superficial people," Dad said with more than a hint of sneer. "As long as our guys look and act entitled enough, they should get away with it. It's those who appear to be poorer that they're going to take a closer look at."

The door opened and I caught a flash of Eduardo's camo uniform in my peripheral vision. My dad beckoned him over as I continued with the presentation. "Now, we should carry out these missions roughly two weeks apar—"

His life is yours to take.

The once-comfortable room temperature dropped to an icy chill, making every hair on my body stand up. Stunned, I looked at Hades. The dog's whole body was tensed with alertness, his nose pointed directly at my dad's young recruit.

The god had awoken.

"What?" I whispered, fear and confusion locking up my limbs.

Reap what has been sown. His life is yours to take.

"Ah, Reaper?" Vance and Josh peered at me, the puzzlement on their faces a clear indication they didn't feel the cold heaviness of this god's command. "Are you alright?"

My gaze shifted to Eduardo, the skinny teenager staring back at me blankly.

You will carry out my command, came the voice of Hades. *Take his life. Now.*

"What the fuck?" I said numbly, fully aware that I appeared to be talking to myself like a maniac. "Him? He's just a kid—"

You are a human instrument and you do not question me. You obey. Reap. Him. Now.

"He hasn't even done anything! Why would you—"

Eduardo moved faster than I could blink. I only saw the silver flash of a blade before he buried it in my father's gut.

My dad wheezed, his breath laced with pain as he clutched his stomach, eyes wide with disbelief.

"No—"

Either from shock or disbelief at what was happening, I moved too slow. And Eduardo, too fast.

Sharp pain sliced through my ribs, blooming out from a central point as the blood spilled over my palm and fingers. Eduardo's eyes, right in front of mine, were empty, soulless, his face devoid of any emotion as he withdrew the knife from where he had stabbed me.

"Help!" Josh yelled. "Protect the governor! Where is security?"

My knees buckled, head already swimming as I saw Josh scramble over the table to shield the governor from getting stabbed. Eduardo jumped on the conference table, boots stomping over our maps as he walked across the surface and slashed down.

The blade caught across Josh's forearm as he held it up to shield his face, his cry full of fear. My vision blurred, something solid hitting me, which I realized was the floor. Blood soaked my hands and clothes, staining the floor and filling my nose with the smell of copper. Dad had fallen too, his blurry form leaning against the wall with his hands pressed over his wound.

No, not like this, I pleaded. *We cannot go out like this.*

I heard the sounds of a struggle, punches and groans and cries of pain. Blurs of movement flew over the long table, Josh and Eduardo locked in a fight, wrestling for their lives.

"Reaper, do something!" Josh sounded like he was underwater. "He dropped the knife but I can't—agh!"

A thump and Josh went silent, his body eerily still as it draped over Eduardo's. I couldn't see the governor, fuck I could barely see shit. My arm felt like a sack of bricks as I fumbled for my holster, finding sweet purchase on the grip of my handgun.

Eduardo was too busy shoving Josh's lifeless form off of him and the table, sending the governor's assistant to crumble onto the floor in an awkward position. The fucking traitor dared to glance at me and smirk before jumping off the table and landing on his feet like a cat.

I didn't move, worried I'd be too slow and he'd stab me again before I could pull the trigger. My dad's panicked breaths against the opposite wall began to slow and I prayed it wasn't too late. I needed this fucker to turn his back on me, to write me off as good as dead.

I took a painful, rattling breath and coughed, letting the blood from my lungs coat my lips and tongue.

Looking pathetic and close to death did the trick. Eduardo snorted derisively, turned around and lowered to his hands and knees. He began crawling his way under the table, where the governor had hid.

"No, no! Please!"

My arm was so fucking heavy and couldn't stop shaking. Each breath felt like another hundred small knives in my lungs. My vision was going dark and I could barely make out the shapes in the room. There was a very real chance I could accidentally hit the governor if my shots went wide. But it was a chance I had to take.

I raised my gun, willing my arm to be steady and the fuzzy shapes in front of me to sharpen into focus. The governor was about to lose his life and I couldn't afford to wait for a miracle. So, pointing under the table, I used the last of my strength to aim and pull the trigger.

A cry of pain rang out. It didn't sound like the governor's so I kept shooting. I emptied my gun, shooting half-blind until my ammo ran out and my arm fell like a concrete block to the floor.

Hades had been silent and uninvolved through the

whole exchange. The black dog just stood off to the side, watching, as if waiting for his chance to step in and escort a new batch of souls to the underworld.

He came over to me after I stopped shooting, while I hung between alertness and unconsciousness. While my surroundings had gone blurry from pain and blood loss, his face in front of mine was the only thing in razor-sharp focus.

You will not hesitate on my command again. When I give the order, you will *obey.*

MARIPOSA

"If you don't have a scalpel out in the field, use anything you can find with a sharp edge," I said to the small group of new medics. "A pocket knife will do, even a shard of glass can get the job done. But you *must* have some way to sterilize it, whether that's rubbing alcohol, a lighter, or a flask of whiskey."

A few chuckles arose from my group, but I kept my face solemn. "It might be funny to think about, but you won't have time to think out there. Whatever you have on-hand might be the thing that saves someone's life. Got one of those little teddy bears on a keychain to remind you of your kids, maybe? Guess what, you might end up dousing it in whiskey and shoving it into a bleeding hole in someone's arm because you ran out of gauze."

The doors burst open then, Rhonda coming in fast and leaning heavily on her cane. "We've got four incoming with multiple stab wounds. One deceased with multiple gunshot wounds."

Stabbings and gunshots? What the hell?

A mix of adrenaline and fear coursed through me as I nodded and turned back to the new medics waiting for my instruction. "You heard her, get your asses to the ER."

We all sprung into action, running down the hallway toward the stairwell. Jogging down the steps two at a time, I tried to stamp down my worry. Multiple stab wounds weren't supposed to happen in a place like Four Corners. Who and what could have caused this?

"Two medics per patient," I instructed, opening a faucet just outside the emergency room doors to scrub my hands vigorously.

Everyone around me did the same prep in solemn silence. Washing hands and putting on gloves, donning masks and surgical caps before heading in to save some lives. I followed after my students, eyes scanning the room to assess the damage when a horrifying realization dawned on me.

Governor Vance was conscious, sitting up and looking pale as the medics cut away his blood-soaked shirt. Forgetting myself, I ran to his side in a panic.

"Governor!" I cried, my voice muffled through my mask. "What happened? Who did this?"

"Oh shit, this is the governor?" a student asked, his eyes going wide.

"Keep working on him, you're doing fine," I said before addressing Vance again. "You're going to be okay, sir. Seems you made off with the fewest injuries."

"Josh!" The shocked man looked all around the room as if searching for his assistant.

Another medic gently pressed back on the governor's shoulders. "Sir, I'm going to need you to hold still and remain calm—"

"I think he killed Josh!" Vance cried out in a panicked sob. "He stabbed General Bray and Reaper too, but—"

"Reaper?" I repeated, my own voice rising with panic. "My husband, Reaper?"

"Reaper shot him. I don't know if he made it, I'm sorry. It all happened so fast—"

I pulled away, frantically looking around the room in search of my husband. Josh seemed to be in the worst shape, Dr. Brooks and another doctor were tending to him along with two of my medics.

"Finn!" I ran to my father-in-law's gurney, making sure to stay behind the medics who worked quickly to slow his bleeding.

"Hey, sweetheart." He smiled, despite looking pained and pale. "I meant to come visit you at work, but not like this."

"What happened?"

"Eduardo," he hissed, grinding his teeth. "Fuck, it's my fault. I was too trusting—"

"You couldn't have known," I said. Now I knew where my husband's tendency to shoulder all the blame came from.

"I'm alright, Mari," Finn insisted. "I've had worse. Go find your man."

"Okay," I nodded, stepping away. "I'll be back to check on you." He was stable, his single stab wound was being tended to quickly and blood bags were being set up for his transfusion. That only left…

Reaper was lying on a gurney, his body still and pale as two medics hovered over him, bloodied and shirtless.

"Talk to me," I snapped, shoving my way over to my husband's side.

"He lost a lot of blood quickly. The weapon nicked the SMA and his lung—"

"Why aren't his transfusion lines set up yet?"

"We're finding out his blood ty—"

"He's O-negative. Grab the blood and set up the drip now."

The medics rushed to follow my instructions while I took over pressing down on his wound. They had already packed it to slow his bleeding, but he was covered in blood from the chest down. It was still wet on his hands and dripping onto the floor. Damage to his superior mesenteric artery explained the heavy blood loss. I'd have to assess the damage to his lung once the artery was treated. The blood around his mouth indicated he'd coughed some up.

"We're getting you topped up on blood, love," I whispered, hovering over him. "You better hang in there, or Hades is about to get an earful from me about bringing you back."

My surroundings melted away as I got to work, checking for liquid in his lungs as his blood drip was set up. Once the coagulants did their job and we got his bleeding under control, I sutured his wound closed while keeping an eye on his vitals the whole time. They never dropped to dangerous levels, but that didn't mean I wasn't going to watch them like a hawk.

Dr. Brooks came up behind me at some point with a pat on my shoulder. It must have been hours later. The room had been cleaned up, patients were resting, and most of the medics had gone home.

"Take a rest, Mariposa," the doctor told me kindly. "You led the new medics well through their first big ER rush."

"I'll stay, if that's okay," I told him. "This is my husband. And the general is my father-in-law."

Dr. Brooks nodded in understanding. "Governor Vance is sending word to Josh and General Bray's family. Is there anyone you'd like to notify?"

"Yes." I smiled tiredly. "A few people."

"I *KNEW* there was something fucking fishy about that kid."

"Stop pacing like that." I reached for Gunner's hands from where I sat between Shadow and Jandro. "You'll wear a hole in the floor."

Reaper had woken up a few hours later, opting to share an overnight hospital room with his father. Several of us packed in, bringing extra chairs for everyone who rushed over when they received word.

And it pretty much was *everyone*.

Jandro, Gunner and Shadow rushed over the moment they got the news at the B&B, but not before telling Noelle and Larkan. And course, Reaper's mom rushed over as soon as she got word about Finn. While it wasn't exactly how we wanted Reaper's parents to meet the rest of the guys, all of them being here made me feel supported in light of what happened.

The information sat like a brick in my stomach. Someone had tried to kill the leaders of the Four Corners territory.

"I keep turning it over in my head," Finn sighed, his IV-arm wrapped around his wife who'd climbed into the hospital bed with him. "Fuck, how many meetings had he sat in on? How much did he know and supply to whoever he was working for?"

"Was there any sign of him being a spy?" Gunner asked. "Anything at all?"

"Gun, maybe now's not the time," I said. "They need to rest."

"It's okay, Mari." Finn offered me a weak smile before answering the question. "But no, there was none. I checked his paperwork, like I do all my recruits. No signs of him being pro-Blakeworth regime, and no reason for him to be. He freaking escaped by getting pushed out the back door while his home was raided. Either he's hidden his support for a dictator who ordered the execution of his family or," Finn paused to take in a shaky breath, "or he was indoctrinated here in Four Corners."

I didn't realize I was holding my breath until Shadow rubbed my back, encouraging me to release the air.

"How could any pro-Blakeworth people get in

here?" Noelle demanded, leaning into Larkan who wrapped around her protectively.

"The checks at the borders are thorough, but they aren't perfect," her father said. "And you have to remember the relationship between Vance and Blake wasn't outright hostile until they took Kyrie. I wouldn't call it friendly, but the two territories were cordial. There may be some pro-Blakeworth stragglers laying low."

"We have to assume there's more in the territory," Jandro said. "Plotting in secret, fucking cloak and dagger bastards. That kid definitely wasn't working alone."

"We have to find out who gave him the order," Reaper agreed, shifting in his hospital bed.

"I'll get with the Sons and start keeping eyes out," Shadow offered with a low growl.

"I'll alert Demon guards too, but listen. Are we certain it's Blakeworth?" Gunner resumed his pacing, despite my telling him not to. "And not Tash? I mean, he stabbed you two first. Tash has wanted Reaper's head on a stick since the Sandia outpost." Reaper's mom shuddered and Gunner immediately froze. "Shit I'm sorry, Mrs. Daley. I'll watch what I say."

"It's no secret that I'm wanted." Reaper shrugged. "But Governor Vance was the most important person in that room. I think he was just trying to get Dad and I out of the way to get to him." He looked to his father for confirmation.

Finn nodded. "If your biker gang is as notorious as you say it is, I think he would have made sure to finish you off if you were the main target."

Poor Alisa was looking more and more distraught the more her husband and son discussed.

"Alright, guys." I clapped my hands and rose to my feet. "We'll see about discharging you in the morning, and you can discuss the next move then. But right now it's time for the patients to rest." I forced a grin. "By orders of the SDMC medic and president's old lady."

"Are you coming home with us?" Shadow asked hopefully. "Or staying?"

I leaned over to push his hair back and kiss the scar on his eyebrow, and then his lips. "I'm staying here to oversee all the patients' care. I'll be home tomorrow though."

"Good." His mouth lingered on mine, hands brushing my waist as he stood up. "You make sure to get some rest too."

I reached on tiptoes, arms stretching up to wind around his shoulders. "I will."

"I'll take you home, Lis." Jandro helped Reaper's mom out of Finn's hospital bed. "And bring you straight back here in the morning, okay?"

"Thank you, son," she said wearily before turning around to kiss her husband goodbye.

"Don't worry about a thing," I assured her. "I'll be here and I'll have these guys checked on round the clock."

She surprised me by pulling me into a hug. "Thank you, Mari. We're so lucky to have you watching them over them. I leave my boys in your capable hands."

I returned her affectionate squeeze before saying my goodbyes to Jandro and Gunner. The room quickly emptied and Finn fell asleep almost immediately. His injuries weren't as bad, but he was older, and would likely need more time to recover than his son.

Reaper, on the other hand, was wide awake and staring at the ceiling. He barely took notice of me crawling into the hospital bed with him, much like his mother did with his father.

"What's on your mind, president?" I whispered with a small kiss to his shoulder.

"Hades told me to kill him," he replied flatly. "He told me to, and I hesitated. Everyone in that room got hurt because I was slow to act."

"Oh Reaper," I sighed. "Please don't turn this into another situation where you're blaming yourself."

"The moment the kid walked into the room, Hades just *knew*," he went on, staring blankly in front of him. "He knew it was going to happen and gave me the order."

"Do you think this is what Daren was talking about?" I asked.

Reaper's eyelids closed, his head shaking slowly from side to side on the hospital pillow. "I don't think so, but…maybe. I don't know anymore. He mentioned a *she* and it was only men in the room. I'm still going nuts trying to wrap my head around it."

"Stop thinking about it." I brushed kisses from his temple to his forehead. "Just for tonight, and rest for me."

"I can't. Not if you're still in danger."

"Yes, love. You're my hero, but…" I kissed his eyelids, encouraging them to stay heavy and closed.

"You saved three people's lives today. Take a night off and protect me after you've recovered."

"Damn you, woman…" His growl had little bite as exhaustion and pain medication finally took him under, his breaths growing deep and steady with sleep.

"I love you, too," I chuckled, planting a final kiss on his cheek before sliding out of the bed and smoothing the blanket over his lap.

Freyja reclined at the end of the bed near his feet, her paws tucked into her body, eyes large and seeing all that I could not. I needed to check on Josh and Vance, but paused on my way out of the room.

"Thank you," I said. "For healing them."

She answered me with a deep purr that echoed throughout the room.

FIFTEEN

JANDRO

"Where are you going?" Reaper grimaced as Mari changed his bandage. She cleared everyone in the stabbing to go home yesterday, but not even Reaper missed an opportunity to be babied by her. She laid him up in bed in our room here at the B&B, and made sure he didn't have to lift a finger for a damn thing.

"Just the country roads right outside of town," I assured him from where I watched in the doorway.

"Someone else should go with you," he said. "Gunner or Shadow, at least."

"Gun's setting up patrols with the Sons around City Hall," I reminded him. "And Shadow has a tattoo appointment."

"Then consider doing this another time," he huffed. "Mari can learn to ride whenever, preferably when we don't have fucking assassins in the city."

"We'll be fine," Mari told him, cleaning up her

supplies as she finished dressing his wound. "And still close by if anything does happen."

"Well, how long you gonna be gone for?"

"No more than two hours," I said. "Just a quick spin, then she'll come right back to dote on you, your Majesty."

Reaper frowned, the lines in his face deepening as Mari cupped his cheek and leaned her forehead on his.

"I need a break, love. It's been an intense couple of days and Josh still needs to be monitored. Just two hours on the bike for some fresh air, then I can get back to my patients."

The tension in his face smoothed just slightly. He brought his hands to the sides of her neck, staring at her for a moment before catching her mouth in a warm kiss.

"You know it's not about that. I just want you safe."

"There are few places more safe than with Jandro on an empty stretch of road," she said, pulling away slowly. "You rest up and don't worry, *Rory*."

"Ugh, fine. Get gone if you're gonna call me that." He swatted her side, prompting her to get up and duck under my arm on her way out of the room. When I turned to follow her, Reaper called out, "Hang on a second, 'Dro."

I approached his bedside in a few steps. "Yeah?"

The hard scowl returned, all the relaxed ease from Mari's presence gone. "Don't let her out of your sight for a second. Not even to check fluids on the bike. That's an order, do you understand me?"

"Yeah, man. Of course, but," I stared back at him,

puzzled, "you know she's safe with me. Is this about the assassin or something else?"

He leaned his head back on the headboard, pinching his forehead with a groan. "I don't fuckin' know anymore. I'd much rather she stayed here but if you're gonna go, just do it and get it over with."

"Alright, dude." I turned to leave the room, choosing not to indulge in his overprotective crap today. "We'll see you in a couple hours."

Mari was already in my driver's seat, helmet on and her slim fingers wrapped around my grips.

"Go ahead and turn her on," I said, squeezing in behind her. The bike growled to life after only a bit of protest from the initial spark. That was a small concern. I really had to take cold weather maintenance into consideration up here. "Let her idle a bit and warm up."

After a few moments, I coached Mari through easing back and out onto the road. The traffic was light this morning, despite Reaper's concerns. Vehicles were still few and far between for most citizens, so most of them carpooled or walked the short distance to where they needed to be. Four Corners was still small enough to get to most places on foot, although that wasn't likely to be true within the next few years.

I directed Mari outside of the town limits to the mostly-abandoned country road which had been a highway at some point. She would have been fine in town and probably would learn more navigating city streets, but I did promise Reaper.

"It's all you, *Mariposita*." I patted her waist. "Take us away."

She relaxed into the seat, cautiously accelerating on the long, empty stretch of road before us.

"Go faster!" I yelled over the engine with a swat to her hip. "I wanna see you make a dust cloud."

"Fuck off," she shot back, but she was laughing. I missed the pretty sound and realized I hadn't heard it in a few days.

I swatted her again, adding, "hyah!" like she was a horse and she shrieked with laughter.

"Stop, you'll make me wobble the bike!" she cried.

"Nah, girl. You're rock steady." But I calmed and settled down behind her. "Here comes a bend in the road. Remember to lean into it."

She took the turns beautifully, each one smoother than the last as she became more confident in her balance and handling of the bike. We took a few laps of the roads looping around Four Corners main city. While she drove, I took a few moments to enjoy the scenery, something I rarely got to do while in the driver's seat.

Gigantic, snow-capped mountains lined the horizon to the north, red rocks and cliffs to the south. *I could get used to views like this,* I realized. I had my doubts about settling in Four Corners when we first ended up here, but even my nomadic heart was getting attached to the little place.

I dropped my chin to Mari's shoulder after our fifth loop, placing a small kiss on her neck. "We gotta head back, babe. Take us home?"

I felt the sigh leave her body, her fingers wrapping around mine at her waist before she turned at the next intersection heading toward town.

"How'd I do?" she asked, her speed decelerating as we approached the city limits.

I chuckled, bringing both arms around her waist and leaving a bigger kiss on her nape. "You were born to ride, *Mariposita.*"

"Really?"

"Are you really surprised?" I asked. "You belong to three, almost four men who've made their lives on these roads. I had no doubt you'd take to the bike quickly."

"Oh hey, look." She pointed up ahead where a rusted car was parked on the side of the road, someone bent over in front of the vehicle and looking under the raised hood.

"Probably out of gas or something," I remarked. "Go ahead, let's help out." If I was going to stay here, I might as well be neighborly. Hell, even Shadow was starting to rack up a list of tattoo clients by word-of-mouth, and I didn't have my own mechanic's shop yet.

Mari pulled up next to the car, an unremarkable old sedan that had seen better days. The driver peered at us from underneath the hood, a middle-aged guy in a dark blue shirt. I spotted a bright vest and a hard hat in his passenger seat, indicating the guy was probably off to a construction job.

"Need some help?" I swung a leg off the bike and started toward him.

"If it ain't no trouble." He looked back down at the car in front of him. "It just stopped runnin'."

"Any weird sounds when it stopped?" I asked. "Rattling or clicking?"

"Nah, I don't think so."

"See any smoke coming out from under the hood?"

"Nah."

"Where were you at on gas?"

"Just filled up the tank this mornin'."

I rubbed a palm over my head, shooting an annoyed look at Mari still sitting astride my idling bike. The worst part about diagnosing car issues was having to pull the answers out of the owner like teeth.

"Alright, when's the time you topped off the oil?" I crossed my arms, trying to keep my tone patient.

"Uh…" The guy's hand shook slightly as he wiped at something on his pants. "Not sure."

"Okay, man," I sighed, not wanting to be dealing with this. "I can give you a lift into town, just gotta get my wife home first—"

"Run," he whispered.

"What?" I watched him closely, the tremors now taking over his hands. His pupils became pinpricks, filled with fear.

"I'm sorry. I didn't want to but…just *run!*" He screamed the last word at the top of his lungs, scrambling to the side of his car and ducking down as if to hide.

"What the…"

I whipped around, hearing the low rumble of another engine just as Mari cried, "Jandro, someone's coming fast!"

"Go, go!" I jumped onto the bike behind her, drawing my handgun from my holster. "Head away from town, top speed!"

She accelerated hard, jerking the bike into motion as

two figures cut a corner, driving off-road on sport bikes heading straight for us. I cursed under my breath, raised my firing arm and took aim. They'd catch up to us in no time on those fucking crotch rockets.

"Fast as you can go, babe. Don't slow down even a tiny bit," I told Mari.

"I don't want to crash!"

"Better we crash than get taken by them."

The two riders, all decked out in black, had reached our stretch of road and were coming up on us fast. I fired off a shot at the one in front, but it went low, hitting the frame of the bike with a metallic *plink*. Mari was weaving the bike slightly, her balance off-kilter at such high speed.

"I need you to keep her steady for me," I said. "I got them, you can do it."

"Who are they?" she demanded, panic choking her voice.

"Tash's people," I said through gritted teeth. "We're no one important, so they have to be."

Deja vu set in as I turned in my seat, shielding Mari with my body as I took aim at the enemies right on our tail. This was too reminiscent of our ambush from Razor Wire. My dumbass didn't think to bring extra ammo, so I had to be careful with my shots.

The riders couldn't zig-zag much, but they hunched low over their crotch rockets. Black gear on back bikes made it hard to get a clear shot. The rider in the rear straightened up and began firing rapid semi-automatic rounds.

"Fuck!" I pushed Mari's head down low over the

dash, bowing my body over hers. "Don't slow down! No matter what, do not slow or stop!"

"Well don't get fucking hit!"

I decided not to tell her about the burning graze on my calf, my pant leg already wet and dark with blood. It felt like little more than a bad scrape, but I knew that was the adrenaline talking. Mari didn't need to worry about me right then. More than anything, I needed her to just drive.

When the onslaught of bullets finally ceased I returned fire, but the shooter had ducked down, shielded by the rider in front.

Fuck, fuck, fuck. My aim was shit and my shots limited. I was running out of options, especially with two of them to deal with. I'd have to do my damn hardest to make this a two birds with one stone situation.

"Slow down just a touch," I told Mari.

"You said not to!"

"New plan, babe. Just trust me and ease up a little bit. Then when I tell you to," I leaned close to her ear, making sure only she could hear me, "hit it hard, back to full speed. Got it?"

She nodded and slowed as I asked, allowing the crotch rockets to gain significant ground on us. I could practically see the smugness in the riders, thinking we were surrendering. To add to that illusion, I waved both arms above my head.

"Drop the gun, Steel Demon," the first one ordered through his helmet, almost close enough to touch if I reached.

"Okay guys, I will." I lowered my hands slowly, finger well away from the trigger. "Just promise you won't hurt my wife, okay?"

The first one signaled to the rider behind him, who held up his semi-auto again and I sucked in a breath. My leg wound stung, the blood now making a dark trail on the road. *Hades, Freyja, Horus, whoever the fuck is listening, please don't let us go like this.*

"Please," I tried again. "We'll pull right over and I'll go with you, but do not touch her."

The rear rider tapped off a few rounds and more burning pain shot up my leg. I groaned and doubled over, grasping on to the seat to stay on.

"Jandro!" Mari cried.

"We don't need either of you alive, so fuck your demands!"

"Now, Mari!" I yelled.

She accelerated hard and my heart stopped for a moment, thinking I would tumble off. But I held on, squeezing both sides of the bike with my knees as I raised my gun, waiting for the crotch rockets to speed up after us. The shooter copied my movement, raising his weapon and firing off more rounds. An explosion of heat and pain hit my left shoulder before I fired, aiming low at the front rider's tire.

With a loud pop, the rubber shredded and burned. Just as I intended, the bike wobbled and slowed too fast for the rear rider to react. The shooter crashed into his partner with a crunch of metal, my body growing cold and heavy as bikes and bodies skimmed across the road.

"Double back, Mari," I panted, blood now coating the entire left side of my body. "Turn around."

"No! I have to get you to the hospital."

"Turn the fuck around!" I repeated. "We have to make sure they're dead."

I could feel her worry, her intense need to take care of me, but we had to have that sweet nurse and patient moment later. Thankfully, she did as I said and made a wide U-turn. Sure enough, one of our pursuers was stumbling out of the wreckage, dragging a lame foot behind him as he stepped over folded metal and the remains of his friend. His face was still hidden behind the black helmet visor as he raised his weapon.

"Bend down, stay low." I pressed on Mari's back until her chest met the dash, and not a moment too soon. The rider unleashed rapid gunfire on us.

I bowed over Mari to cover her, but her panic and lack of visibility took over. She made us sway to the side, wanting to get away from riding straight into gunfire.

"Babe, brake! BRAKE!" I yelled.

She braked too hard and we were suspended in midair for a split second before hitting the ground hard. I wrapped around her midsection despite the shooting pain up my shoulder, and rolled us away to minimize injury. My eyes shut tight and I thought my teeth were going to crack from how hard I was biting down. Every bump against the ground felt like my leg and shoulder were getting hacked off by a butcher knife.

We finally came to a stop. Her helmet had fallen off and I'd dropped my gun when I grabbed her. The world spun and I was so fucking tired. I'd probably lost a lot of blood. The one thing in sharp clarity was the black figure walking toward us.

"Run." I slid off of Mari and shoved at her side with my good arm. "Get Gunner and Shadow."

"I'm not leaving you!" Her shaking hand fumbled across my chest, reaching for my shoulder to put pressure on the wound.

"Esposa," I groaned, pulling her hand away and bringing her blood-soaked fingers to my lips. "They can either kill us both, or just me. You have to tell the others—"

"Then let it be both of us! Because I am not leaving you here."

"Mari, I'm sorry I don't have time to be romantic, but this is bigger than us. You have to run!" I tried to shove her more forcefully but the weakness was settling into me everywhere now. She barely moved.

Instead she crawled over me, laying on my back to cover me as the black-clad rider approached.

"Mari, don't," I pleaded. My strength was leaving me with every breath, but I could not allow her to die with me out here. Not when she had three other men to love, and a whole town that needed her.

"Do you have another weapon?" she whispered. "Anything at all?"

"Knife. Inside left pocket. But babe—"

She started fumbling over the front of my shoulder, reaching into my cut to feel for the knife just as our attacker tossed his magazine and loaded a fresh one into his gun. If he wasn't so close, I would've made some crack about bringing knives to gun fights.

"Stand up," he ordered Mari, pointing his barrel straight at her.

"Listen, I'm a medic," she said, her voice taking on that calming but authoritative tone as her fingers brushed the handle of my knife. "I can help your friend if he's still alive—"

"He's not. And you're nothing but rotten Steel Demon cunt as far as I care. Stand the fuck up."

"I can help that foot of yours too." She nodded toward his bad ankle, her fingers wrapping around the blade handle. "But if I get up, he's going to bleed out."

"Do I look like I care, bitch?"

Mari began sliding the knife out of my pocket, but my eyes were on that gun pointed straight at my woman. His gloved finger rested on the trigger and that fucking barrel was less than a foot away from her head. Bleeding out or not, I'd spend my last few breaths taking that fucker down if he shot her.

"I'm not gonna ask you again." His trigger finger squeezed just a hair, enough to make my heart stop. "Stand the fuck up."

Mari pressed her knees to either side of my body, her left hand flattening on the ground to push herself up. I felt the knife withdraw from my chest pocket and held my breath. I had no idea what her plan was, but he wouldn't hesitate the moment he saw her holding a weapon. Each second felt like an hour as she slowly rose to standing, my body braced for the sound of the shot. When none came, I turned my head against the ground, squinting up to look.

Mari stood over me with her hands up and no knife

in sight. I blinked in confusion, then the fear overtook me as our attacker leaned in and pressed his gun barrel directly against her sternum.

"General Tash wishes the Steel Demons a long and prosperous life," the rider sneered under his helmet.

"No." I thrashed on the ground, reaching for a leg, a kneecap, anything. "No, not her!"

I got a swift kick to my stomach for my effort, the air leaving my body in a violent rush, but it was the gunshot ringing in my ears that felt like the killing blow.

"No..."

I could barely whisper, let alone scream. All I knew was Mari no longer stood above me. *No, no, no. Why, Mari? You should have fucking run.*

It felt like forever before I could get my good arm under me so I could lift my head and look around. The world seemed to go silent, my senses dulling as I scanned the ground for my wife, or what was left of her.

I tracked the movement at the corner of my eye, turning my body painstakingly, slowly. Two black figures seemed to be wrestling on the ground, fighting desperately for the upper hand.

"Mari..."

My vision was going so blurry, I couldn't tell which one was her. I heard her grunts of effort and cries of pain, and ragged breaths and curses that sounded like a man's. I tried to drag myself closer to help, but my own bodyweight was too heavy. I tasted salt and dirt and blood. I couldn't reach my wife. I couldn't save her.

Another shot rang out and the figures went still.

GUNNER

"These dumb fucks," I sighed, dabbing an alcohol wipe at the cut on Mari's cheek. "Getting themselves shot and stabbed days apart. It's shameful, really."

"It's increasing my workload, that's for sure," she sighed. "Okay, that should be good. Now let it dry, then put the ointment on."

She sat on the counter in Jandro's hospital room, legs swinging back and forth like a child awaiting a check up. Her injuries had been minor compared to the VP, who was laid out in the hospital bed, his left shoulder and chest wrapped in gauze, his arm in a sling, and his lower left leg equally wrapped up tight and elevated on a pillow. Freyja sat in a dark loaf at the foot of his bed, green eyes observing the room.

Club members on the fringes of town had heard the gunshots and went to investigate. Members of General Bray's border patrol went to check it out as well. They found the motorcycle crash with two confirmed dead, Jandro nearly dead, and Mari working to slow the bleeding on his leg and shoulder until he could get rushed to the hospital.

Jandro went into emergency surgery immediately, with Dr. Brooks and his team firmly shoving Mari out of the operating room so she could rest and recover from shock. Unsurprisingly, she refused to have any of her own injuries looked at until Jandro was released from surgery a few hours later. Shadow, Reaper, and I rushed over as soon as we heard the news, taking Mari off the hands of the frustrated medics who had been trying to look after her.

"Don't leave us in suspense now, baby girl." I dabbed ointment carefully over the scrape on her face. "How'd you win with a knife at a gun fight?"

"I'm still not sure," she laughed tiredly. "I pulled it out of Jandro's cut when I was on top of him, and tucked it into my waistband like you showed me."

"That's my girl!" I grinned and kissed her temple.

"I stood up with my hands raised and he put the gun right up against me." She touched a finger to her sternum. "I was so fucking scared, I didn't think I'd get to the knife at all."

Across the room, Reaper groaned and scrubbed his hands down his face. He'd bitten his tongue so far, but I knew he was full of pent-up *I-told-you-so*'s. After this, I had no doubt he'd only be extra protective of Mari.

"Then he said, 'General Tash wishes you a long and prosperous life'."

"That fucker," I cursed under my breath. It was what the general said after every meeting back when we traded goods.

"And then Jandro moved." She looked over to the man in the hospital bed, chewing her lip. "Like he was trying to grab his leg or something, and the guy kicked him. I took that as my chance to pull the knife."

"Good girl," I praised, my grin returning. "Where'd you get him?"

"Well I shoved his arm first to get the gun away from me, so I just nicked him here." She dragged a touch along the side of my ribs. "It caught him off-guard and I didn't want him to regain balance, so I jumped on him and we went falling."

"How'd you get the gun away from him?" Shadow asked. He sat next to Reaper against the far wall, but was entranced by her story as I was.

"I honestly don't know." She shook her head. "It's such a blur. I just remember being so desperate to keep the gun away. He had a smashed ankle too, but was still a lot stronger. If I kept wrestling him on the ground, I know he would've been able to overpower me. At some point I just had my finger on the trigger and pulled it. For all I knew, I could've been pointing it at myself."

"You did good, baby girl." I pulled her into me, rubbing her shoulder as I kissed her forehead. "You saved your man, and probably all of Four Corners, again."

"Jandro took care of the first one," she sighed, leaning into me. "If it was just me, I would've kept riding."

Shadow stood and crossed the room in two long strides as Mari pulled away from me. I stepped back to give them space, the two of them in their own world for a moment as Shadow nudged his hips between Mari's legs and placed his hands on her waist.

"I'm proud of you," he said, forehead leaning down to hers.

She tilted her face up to return the contact, a small smile lighting up her face as her petite hands glided over his ribs. "Thanks, love."

I did that thing Reaper always told me to do—check myself for jealousy and try to figure out why. With a woman like Mari, it was most likely my own head trying to find something wrong, rather than anything she was doing.

But I was pleasantly surprised to find none, watching them embrace and kiss quietly. Shadow had been just as worried about her and Jandro, if not more. If the situation had turned out any worse, he could have lost his two favorite people in one swoop. The relief was clear in how his shoulders sagged when Jandro was wheeled out of surgery, and now, leaning over Mari like he wanted to shield her from the world. A world that seemed determined to take us out, no matter where we ended up.

"Gun, what'd you find out about the fucker with the car?" Reaper stood, stretching his arms over his head with a grimace. His stab wound was healing just as quickly as we expected, the fresh scar tissue still itching. Mari had already okayed removing his bandage while we were waiting on Jandro.

"Just some poor Four Corners worker that was bribed," I said. "He swears up and down that he never wanted to be bait in the first place, but they wouldn't take no for an answer."

"They all say that," Reaper growled.

"It's true," Mari piped up. She hopped down from the counter, her arm still around Shadow's waist as she leaned into his side. "He was visibly nervous from the start, and told Jandro to run." She released Shadow to stand next to Jandro's bed, and reached for the VP's hand. "If he hadn't given us a head start, we might not have survived."

"If he hadn't been there at all, you wouldn't have been hunted by those fucks," Reaper spat.

Mari turned her head sharply to look at him. "If they hadn't gotten him, they would've preyed on somebody else. I believe he was a victim in this too, Reaper."

"I'll take that into consideration," Reaper said carefully back to her, his rage clearly on a short leash. I didn't blame him, even if what Mari said made sense. My instinct was always to spill the blood of anyone who hurt my woman, and my brothers.

"You gotta stop doing this, man." I turned to Jandro, trying to lighten the mood. "You, burned up and shot. Reaper almost blown up and stabbed. Shadow harpooned and poisoned. I'm due for something bad."

"Yeah," Jandro mumbled drowsily, proving he wasn't knocked out after all. "'Bout time your pretty face got fucked up."

"Hey, I was *almost* sold into sexual slavery. That shit is traumatizing."

"Right. If you take out the *almost*, I'd believe you."

Rapidly approaching footsteps in the hallway ended our ribbing, with General Bray poking his head through the doorway. "Hey guys. Is this a good time?"

"'Course, Dad."

Reaper turned to give his father a brief hug, but it was Mari, approaching with her arms open, that made the older man's eyes light up.

"Oh, sweetheart." Bray sighed heavily with relief as he hugged her against his chest. "My heart stopped when I heard. I'm so glad you're okay."

"Thanks, Finn," Mari mumbled against his shirt. "Me too."

He released her, sauntering over to Jandro's bedside. "And I'm glad this guy's alright too, I guess."

"Ain't getting rid of me yet," Jandro said.

"You're hard to kill, man," Bray teased, leaning over and squeezing his good shoulder. "But thank fuck you were there." He turned to smile goodnaturedly at me and Shadow. "And it's a damn good thing you guys taught her how to defend herself. It's important, even though there's four of you."

"We should keep her trained." I nudged Shadow with my elbow. "She can learn some assassin tricks from you too."

The big guy nodded in agreement while Jandro groaned from the bed. "Don't give her too many ideas. She'll kill us in our sleep when we're being dickwads."

"By the time I'm done with her," Shadow crossed his arms, a smile quirking on his lips. "She'll kill us on a busy street in broad daylight."

"I already know how to kill you in your sleep," Mari snickered. "And how to make it look like an accident."

"While I'm glad to see you're all in high spirits in spite of what happened—" Finn began.

"Not all of us." Reaper mumbled. That was par for the course for him. He wasn't satisfied with the two riders' deaths. His old wounds with Tash—the first attempt on our lives, Dallas's death, and being driven out of our home—it all had to have been sitting on his shoulders like a massive boulder right then.

Finn walked over and placed a hand on his son's shoulder, sympathy etched in his face. "I didn't just come by to say hello. The attack has floated all the way up to the governor and he wants to meet as soon as possible. Right now, if you can. He's ready for action."

Reaper nodded. "Finally. Mari." He beckoned our wife forward. "You're coming, too."

Her eyes shifted from him to his father. "Are you sure that'll be okay? I should probably stay with Jandro."

"I'm not letting you out of my sight again," the president growled. "Fuck it if the governor doesn't like it."

"I don't see it being a problem," I mused, looking at Finn who answered with a shrug. "Vance gets that we don't leave you out of our business. I don't think he'll say no."

Shadow approached Mari, drifting a hand along her lower back. "I'll stay with him. You go to the meeting."

She looked straight up to meet his eyes. "Are you sure?"

"Yes." He returned her gaze, warmth and adoration in his eyes. "They can brief me later."

They parted with a kiss and a slow untangling of limbs, eyes only for each other until the last moment, when she came to walk between me and Reaper.

"You guys are fucking cute," I teased her as we followed Finn down the hallway to the elevator.

"Yeah, well, so are we." Her fingers slid through mine and then Reaper's on the other side of her as we stepped inside.

Reaper pressed the button for the lobby while I brought the back of Mari's palm to my lips and kissed her there with a grin. "But does he measure up in the bedroom?"

The cut on Mari's cheek deepened to a dark red as her skin flushed. "We haven't made it to that point yet."

"What?!" I looked over her head at Reaper, bewildered.

He shrugged, bringing both of his hands up. "Don't look at me. They wanted to take it slow."

"But...*why?*"

"Because we just *do*, Gunner. It feels right for us."

"You sure about that?" I teased a hand along the back of her neck. "You seem a little frustrated, baby girl."

She just glared at me as the elevator dinged and the door slid open. Finn, who had stayed politely silent during our whole exchange, stepped out first, holding the door open with his arm for us.

"What do you make of this, General?" I asked him. "Did your wife take it slow with one of her men?"

"She did with Nolan," he confirmed with a small smile. "The ah, physical chemistry she had with me and Carter was instant, explosive—"

"Fuck, really?" Reaper released Mari's hand to slap his palms over his ears.

"Lis and Nolan were a slower burn, physically speaking," Finn continued. "Their connection was more emotional, almost platonic at first, like they were best friends. They'd spend hours just staying up late and talking. It might've been weeks before they even kissed."

"That's really sweet," Mari said. "I'm sorry you all lost him."

"Thank you." Finn smiled at his daughter-in-law. "It's been over fifteen years now, so it's not as sharp. But it still hits Lis and I sometimes."

We all piled into the black SUV waiting for us outside. A thread of annoyance started to make a knot in my chest as Finn's lieutenant drove us. Jandro had just come out of surgery. Mari was in danger of dozing off, leaning heavily on my shoulder. The governor had barely given them any time to rest and let the shock wear off before calling this meeting. Tash's forces needed to be dealt with immediately, yes. But the timing of this didn't seem appropriate.

I shoved my discomfort down, wrapping an arm around Mari's shoulder and pulling her closer to me. We'd all make sure she rested well tonight. It was the least our wife deserved.

"Where are we going?" Suspicion laced Reaper's voice.

"To meet the governor, like I said," Finn answered coolly.

"Where?" Reaper demanded again. "We've just passed City Hall *and* his house."

"You'll see, son."

"Dad." Reaper's teeth ground in his jaw. "I'm not

the mood for fucking surprises. Can you just tell us what's going on?"

"You'll like this surprise," Finn answered. "Just relax."

Reaper grumbled in his seat, only quieting when Mari lifted her head from my shoulder and turned to snuggle against him.

We drove over the small bridge crossing the lake to the new development on the other side. No streetlights had been erected yet, let alone paved sidewalks, so the SUV's tires rolled over bumpy gravel with just the head-lights to guide our way.

The car came to a stop just as our headlights picked up a figure standing in the middle of the road, who I quickly figured out was Governor Vance. It was pitch black outside, the temperature dropping fast, and he was waiting for us in a construction zone away from the main part of town? My suspicion started to match Reaper's, hand brushing the gun at my hip as we started climbing out of the back seat. Everything about this was fucking fishy.

"Mariposa!" Vance beamed at the sight of her, his smile rivaling the brightness of our headlights. "I'm so glad you came out for this, dear."

Reaper's arm shot out to the side, blocking her from getting any closer. "What is *this*, Vance? A meeting out in the freezing fucking darkness?"

"Ah, yes." The governor's eyes shifted to General Bray still behind us. "That may have been a small fib. I wanted you and at least one or two of your men out here for this."

"*This* being what, exactly?" I stepped up to Mari's other side, another shield for her in the event of any danger.

"Josh!" Vance called out to the darkness behind him. "Go ahead."

I heard a series of clicking sounds, like breaker switches being flipped. And then, blinding brightness.

"Ah, fuck!" I brought a hand up to shield my eyes, squinting at the brightly lit house in the distance.

"It's yours," the governor declared. "And this time, I'm not taking no for an answer."

When my eyes adjusted I lowered my hand, blinking as I took in all the details. The house the governor showed us the night of the dinner party had transformed, or expanded at least.

The first story had been widened out from the center—a sunroom lined with windows facing south, and what looked like an additional garage or workshop with a roll-up door on the opposite side. Through all the windows, cozy warm light glowed, lighting up the sparse furniture and fixtures already inside.

"We added two more bedrooms downstairs for three total on the bottom floor," Finn said in our stunned silence, walking up from behind us. "And with the three up top, it should be plenty of room for all of you to have your own space."

"Wha...what?"

"You've been in Four Corners over two weeks already," Vance laughed at Reaper's stunned look. "And have saved us all more times than we can ever repay you for. Take the house. I insist." The governor reached deep inside his coat and produced a set of keys.

"You can't tell us you're good and settled crammed into *one* room at the B&B," Finn laughed, bringing a hand down on Reaper's shoulder. "Take the house, son. Make a life here." His grip squeezed, not letting go as his voice grew heavy with emotion. "Let an old man watch his only son grow old and have his own kids, huh?"

Mari approached the two of them, hugging around Reaper's waist as she stared at Finn with an awed smile. "I bet you orchestrated this ruse, huh?"

"We started building the extension and were gonna surprise you anyway," her father-in-law grinned. "But it was the governor's idea to present it to you now, after what happened."

"I understood your hesitation when you told me the first time," Vance nodded at Reaper. "But after that day in the conference room, and now with what happened to your sweet wife and VP," he shook his head. "Four Corners *needs* the Steel Demons. The house is yours. My trust is yours. And still, it feels like too little for what you've given us."

Reaper looked down at Mari, his arm around her shoulders. "What do you think, sugar?"

"It's a beautiful house." She leaned her cheek on his chest. "Let's take it."

"Gun?" Reaper lifted his gaze to me.

I shrugged, but couldn't stop the grin from spreading across my face. Hell fucking yeah, I was ready to leave the B&B and actually *live* somewhere.

"Whatever the wifey wants."

Mari's excited giggle was drowned out by Finn's laughter as he grabbed my arm and pulled me into a bone-crushing hug.

"Congratulations, son," he said on my shoulder. "Happy to have you in the family."

"Thank you." I returned his hug, leaning into probably the only display of fatherly affection I'd ever received. "Thank you, sir."

"None of that *sir* business," he chided, pulling away. "Well, maybe only when we're at work," he added with a wink.

"We'll throw a housewarming party soon," Reaper said, releasing Mari so she could hug me. "Invite the whole club. Hell, we'll have Larkan's patching in ceremony at the same time."

"Oh, finally!" she declared, her cheek nuzzled against my chest.

"We gotta tell Jandro when he's not all doped up," I said, rubbing warmth into her back.

"And Shadow." Mari's eyes widened like she had mistakenly said that out loud, but didn't take it back as Reaper and I sandwiched her between us.

"Something you want to tell us, sugar?" His tone had finally lightened, arms wrapped around her shoulders from behind as he kissed the top of her head.

Mari held on to his forearm across her chest. "I want Shadow to move in with us," she said, her voice firm.

Reaper and I exchanged a fast look. "Okay," he said. "Does that mean…?"

"He's mine," she answered, gripping his forearm tighter. "I'm keeping him. I...*love* him."

"Alright then." Reaper squeezed her against his chest, planting another kiss in her hair. "He's moving in and picking a room."

"Baby girl." I teased her nickname with a hint of warning, hooking my fingers in the belt loops of her jeans. "You know what I'm gonna say."

Her eyes narrowed at me in warning. "What, Gunner?"

I leaned in close and whispered, "What if his dick is small?"

"You *asshole!*" she shrieked, swatting me. "Don't be like that!"

"Sorry, I had to!" I laughed, blocking her blows with my arms.

"And anyway," she grinned smugly. "I already know what his dick looks like."

"Oh, right," I said sheepishly. "I forgot that...that happened."

"Let's get the fuck out of this cold," Reaper huffed, dragging Mari back to the car. "And celebrate our last night sleeping in the B&B."

"Works for me." I followed them after stealing one more glance back at the house.

Our house.

SEVENTEEN

SHADOW

___

For the first time ever, my workout felt lonely without an audience.

I set the barbell down after my last deadlift, slightly mystified that I didn't have a cat wrapping around my ankles to watch out for, or the sneaky glances of a woman from the window.

My woman. The thought bubbled up inside me before quickly bursting. *Don't get ahead of yourself. She could still decide that she doesn't want you.*

The night after their meeting with the governor, Mari came back to the hospital in the morning to check on Jandro. She told me to head back to the B&B to rest, and that she'd brief me on what they talked about later. I came back and got a few hours of sleep in my room, then woke up to the whole place being empty. I had no tattoo appointments or anything pressing, so I started my day with a workout like usual.

I could name this feeling now, this tugging in my

chest when Mari wasn't around and I couldn't get her out of my head. It meant I missed her.

Getting closer to her only made the sensation stronger.

People being around me used to be an intrusion, their noise poking holes in the shield I wrapped around myself. I couldn't pinpoint when the shift started, it must have happened so gradually, but I started finding myself more comfortable in the company of others. People that weren't her, nor those closest to me in the Steel Demons. I could walk into a room full of strangers and feel… okay. Not *good* by any stretch of the imagination, but like I could survive it.

I headed inside, using my discarded shirt to wipe my sweat before tossing it in the laundry pile in my room. My pill bottle caught my eye on the nightstand. I'd have to get a refill of sleeping pills soon. Those little tablets were one of the biggest reasons I attributed to feeling more like a normal person.

The monster within me, created by years of torture and isolation, had been quiet lately. It might never go away completely, but it had been lying dormant over the past several weeks. I slept through the night without issue, the nightmares starting to feel like a distant memory. I craved Mari's touch and sought it out, rather than retreat into myself. The absence of that dark, oppressive force made everyday life so much less exhausting.

I was no longer terrified of riding out to the hospital to get a refill of the pills, of potentially talking to someone besides Mari, another woman even. If she was there, I might even linger. Talk to her for a few moments, maybe even get a kiss before I left.

A huff of laughter escaped me as I undressed for my shower. I was fucking fantasizing about doing something that used to set me so far back with fear. I had made my own prison, I realized, by feeding into the narrative I'd been told all my life—that I was an evil force upon the earth because I was a man. I deserved to be caged up and cut with blades because men were the reason civilization went into Collapse. Men were the reason so many girls and women were snatched from their homes and rounded up like cattle. I was dangerous and deserved a life of torture simply because I was born.

Even after being taken away and finding my life in the SDMC, I still believed it. No one told me those things anymore, they didn't need to. I told them to myself, because it never occurred to me I could be anything different.

That I might matter to someone.

I turned on my shower and stared in the bathroom mirror while I waited for the water to heat up. The steam on the glass smoothed out the complexion of my skin, softening the textures of scar tissue. If only I could swap places with my reflection.

My fingers drifted up, rubbing over the fading bruises on my chest where Mari had bit and sucked on me there. A hickey, she called it.

I recalled how it felt, the small bloom of pain under the heat and wetness of her mouth that I'd become addicted to tasting. Pain—a sensation I'd forgotten about and hadn't felt in years. The way her teeth pulled at my skin and sent the feeling like small shock waves all over my body. I recognized the sensation but never felt it like that, never thought it could be something I'd crave.

Staring at them in the mirror, I contemplated tattooing over those bruises. Just tracing over the small blotches of purple and red, so her mark on me would never fade.

She'd be willing to leave more on you, if you just asked.

My heart sped up at the thought. Turning away from the mirror to step into the shower, I thought of my conversation with Jandro at the bar the other night. As close as he and I were, I'd never really talked to him like that before. Most of our heart-to-hearts consisted of him talking *at* me, with me doing my best to ignore him.

But this time I listened.

Mari loved him. She kept him and made him hers. I desperately wanted that for myself, and needed all the help I could get with the odds stacked against me.

As well as things were going with Mari, I still felt like I was fumbling around in the dark. The lingering fear of scaring her, or possibly hurting her, halted me from taking anything further physically. Plus the uncertainty from having never done that with someone I actually cared about. I knew how to proceed to the act of having sex, but would never forgive myself if I saw that same fear in her eyes that I'd seen so many times before.

I had to talk to her. Ask her what she wanted. Let her lead me through it like she did with kissing. I just had to remind myself that she didn't hold my inexperience against me. She didn't think I was stupid or ugly. And she would want me to enjoy it too.

Easier said than done.

I finished my shower and had just put pants on when the knock came to my door, heavy and urgent.

"Yeah?" I called, rummaging around for a clean shirt.

"Reaper's calling church," Gunner's voice answered through the wood. "The whole club at City Hall."

I paused in my search and pulled the door open. "When?"

"Right now, as soon as we can get everyone together. Reap's on his way to pick up Mari and Jandro from the hospital now." Gunner's eyes lowered from my face, hovering at my collarbones. "Nice hickeys, dude."

"Shit." I slapped a hand over the marks on my chest, much to his amusement. "Is this about the assassins?"

"Yeah." His expression turned solemn. "Reap's not fuckin' around anymore. We're hitting them back, ASAP."

"Okay. Anything from the meeting last night I should know?"

Gunner only smiled as he turned away. "I'm sure you'll find out everything you need to know today."

———

THE CONFERENCE ROOM was already crowded by the time Gunner and I arrived. Normally, the press of so many bodies in a confined space would drive me to a panic attack. But as I squeezed my way in, I felt okay with only a few deep breaths. Not great by any means, but good enough to not look for an immediate escape route.

It wasn't just Steel Demons in the room—their women too. Tessa, Andrea, and Noelle stood huddled together, with Big G looking sour across the room from his ex-wife. General Bray's soldiers also lined the walls, standing at attention. The governor and Josh, bandages on the assistant's face and hands, talked with General Bray near a window.

I even spotted the Sons of Odin, the black raven and horned viking helmet on their cuts, to the right side of the room as they mingled.

"Shadow," T-Bone greeted with a lazy smile.

"Who invited you fuckers?" I returned.

They laughed as we all clasped fists and slapped each others' backs. Maybe I was starting to get the hang of this sense of humor thing.

"We're honorary Demons as far as I see it," Dyno grinned. "Saved your sorry asses enough times."

"Since you're Grudge's brother, you're a Son too," T-Bone said.

"Mari hasn't tested us to see if we're blood-related yet," I remarked. "Not that it matters."

"Mm-mm!" Grudge shook his head emphatically.

"Glad you agree, brother." I knocked my fist against his and went to stand next to him against the wall.

"Speaking of, where is your little lady?" T-Bone stroked his beard as he scanned the room.

I nearly corrected his assumption that she was mine, but decided against it. "Coming with Jandro soon."

Reaper's voice cut through the murmurings of conversations from the room only moments later. "Make a path, move! Give the VP some fucking room."

People jumped quickly out of the way, all talking fading to silence as they made their way inside. Over everyone's heads, I could see Mari holding on to Jandro's good arm, the other one still in a sling. Somehow, he still managed to get both arms through the holes of his cut.

His steps were slow and slightly unbalanced due to the walking boot encasing nearly the entire bottom half of his leg. Reaper walked on his other side, his eyes scanning the faces in the room as if daring anyone to say something out of line. But everyone only looked on with respect as the three of them made their way to the conference table.

Because of all the extra people here, this wasn't a church meeting in the traditional sense. But a gavel and a block still waited for Reaper at the end of the table, where he took his seat with Hades at his side. Mari helped Jandro settle into the seat next to him, then stepped back to stand with the others lining the wall.

Jandro nodded at me, indicating I should take the seat next to him. Mari smiled at me as I approached the chair, and Gunner took his place on the other side of Reaper. Our president hit the gavel once, the clack of wood echoing throughout the otherwise silent room.

"Thank you all for coming on such short notice," he began, his voice softer than any church meeting I'd attended before. "I invited you all here because this matter affects all of us." He paused for a deep breath. "Four Corners is in danger. And the people who want to topple this place are trying to do it from the inside."

Stony faces looked back at all of us sitting. Either everyone already knew, or at least suspected this, or was trying to look unafraid.

"We're facing a general who has also used MCs to do his dirty work for him," Reaper went on. "If we come at him with military force, he'll be ready. Expecting it, more likely. What we need to do is slip under his defenses, just like he did here. The only thing is," Reaper sighed, leaning back, "he'll recognize most of us. Fuck, any traveler approaching his territory from this direction will be regarded as suspicious. So we need to get creative. It's not just scouting we need anymore. We need to know what General Tash is thinking, planning, even feeling. We need someone to plant inside who can get us information. And we'll need them to stay there, for an extended amount of time."

My president took a moment to meet the gaze of everyone in the room. "This isn't going to be easy. I will order someone to do it, although I'd much rather not do so. I wanted to put it out to anyone, see if there's any volunteers or another solution that I'm missing. But no one is leaving this room until we have a mission set in stone."

Slick stepped forward. "How will this inside person get information to you, president?"

"We'll have rendezvous points where you can leave coded messages for either Horus or Munin to pick up."

"And how long will this assignment be?"

"As long as it takes," Reaper answered flatly. "Until we have enough information to invade Tash and wipe him out. Could be months, could be years."

"You're not going." Jandro cut Slick off from asking another question.

The youngest Demon's mouth flapped open. "Sir, I'm—"

"You've prospected for us long enough for one of Tash's inner circle to recognize you. Really, that goes for just about everyone rolling with the Demons, whether they have a patch or not." Jandro nodded his head toward Larkan. "Same for the Sons. Too recognizable."

"But not their women," Mari pointed out.

All four of us at the table whipped around at the same time. "You are *not* going," Reaper snarled. "It's completely out of the question."

"I know." Mari folded her hands demurely. "Tash's guards would recognize me from the Sandia outpost."

"What she says is true, though," Gunner piped up. "A woman might be our best chance of getting close to Tash and arouse the least suspicion."

Reaper made a noise of disagreement. "I don't like it. It's fucking dangerous."

"It'll be just as dangerous for a man," Gunner replied. "If not more so, because he'll be more likely to be interrogated the moment he steps foot in the territory."

"I'll do it."

Everyone's heads swiveled to the woman who spoke.

Andrea, Dallas's widow, stepped forward, her face a calm, blank mask.

"Drea, no." Behind her, Tessa's face was white as a sheet, her arms holding her infant daughter starting to tremble.

"Andrea." Reaper's voice was heavy as he addressed her. "Not you. Tessa's right."

"You're both wrong," the woman retorted. "None of Tash's people have ever seen my face. I can charm his soldiers and make them tell me their secrets. It was what I did before Dallas and I got together. I'm the best person to do this, president."

"Your children need you," Reaper argued. "You're all they have left. It's not right for their mother to just leave them for months, if not longer. And that's *if* we get you back after this is over."

"They're big enough to get by without me, and to remember me if I don't return. The Steel Demons will look after them." Andrea remained tight-lipped, insistent. "Or did you forget that this club is a family, Reaper?"

A few beats of silence fell over the room, no one daring to interfere.

"No, I haven't forgotten," Reaper answered. "But they just lost their father, Drea. To lose their mother right after—"

"And *I* lost my husband," she cut him off. "One of your best, and the love of my life. He would *never* be hanging back, never have a second thought about hitting Tash where it hurt. If you called for battle, he'd be leading the charge."

"I know." Reaper closed his eyes, his shoulders sinking with the weight of Dallas's death. "I know, Drea."

"He wouldn't want me to hang back either," she added. "To sit here waiting for news, when I could be doing something for the good of all of us. When I'm the *only* one who can."

"There could still be someone else," Reaper protested.

"There isn't. All of your men will be recognized. The other women either don't have the skills I do, or their children are too young. I'm prepared, and I—" Her voice shook for a moment before she steeled herself with a breath. "I'm ready to avenge my husband."

Reaper didn't respond, the silence stretching on long and uncomfortably. Finally, he sighed and touched the handle on his gavel. "Are there any objections to Andrea carrying out the mission?"

Noelle and Tessa each held one of Andrea's hands, their faces twisted up in grimaces as they tried not to cry. The men in the room looked worried, some of them shaking their heads, but no one spoke up to object. Even Governor Vance and General Bray just observed the room silently.

As the seconds ticked by with no objections, Reaper lifted the gavel and brought it down with a firm crack on the table. "You honor us, Andrea," he said solemnly. "You honor your husband and your whole Steel Demons family."

The woman nodded sharply and stepped back into the crowd. "Just tell me when to go."

Reaper nodded, folding his fingers on the tabletop. "That brings us to the next step in our plan—getting you inside. At least one person should go with you, to ensure you get to the border with no issue and report back that you got safely inside. After that, you're on your own."

"Understood." Andrea said.

"Do I have any volunteers on taking Andrea to New Ireland?" Reaper asked the room. "Being unrecognized is not as essential. Ideally, you should be able to hang back while she gets inside, but the risk of death or torture is still high."

Much to everyone's surprise, Big G stepped forward. "I'll take her."

"G!" Poor Tessa looked like she was going to crumble to the floor. "What the fuck are you doing?"

"And why you?" Reaper peered at him shrewdly.

The large man released a breath, taking a moment to glance back at Tessa and Andrea huddled together.

"I know I've been on your shit list lately, president, and rightly so. Everyone here knows I'm not the best husband, and far from the best father. In your eyes, I haven't been the best Demon either. So let me correct that." He straightened, puffing his chest out. "Let me take this as a chance to start righting my wrongs. If I don't come back, I want my kids to remember me as a Demon who helped us win."

Reaper's eyes flicked to Andrea. "Do you have any objection to him taking you?"

She regarded Big G with a cool indifference at first, then looked at Tessa with a silent question I couldn't read. "No objection, president. I'm fine with it."

"Does anyone else object to Big G escorting Andrea on the mission?" When no response came, Reaper smacked the gavel once again. "Moving right along here," he sighed, scrubbing a hand down his face. "Now we need at least two scouts to oversee and hang farther back in case anything happens to either Big G or Andrea, and to step in and engage the enemy if necessary. Shadow?" He looked down the length of the table at me.

I knew this would be coming. In all likelihood, the mission would be carried out at night and he'd need me to see in the dark. I was also the most silent rider and least likely to get caught if it came to a fight.

"I accept, president." My answer came without hesitation, a heated thrill lighting up my senses. I hadn't been on a true mission since Blakeworth, and was eager to take out more enemies who threatened us.

My ears picked up a small sound, like a gasp behind me. Mari? My hands closed into fists on my lap, the reminder of her making me all the more determined to carry out my duty as a Steel Demon. She had been hurt, nearly killed by the enemy. I'd pick off any man who would follow through on an order to shoot her.

"You're leading the scouting team, then," Reaper said. "Who would you like to take with you?"

My gaze lifted to the Sons of Odin across the room, Grudge meeting my eyes.

"I'll take Grudge with me," I answered. The silent Son grinned as he stepped forward.

"Anyone else?"

It didn't take long for me to make a decision. "No, president. The two of us will get the job done."

"Excellent." Reaper smacked the gavel once again.

The rest of the meeting was less emotionally taxing. Maps were pulled out to decide on the best route to get Andrea into New Ireland. It would be a long, winding journey to make it look like she was coming from the northeast and not directly west. General Bray and his lieutenants also gave input on the best rendezvous point, somewhere outside the territory where Andrea could leave the coded messages for us to find.

The sun was setting by the time Reaper concluded the meeting. "Are we ready to do this tomorrow night?" he asked the room. When no one objected, he smacked the gavel down for the final time that day. "Church is adjourned. Those who need to, come back here at sunset tomorrow night."

I rose from the table, but stayed back while everyone filed out of the room. Reaper and Gunner helped Jandro out, while Mari came to stand next to me at the table.

"I won't ask you to stay." Her soft voice was nearly a whisper in the large, empty room. "But it doesn't make me worry any less."

Turning toward her slowly, I reached for her waist and pulled her closer without a single dissenting thought in my mind. Touching her had become normal, natural. Something I *needed.*

"You don't have to worry about me." I slid my hand up her back until my fingers touched the ends of her hair. "I didn't know what to expect in Blakeworth. But with Tash, I know exactly what to expect."

Her expression didn't change. If anything, the tension in her forehead grew even deeper. "Just make sure you come back. Even if Grudge has to drag you behind his bike through the desert."

"It won't come to that," I promised her. "We'll be back in four days at the most."

"You better." Her fingers slid between mine, slender and twig-like through my massive paws. "You can't miss the housewarming party."

"Oh, yeah." I heard others talking about how she and her men decided to move into the house the governor had offered them. "I wouldn't miss it. Congratulations, by the way," I added stiffly.

Her smile up at me was bright. "Congratulations to you too."

I frowned. "What do you mean?"

"Shadow." Mari propped her chin on my chest, sliding her arms around my ribs. "It's your house too."

"It is?"

She nodded.

"But." My chest was tight, my mind going off in all kinds of directions I didn't dare voice aloud. "I thought it was only for you and your men."

Mari grinned wider. "It is." She stretched on her tiptoes, leaning up until her lips came within kissing distance of mine. "You're mine, Shadow." Just as quickly, her feet planted on the floor again, the nervousness visible on her face. "That is, if you want to be."

My body felt it, but my brain seemed slow to catch

up. I felt light, almost like I was floating. My pulse hammered and I wanted to laugh to release the sparks building in my chest. But my brain, my stupid brain, wouldn't let me believe the words she said.

"I'm…yours?"

She nodded. "Yes, I want you to be."

"Why?"

"Because," she laughed like it was obvious. "I love… how you make me feel. I admire your creativity, your loyalty, how sweet you are with me and my cat. When I'm not wrapped up in you, I wrap myself in your hoodie." Her touch slid down my arms, finding both of my hands. "I want to say good morning to you *every* morning."

I leaned my forehead down to hers. My stubborn brain was finally reconciling with my body's reactions. This brightness sparking under my skin, the smile I couldn't stop from spreading on my mouth. She wanted me.

Me.

"I…want to be yours." I placed her hand over my racing heart. "I still feel clueless about so many things, but I'll do my best to be a good partner to you. One you deserve." I brought her hand to my lips and kissed her small palm. "And you can have all my hoodies as long as you watch every sunset with me."

Her grin reflected mine. "Deal." She pulled away from me until her hands tugged mine toward the door leading out of the room. "Let's watch one now, before you leave me."

I tugged her back to me, catching her against my

chest from the force of my pull. "I'll never leave you." I pressed a fast kiss to her mouth before releasing her. "Not without a promise that I'll come back."

"Hm." She practically skipped out the door, tossing a playful glance over her shoulder at me. "I'm gonna hold you to that."

EIGHTEEN

MARIPOSA

"Get some antifreeze and put it in someone's drink if you need to kill them without being detected."

Andrea threw her head back and laughed, nearly falling out of her armchair. "How many times have you had to do that, Mari?"

"I plead the fifth," I snickered. "Oh wait, that doesn't exist anymore. Damn it!"

"You can always 'accidentally' smother a guy to death while you're sitting on his face," Noelle suggested. "Although, you'll need his limbs tied down, so make it like a kinky bondage session first."

"Better to use a pillow," I interjected. "You don't want things getting bitten off down there if he catches on."

Andrea howled with laughter, and even I couldn't smother my giggles entirely. The only one we couldn't seem to drag out from the dumps was Tessa, who barely cracked a smile as she rocked Vivian against her chest.

None of us could blame her. The father of her children and the woman she just rekindled a romance with were leaving on a dangerous mission in a few short hours. The probability was high that neither would come back soon, if ever.

The four of us were in one of the City Hall lounge rooms, usually reserved as sitting rooms for the male dignitaries to drink and smoke cigars. But us girls wanted to chat and get together before sending Andrea off.

And Big G. And Grudge and Shadow. My *Shadow,* I thought worriedly. We watched last night's sunset from a City Hall balcony until darkness and cold settled in. Our new house wasn't entirely furnished yet so we still had to spend another night in separate rooms in the B&B. By the time he returned from the mission, his new home would be moved in and ready.

Our new home.

"Don't look so sad, sweet cheeks." Andrea stood from her armchair, wobbling slightly from the drinks we'd all been consuming, before planting herself next to Tessa on the loveseat and pulling the young mother into a forced cuddle.

"I don't know how you all can be laughing right now." She leaned her head on Andrea's shoulder. "What if I never see you again?"

"Then we can remember the good times we had." Andrea planted a kiss on her forehead. "However brief they may have been."

"I've always laughed at the worst fuckin' times." Noelle helped herself to more whiskey from the coffee table. "Drove my moody-ass brothers nuts. Helps me deal with shit, I guess."

"That's really common, actually," I told her. "Cracking jokes at seemingly-inappropriate situations is a widely-studied coping mechanism."

"Alright, smart girl." Andrea wadded up a cocktail napkin and threw it at me. "What else should I know about potentially ending or saving lives?"

"Do you know how to give CPR?" I asked.

"Sure do. I taught myself from a book actually, when my son was born." Andrea's face turned thoughtful, her hands stroking lightly over Tessa's arms. "I should…I should see my kids one last time."

None of us were about to tell her no, as she slid out from behind Tessa and headed for the main doors of the building. She had said goodbye to her children right before coming here, but the finality of the situation seemed to sink in as the time grew near.

"Poor Drea." Noelle curled her feet underneath her. "It has to be so hard to do this."

"I told her that," Tessa said in a small voice. "She just said that was exactly *why* she had to. And that it's what Dallas would have done."

"She's being so brave," I said, swirling my *reposado* in my own glass. "I have to hand it to Big G too. He really stepped up."

"Yeah, *now* he does," Tessa scoffed. "Like I wasn't feeling shredded up about this enough."

"You still love him?" Noelle asked, never able to put a filter on that mouth.

"Not like I used to, but I still care about him." Tessa

cradled Vivian's head against her shoulder. "He's my kids' father. There's always gonna be *something* there."

"It is nice to see him take initiative instead of just tagging along on the rides," Noelle relented. "Hopefully this is the start of him acting like a grown-up."

"If he comes back," Tessa mumbled.

"He will." I reached over and squeezed her knee. "He's stubborn as hell and built like a stone chimney. And he won't miss out on being here for his kids."

"What about your tall, dark, scary one?" Noelle turned to me, the alcohol making her extra chatty. "Scared for him?"

"He'll get it done," I answered, the tequila now jostling in my stomach.

"Not what I asked, sister." Noelle nudged me with her foot.

"Of course I'm scared," I sighed. "Why do you think I'm drinkin' with you two bitches?"

A sharp peal of laughter burst out of Tessa first, waking up a fussy, distressed Vivian, while Noelle just stared at me agape.

"Aw, shit!" Tessa fanned her face. "I needed that laugh."

"Someone's feisty on that tequila." Noelle chuckled. "I get it, sis. Sometimes cluckin' around like hens is the best therapy for when our men are out there doing stupid shit."

"Or women," Tessa corrected as she shushed Vivian.

"Or women, yes."

"It's different now." I rolled my glass between my

palms, talking more to myself than either of them. "Back in Blakeworth…he wasn't mine, then. Not officially."

"Please tell me you've fucked him." Noelle, of course.

"Aside from the first time?" I shook my head. "No."

"What the shit!" Noelle flailed her arms and legs out dramatically, sliding from the armchair to the floor. "You had your whole romantic evening with him and didn't get some scarred, giant dick? Why the fuck not?"

His dick isn't scarred. I bit my tongue and chose against the snarky answer, despite what my tequila-driven urges wanted me to say. "I just wanted to have that moment with him, watching the sunset together."

"Bo-*ring,*" Noelle groaned. "Who says you can't watch a pretty sunset and get pounded at the same time?"

"No one," I laughed. "I dunno, it just didn't seem right at the time. I'd rather do it when we can relax and not have this dangerous mission hanging over our heads, you know?"

"Nah, I'm with Noelle on this one," Tessa chimed in. "There's no better sex than might-never-see-you-alive-again sex."

"Thank you!" My sister-in-law flipped her hair smugly.

"But," Tessa added, "the holy-shit-you're-alive-and-back-in-one-piece sex is pretty epic too. That's how this little lady was made." She patted Vivian's back.

That last statement seemed to do it. Tessa's face screwed up in a grimace, her lower lip wobbling as she willed herself not to cry. Noelle and I slid over to her at the same time, sandwiching her between us to wrap mother and baby in a cocoon of love and support.

"It's okay, mama." Noelle rested her cheek on the back of Tessa's head as she rocked her gently from side to side. "It sucks. It's not fair. Let it out."

"Why does it have to be *both* of them?" Tessa sniffed, accepting my tissue. "Goddamn it."

"We're still here," I said. "I know it's not the same, but we're here for you, honey. You're not alone."

"I know." She sniffed again, dabbing at her eyes. "Thanks, guys."

"And it's not forever," Noelle reminded her. "They'll be back. Both of them."

The three of us remained linked around each other until Andrea returned, her own eyes puffy and nose running. We opened our arms and brought her into our cuddle pile like she had never left. There we remained until one of Finn's lieutenants informed us that it was almost go-time, and that Andrea was needed in the conference room.

My heart beat a hard rhythm in my chest as the four of us stood up, hands linked as we followed him to the secured conference room. Noelle glanced at me, blinking back her own tears, but her mouth was hard and determined. I tried to funnel some of her strength to myself. We'd stay with our people until the last possible moment.

The room was already bustling with activity when we entered. Shadow, Jandro, Grudge, and Finn spoke quietly at one end of the table, leaning over a map in front of them. Big G, Reaper, Gunner, and another member of Finn's army spoke on another side of the room.

A few faces looked up as we stepped into the room. Some were friendly, others tense. It was no secret that most of Finn's people disagreed with how this mission would be carried out. But they'd never seen how an MC operated before.

"Ah, the woman of the hour," Finn greeted Andrea with a warm smile. "If you're ready, we'll just go over a few things one final time."

She nodded and broke away from us with a last squeeze of our hands. As Finn led her to look over the map, Shadow made his way over to me.

He was dressed from head to toe in black, for once not wearing his Steel Demons cut, but a plain one with no insignia. Under his cut and long-sleeved shirt, a stab-proof vest created a slightly bulky rectangle over his torso. It did nothing to diminish his intimidating stature, as evident by people getting out of his way as he crossed the room. Nor did it decrease the heat lighting me up as he got closer. I closed my fists until my nails bit into my palms. It was all I could do to not drag him off to another room and rip every piece of armor off of him.

My newest man didn't stop until his gloved hand reached my face, the other one drawing me against him by my hip. Our lips came together in the most fluid, natural way, like we were made to be linked together. My palms rested on his wide shoulders, toes barely touching the ground like his kiss would send me floating.

With the vest between us, it felt like I couldn't get close enough, no matter how much I pressed my body to him.

"Wait," he said when we parted for a breath. With a turn of his head, he bit the fingertip of his glove to pull it off. The warmth of his bare hand against my cheek drew a shaky sigh from my chest. It hit me hard then, that this would be the last time in days that he'd touch me.

I leaned into his palm, reaching for another kiss, which he freely gave. The whole room was probably staring at us, but fuck if I cared. I wrapped around his neck tighter, tongue melding with his as I realized *he* didn't care if anyone watched us either.

"Keep kissing me like that," I whispered, forehead pressed to his. "And I really won't let you go."

He let out a soft hum as he kissed me again, slow and decadent, scar-tissued fingers caressing my cheek. "I'll be back before you know it."

"Not soon enough."

Our surroundings melted away, and I committed all of my senses to memorizing this man. Everything, from the slight flavor of coffee on his tongue to the scent of gunpowder and leather on him. The texture of his skin under my lips and hands and those mismatched eyes drinking me in like he wanted to memorize me in the same way.

"Tell me what you said last night." My hands trailed down and slid under the stab-proof vest. "I need to hear it again."

Shadow pulled his other glove off and cupped my face with both hands bare. "I'll never leave you." His breath hitched in his chest as he hesitated, then continued. "Because…I'm yours."

"Say it again," I pleaded shamelessly, desperately. My chest already ached with missing him. He didn't have the most dangerous job on the mission, but I knew my stomach wouldn't stop clenching until I saw his motorcycle riding into Four Corners again.

"I'll never leave you," he repeated. "I'll always come back."

Jandro walked up next to us at that point, hands behind his back and his face apologetic. "It's time, man."

Shadow nodded and slowly unwound from me, our fingertips the last to break away from each other. He pulled his gloves back on, then he and Grudge followed Andrea and Big G out the door.

A crowd of no less than thirty people watched their motorcycles take off just as dusk gave way to night. Shadow kept his headlight off, perfectly capable of seeing in the dark, with Grudge keeping his light dim as he followed Shadow's red brake light.

Jandro hugged me from behind as their lights and rumbling engines faded away into darkness.

"Did you tell him?" he asked with a warm kiss on my cheek.

"No," I sighed. "Maybe I should have, but I didn't want it to seem so…final."

"It won't be," he assured me. "You will when he comes back."

NINETEEN

SHADOW

W e rode exclusively at night, with Grudge and I avoiding the main roads. Andrea and Big G took the highways like normal, with us keeping watch from a distance. We even camped separately to not appear as though we were traveling together, which was fine with me. I didn't know Andrea well and didn't care for Big G's company. I appreciated Grudge's silence, although he was a chatty fucker with a pen and paper. And apparently, he loved terrible jokes.

What's orange and sounds like a parrot? He shoved his notepad at me, snickering.

"I dunno, Grudge. What?"

A carrot!

I choked on my drink, going into a coughing fit while he fell over with that silent laughter of his.

"Why haven't you picked up sign language?" I asked him one night. "Might be easier than writing all the time, right?"

I knew from our mission in Blakeworth, he and the

Sons used hand signals to communicate quickly between each other. Beyond that, he made gestures for simple things and wrote down any thoughts that were more complex.

"Hmm." He shook his head and scribbled out a reply. *Nah. T & D would have to learn it too. Then translate 4 me. This is easier 4 everyone.*

"Still might not hurt to learn," I said. "I had a book on ASL back in Sheol. Taught myself the alphabet and a few phrases. Didn't really go deeper than that, though."

Grudge's mouth tightened and he shook his head. He clearly didn't want to be pressed on the subject, so I dropped it, sipping whiskey next to our campfire as he turned to a fresh page.

Miss her?

I swallowed, wondering if there was another word for the uncomfortable pangs in my chest from not having Mariposa around. I missed her while she worked at the hospital for an entire day. I missed her when I was alone at night in the B&B, knowing I wouldn't see her until morning while she was in the next room with her men.

But this feeling, like a tether stretching to its breaking point across the distance between me and her, felt different. It was deeper, sharper. A physical ache in my body that would only be soothed by having her near me again.

"Yes." I opted to give Grudge the simple answer. "A whole fucking lot."

Me too.

I looked at him across the campfire. Grudge often wrote his messages to be brief and to the point, which didn't always make his thoughts clear.

"You miss Mariposa, or someone else?"

He waved two fingers, indicating it was the second thing I said.

"T-Bone and Dyno?"

He shook his head, then waved his hands in a way that seemed to illustrate feminine curves.

"A woman?" I lifted my head from the saddlebag I was using as a pillow. "I didn't know you had one."

He shook his head again, quickly scrawling on his pad to elaborate. *I don't. Just miss one.*

"You should take the advice you gave me," I said, knocking back the rest of my drink. "Just put it out there and be yourself."

"Heh." Grudge made a noise of disagreement and shook his head again, but didn't write out another explanation.

We smothered the fire as daylight approached and took turns watching as the other man slept. When dusk began falling, we hit the road again.

Andrea and Big G doubled up on one motorcycle, taking the winding two-lane main road while Grudge and I kept them in our line of sight along the canyons above. Jandro had fitted our cafe racers with the thickest off-road tires and biggest damn mufflers he could find so we'd make minimal noise.

The two-day ride was a whole lot of nothing, with no direct contact with the other riders except for a quick flash of a mirror to let them know we were still there. It was late afternoon when we came within sight of New Ireland's northeastern border. Although it wasn't the border itself as much as we spotted the Irish flag flapping in the chilly wind.

Grudge and I rode to opposite embankments flanking the settlement. We were each a good hundred yards away from their perimeter, and would have no problem taking out anyone patrolling.

I parked next to some dense brush, took what I needed from my packs, and walked the bike *into* the bush. After grabbing some tumbleweeds and sticking them in at odd angles, I felt satisfied that my bike was adequately camouflaged. Ideally, no one would be walking around here anyway. I loaded the first of my rifles and made my way up to the top of the hill, crouched low and silent as a cat. Right before reaching the top, I lowered to my knees and crawled my way to the ledge until I had a clear view of the gate while lying on my stomach.

Big G and Andrea were, for the moment, out of sight. They were hidden at the base of Grudge's hillside, preparing to approach the gate with their disguises. Grudge flashed me an okay sign, indicating he had eyes on them. Nodding in return, I turned my attention to the final obstacle Andrea would be facing.

Twelve armed guards stood in front of the northeastern entrance alone, while a Jeep filled with more soldiers made its way slowly around the perimeter just outside the gate. This kind of security seemed excessive, almost like they were expecting an attack. I could only speculate that General Tash made many enemies due to how swiftly he trampled over cities and territories. Small uprisings of those he'd conquered had to be expected.

I tried to push away the thought of survivors marching up to this gate, probably wholly unprepared and armed with things like pitchforks. Just ordinary people who wanted justice for the atrocities committed against their loved ones. What kind of fate did they meet against these soldiers? The gravel road, surrounding sand, and perimeter walls were clean, even polished. There were no heads on spikes, no human remains littering the ground, no clues to indicate Tash's abject cruelty. Some unassuming refugee might stumble upon this place and even think they were safe.

Movement below me prompted my index finger to curl around my trigger—just resting, not yet squeezing. Andrea was making her way out, approaching the gate on foot and…

I looked up from my sights and blinked both eyes. "What the fuck?"

Big G was approaching the gate *with* her.

Looking across the valley to Grudge, he seemed just as confused as me. The plan was for Big G to cover Andrea as she went in *alone*. If there had been a change in plans, we sure as fuck weren't notified.

"God fucking damn it, Big G," I cursed under my breath as I pulled a small set of binoculars from my pocket.

Andrea was bound with her hands tied in front of her, Big G pulling roughly on her arm so much that she stumbled to keep up. She was scantily clad, the low-cut dress she wore her only possession. I figured she would make some kind of pitch as a service girl offering to entertain the soldiers, but to my knowledge, she didn't need Big G for that.

Unless he had plans of his own that he wanted to carry out once inside, which was the most likely answer. I muttered curses under my breath as the guards halted them at the gate and began asking questions. Big G acted without thinking or informing others who his actions might affect. The problem with him wasn't so much that he was insubordinate, but that he believed his ideas were much better than they actually were.

It felt like I held my breath through their long, ten-minute exchange standing outside the gate. Big G did most of the talking, while Andrea only answered questions when directly spoken to. My lungs released when the gates began to swing open but tightened up again when, just as I feared, Big G followed Andrea inside.

Grudge and I quickly lost our view of them as the gates slid closed. The two undercover Steel Demons were officially behind enemy lines. My mind raced, wondering what I should do. We weren't given orders for this situation and I didn't have a tactical mind like Gunner. We were supposed to come back with Big G alive or dead, unless circumstances prevented us from retrieving his body.

Anger coiled in my body. The fucker *knew* we were out here, they both did. They knew we couldn't leave.

I had to get back to my woman. I promised her.

Looking across the valley, I made sure I had Grudge's attention before making the ASL sign for *hours* with my left hand, then counted up to 24 with my right.

To my relief, he nodded and made the *okay* sign that he understood. I sighed and shifted my legs underneath me, trying to prepare myself for the long day ahead as I marked where the shadows touched the ground next to me.

One full day. Big G would have twenty-four hours to do whatever the fuck and get out. If he wasn't outside that gate by this time tomorrow, we'd head home without him and he was on his own.

———

IT MUST HAVE BEEN SOMEWHERE around hour twenty when I spotted movement down below. I rubbed my weary eyes and slapped myself awake, just as I'd done for the last several hours. A quick glance to the other embankment confirmed that Grudge was awake and watching too.

I waited with bated breath as the gates slid open, not knowing entirely who or what to expect coming through from the other side. My heart lifted slightly when I saw Big G being escorted out with a soldier on each side. He looked fine, not at all abused or in any distress. I didn't want to relax too soon, but whatever story he told to get in with Andrea must have worked. I couldn't wait until Reaper dragged that information out of him.

His escorts followed him roughly fifty feet outside of their perimeter before halting, their work done as they returned to stand at attention. Rather than continue on to where his bike was hidden, Big G stopped with them.

"Fucking get out of there," I muttered under my

breath. "You big dumbshit, what the fuck are you doing?"

He dawdled, standing casually as he turned to face his two escorts. His mouth moved and his facial expressions looked as if he was cracking jokes, but I couldn't be sure. My finger curled around my rifle trigger, aiming at the empty space between him and the two soldiers. It was unnerving how familiar he was acting with Tash's men. Like they were friends.

My heart beat with ever-increasing punches to my ribcage. Big G was annoying and not very smart. But a traitor? Even if so, would he be dumb enough to act friendly with Tash's guards right in front of us?

The next movement came faster than my eyes could follow. All I saw was Big G swaying his upper body like he was leaning forward with laughter. Next, a gunshot rang out and one of the escorts clutched his chest as he fell to the ground.

All my senses heightened to focus on the scene below me, my whole body as tense as a tripwire. Big G shot the second escort before he had time to react, and then both men were on the ground. The first man who'd fallen had an empty holster.

Shocked stillness gave way to chaos. Shouts and running exploded from the front gate as Tash's guards realized two of their men were down, and the culprit was someone they just released.

Big G shouldered his stolen gun and fired into the soldiers running toward him. In the distance, a Jeep made a sharp U-turn and accelerated hard toward the lone gunman.

"For Dallas!" Big G shouted at the top of his lungs. "For the Sons of Odin! The Steel Demons wish you a long and prosperous fucking life!"

"Fucking idiot," I grumbled through my teeth. "Stupid goddamn fucking idiot."

The windshield of the oncoming Jeep shattered, but not from Big G, who was still focused on the men on foot ahead of him. Grudge had his long-barreled rifle pointed right at the vehicle and began picking off passengers and the driver.

Right, we still had to cover him, despite him outing himself like a fucking dumbass. I took careful aim at another swarm of soldiers heading for him, nailing their squadron leader right in his forehead.

"We're under attack!" someone yelled. "Snipers in the canyons! Get the Jeeps out there!"

Fuck, we couldn't afford to stick around. Why in God's fucking name would Big G endanger us like this?

It's a suicide mission, I realized.

He had to have known he wouldn't make it out of this alive, even with us covering him. But now Andrea was at risk, and we weren't expecting first contact from her for weeks.

Big G's body jerked as he received a bullet to his shoulder. He just switched hands on his gun and returned fire, his strength already leaving him. Grudge and I picked soldiers off as fast as we could, but there was no way we could get all of them. And now they knew our positions, and who we were affiliated with.

Everything about this mission had been fucked up.

If Andrea wasn't subsequently captured because of this shit, I would consider it a miracle.

I pulled away from the ledge just as Big G fell to his knees. More soldiers were swarming in, and there was nothing we could do for him. Half-crawling, half-sliding down the hill on my side, I tried to ignore the feeling of abject failure in my gut. I had done my part, but it felt like I'd barely done shit. And now another one of our own was dead.

That pulled forth a lot of confusing feelings for me. I had never liked Big G, or even cared about him, really. But he was still a Steel Demon, a brother-in-arms. Foolish as his final actions were, he did it for the club. For the ones we lost.

I sprang to my feet at the bottom of the hill and took off running, hoping Grudge was already retreating too. Jerking my bike out of the bushes and weeds, I turned the ignition before even jumping on. I threw a leg over and hit the throttle hard, kicking up rocks and dust as I searched the fading daylight for Grudge.

I didn't dare turn my headlight on, and thankfully didn't need to. My silent brother raced down his hillside like a bat out of hell, hair and beard whipping back as he pushed his bike hard.

"Grudge!" I yelled, maneuvering closer to him.

He glanced at me, then made a panicked motion at something behind me. Before I could check my mirrors, a bright glare reflecting in them nearly blinded me. I looked over my shoulder to see the outlines of three Jeeps in my dust, with gigantic search lights mounted on top of their vehicles.

TWENTY

MARIPOSA

"They'll be okay, sugar." Reaper reached for my hand to stop me from pacing a hole into the floor, but I just moved further away from him to keep doing it.

"It's been five days," I said, not for the first time. "It wasn't supposed to take more than four. Something must have happened."

"Maybe, but it could be literally anything." Gunner moved into my direct path. "There's been thunderstorms out in that area, so they might've had to hunker down. They could've run out of gas and had to hitchhike. Don't worry until we've got something to worry about."

"No word for over twenty-four hours past their ETA *is* something to worry about!"

"*Bonita.*" Jandro tried next. "This is Shadow we're talking about, doing the best at what he does."

"Last time he did that, he nearly died, and guess who had to put him back together?" I shot back.

Without anything left to convince me, I resumed pacing the living room in my beautiful new house, too anxious to enjoy it. Moving and decorating had been my only distractions for the last few days. Reaper, in his persistent paranoia about Daren's dream, did not want me away from my men for even a moment. There was only so much I could do at the hospital without one of them hovering over me, so I took a few days off to get moved in.

Finn and Lis insisted on buying us furniture, introducing us to a lovely family of woodworkers who made everything by hand. In just three days, we had a brand new dining table, chairs, and bookshelves.

In their five years since arriving at Four Corners, my in-laws also accumulated dishes, blankets, rugs, wall-hangings, and other various knickknacks they were happy to pass along to us.

"It's the artist in me," Lis laughed. "I love collecting beautiful things and supporting my fellow craftsmen, but it's no good if they sit around collecting dust."

One of the most precious things she gave to me was a bronze sculpture made by her late husband, Carter. Like her, he'd been an accomplished metalsmith, but preferred creating large-scale sculptures over jewelry. Soon after settling in Four Corners, she and Finn recovered a small collection of Carter's pieces that he'd hidden away in storage.

"Lis, he made this for *you*!" I protested when she wheeled the heavy bronze piece into the house on a hand truck. "It's yours, you should keep it."

"Oh, I have a half dozen with a lot more sentimental value." She brought the hand truck upright carefully. "And anyway, I want all of my children to have something of his." She smiled at me, green eyes glittering. "It's like he's still here, watching over his family. Noelle has a favorite that I'll give to her when she has her own place."

"That's really lovely." I was touched, the will to fight her utterly squashed.

And it was a beautiful sculpture. It looked like a tree, each branch and leaf etched with exquisite details. The trunk however, was that of a woman's body. Not terribly unique subject matter for a male artist, but I loved how realistic the form was. Wide hips and thick thighs, softness to the belly, and even breasts that were not perfectly symmetrical. All the perceived imperfections made it even more beautiful. I considered asking my mother-in-law if she had been his muse for this particular piece, but decided against it.

Together we placed it in a corner between one of the first-story bedrooms and the stairs. I stared at the bronze tree woman now, for some reason fixating on the fact that the man who created her, who brought her to life from a shapeless hunk of metal, was dead.

Tonight was supposed to be our housewarming party, but the last thing I felt like doing was celebrating.

Is this how one of my men breaks my heart? I wondered. *By leaving and never coming back to me?*

I hadn't thought about Noelle's prophecy from Daren in weeks, brushing it off with every affectionate touch and word from my men since I first heard it. But Reaper's increasing fear about his own prophecy brought Noelle's harrowing words to the forefront of my mind. *You're going to get your heart broken. And not just by one man.*

"How long?"

"How long what, sugar?" Reaper once again reached for me from his spot on the couch. I relented this time, taking his hand.

"How long until you send a team to go find them? I want to go with, if it comes to that. They might need medical attention."

My husband sighed, tilting his head back, but at this point he knew better than to argue with me. "One more day. Another full twenty-four hours before we investigate." He pulled me over the couch's arm, sending me tumbling across his lap. "And if you're going, at least one of us will too. No excuses."

"Fine." I curled up against his chest, snuggling into the wall of hard muscle. "Fuck, I just want him to be okay."

"Have faith in Shadow, sugar." His hands braced around my hip and lower back. "He's tougher than all of us."

Gunner came to sit next to us. "I'll send Horus out that direction tomorrow morning, if that'll make you feel better."

I turned in Reaper's lap, leaning until I stretched between him and Gunner, and rested my head on Gunner's shoulder. "You're the best. Thank you."

"Jandro!" Reaper looked around behind him. "Where'd he go? It's not like him to miss a cuddle pile."

"Probably in the garage," I mused.

Like me, Jandro tried to smother his concern for Shadow by keeping busy. First, he assembled a brand-new luxurious chicken coop in our new backyard, then moved on to every tiny, minute motorcycle repair he could think of. It was getting late, and the birds were all tucked away in their insulated chicken-mansion, so I could only imagine Jandro would be off tinkering with something.

I was dozing off, cozy and warm from my men's bodies and the fire crackling in the stone fireplace, when a slamming door startled me awake.

"Riders coming into town," Jandro announced, heading to the sink to wash his hands. "Heard the engines and saw two headlights coming down over the hill."

"Two?" I jumped up from the couch, Reap and Gun quickly following. "Not three?"

"Pretty sure, yeah."

"You didn't see who they were?"

"We'll find out in a sec, *Mariposita*." He dried his hands on a towel and bent to plant a kiss on my forehead. "Too dark and too far away to see shit."

I went back to pacing, this time on the front porch. The air was chilly and I huddled my arms close as I listened for the approaching motorcycles. As the roars grew louder, I discerned that it was only one bike coming to this part of town. A single headlight hovering over the winding gravel road through the new development confirmed what I suspected. The rider could surely see me now, but it was too dark out and the headlight too blinding for me to see him.

Please be him, I silently begged. *Please let it be my Shadow.*

Freyja came out to join me on the porch, her eyes watching the road, but I didn't dare hope until I saw him with my own eyes.

And when I did, I burst into tears.

Shadow only had time to park the bike, but left it running as he jumped off. I took one step down the porch, but he closed the distance swiftly, pulling me into his chest with a squeezing, urgent hug.

"I told you I would." His lips moved over the crown of my head, planting kisses in my hair and wrapping my body in heat. "I'm here, see? I'm back."

"You are," I sniffled into his chest, my hands moving over him as if checking to make sure he was really there. "And you're…" I lifted my head, taking in the state of his leathers for the first time. "…filthy."

"Yeah," he laughed, releasing me to turn off the ignition on his bike. Under the porch light, I could see how he was caked in sand and dirt from the road. "It was a rough couple of days coming back."

"Who came with you?"

"Grudge," he answered. "He went back to the Sons and I came straight here. We uh," he sighed, clearly exhausted, "we lost Big G."

"And Andrea?"

"She made it inside, but…" He shook his head with another sigh. "I should give a full report to Reaper."

"Of course, but not yet." I grabbed his hands, pulling him up the porch to the front door. "You should clean up, eat, and rest. We gave you one of the downstairs bedrooms, I hope that's okay. I brought your stuff over from the B&B, everything's in there."

My fourth man smiled wearily at me as he followed my lead into our home. "Thank you, Mari. I'm…"

"Yes?" I closed the front door behind him and whirled around. "Take your boots off here. You're what, love?"

He just looked at me quietly, my hand still encased in his, rough fingers stroking over my palm.

"I'm so lucky to be yours."

———

THE NEXT DAY was spent spreading the word about Shadow and Grudge's return, and our housewarming party was rescheduled to that night. Jandro had gotten to know a butcher in town, and arranged to have a roasting pit dug in the backyard for a whole pig to serve that evening.

Reaper invited his father and the governor over early in the afternoon for Shadow's report, after he'd gotten a long shower and full night of sleep.

"Are you fuckin' shitting me?" I heard Reaper demand from the kitchen table.

"I wish I was, president," Shadow answered evenly.

"What the fuck, Big G?"

"I asked myself the same question many times."

"Has anyone told Tessa?" I popped my head into the doorway.

"I imagine Grudge has," Shadow said. "Considering they live in the same building."

"Sugar, make sure she comes over tonight." Reaper said, unofficially making me part of the meeting.

"I can ask her, but if she wants to be alone, I won't force her. She was afraid of this happening."

"Do what you can," he urged. "She should be around loved ones."

"I can ask Lis to hang out with her," Finn offered. "Losing husbands may be an unfortunate thing they have in common."

"I'm sorry for your lost man." The governor fiddled with his empty teacup and smiled at me appreciatively as I came to take it away. "It truly is tragic."

"I can't say it's completely unexpected," Reaper sighed. "I think he just couldn't pass up the chance to kill some of Tash's people and didn't think it through, as usual."

"Do you think Andrea's cover is compromised?" Finn asked.

"She is definitely a target, if she hasn't already been caught," Shadow said. "Big G referred to us and the Sons by name. They know she's at least affiliated with us."

"We won't know until the time to make first contact comes." Reaper drummed his fingers on the table. "If there isn't a message from her, that will be our answer."

"And what will you do if that happens?" Vance asked.

"Go back to square one." Reaper rubbed his hands over his face with a groan. "Again."

"Andrea's smart," I said over the running water in the kitchen sink. "She knows how to hide in plain sight and put on a persona. Even if G massively fucked up, she'll adapt and get her job done."

"Really?" Vance piped up. "How did she develop skills like that?"

Shadow and Reaper both hid smiles as I answered. "She was a high-end escort before meeting her husband."

"Ah." The governor's blush was precious. "I see."

The others chuckled at his discomfort while I made my way to Shadow, standing behind him as I wrapped my arms around his neck. "What I want to know is why you took an extra day to get back to me."

"We were covering Big G when Tash's patrol spotted us," he said, hands sliding up to clasp mine resting on his chest. "We had to lead some Jeeps on a goose chase all over wild terrain, and lost at least half a day doing that." His head tilted back to look at me. "Fortunately we were faster, and Jeeps are gas guzzlers."

"Uh-huh." I made a show of sounding skeptical as I leaned down to kiss his forehead. "A very likely excuse."

"I missed you before I hit the road." He reached up to caress my cheek. "I was counting down the minutes until I'd be back with you."

"You're all, uh," the governor's voice cut in, "a very openly affectionate bunch."

Reaper laughed as he stood from the table. "Stay for the party, governor. You've seen how hard we fight." He came over to me, taking hold of my jaw as he pressed a hard kiss to my mouth. "Now you can see how hard we live."

———

THE HOUSE STARTED FILLING up with people a few hours later. Noelle and Lis came over to help prepare food, Gunner quickly sneaking in behind them. He darted into the downstairs bedroom we'd designated as the guest room, and quickly shoved something in the closet.

"Are you up to no good again?" I asked, leaning against the door jam.

"Always, baby girl." He grinned, kissing me in the doorway. "You'll see."

"Well, that isn't cryptic at all."

He just laughed, heading to the front door to let more people in. This time it was Tessa, another one of Andrea's friends, Elise, plus Tessa and Andrea's children. The young mother smiled as she walked in, but I saw the somberness in her eyes.

"Hey, honey." I pulled her into a hug. "Thanks for coming. I'm so sorry."

"You don't have to be." Her voice was raspy like she'd been crying. "I know you weren't the biggest fan of him. She'd never tell me, but I bet Noelle was celebrating."

"She wouldn't, Tess. And anyway, none of that matters." I held tightly on to her shoulders. "He was yours. You made your family with him. It's normal to mourn him, even if he wasn't perfect."

"Thanks, Mari. I am glad the other guys got back safe." She lifted Vivian out of her carseat, heading toward the backyard where the kids had gathered around the roasting pit. "Guess I'll go see what the excitement's about."

"Help yourself to anything." I squeezed her shoulder as she walked past me.

More Steel Demons trickled in over the next hour, the house growing loud and the mood celebratory. The Sons of Odin were among the last to arrive, T-Bone picking me up in a crushing hug as he planted a fat kiss on my cheek.

"Better put her down, T," Dyno laughed. "We're already getting the murder looks."

"Ah, these Demons don't scare me." T-Bone set me lightly on my feet. "They're all teddy bears under them cuts."

"Care to fuckin' repeat that?" Reaper came over, grinning, and already on his third glass of whiskey, which he took care not to spill as he hugged and greeted each of the Sons.

"I said you have a great house, Reap." T-Bone chuckled. "Congratulations."

"Thanks. You guys want a tour of the place?"

Grudge pointed at Reaper's whiskey and waggled his eyebrows.

"Drinks first? Yes, absolutely. Follow me, boys."

He led them through to the kitchen and soon after the party was well underway.

I looked out the kitchen window when I started making a plate of food, ignoring Hades begging for a bite at my side. We had enough room for a small pool in the backyard, and maybe a fire pit. I wanted more concrete out there too, with patio furniture and shady overhangs.

So it could be more like Sheol, I realized.

It would never be exactly the same, but I missed that part of our old home the most—having a place where everyone could gather and just celebrate being alive. The cold kept most people inside at this time of year, but a few kids ran around the backyard playing tag. Jandro talked with some guys over beers by the roasting pit. We had the essence of our old home, it just needed a few touches to make it a true Steel Demons party house.

"Can I have everyone's attention please!" Reaper called from the living room. "Where the fuck is Larkan?"

I followed the crush of people moving into the living room and promptly groaned. "Reaper, get off the coffee table!"

"It's fine, babe. She's sturdy." He bounced on the balls of his feet to demonstrate, sloshing his whiskey in the process.

I just covered my face with a hand while someone laughed and patted my shoulder sympathetically. If he broke our brand new table, it was on him to fix.

"Gun, get the thing. Where's Larkan at?"

"Right here, Pres." The prospect raised a beer from the middle landing of the stairs, his other arm around Noelle's shoulders.

"Get your grubby mitts off my sister and come down here, boy."

Larkan took his sweet time, knowing it would irritate Reaper. He polished off his beer and kissed Noelle, deep and full of tongue, to the sounds of cheers and wolf whistles. His smile as he came down the stairs was smug with a hint of curiosity. Surprisingly, Reaper didn't continue to rib him for it.

Gunner came out of the spare bedroom, carrying the wide, narrow box I saw him with earlier. He couldn't hold back his grin as he stood next to Reaper, facing Larkan and everyone else.

"I know we have traditions and customs and shit, but I'm drunk and I can't remember 'em now," Reaper began, earning laughs from everyone. "Gun, just open it and give it to 'im."

Gunner pulled open the top of the box, revealing a swath of black leather with the Steel Demons' grinning skull depicted. "Try it on, Lark."

Larkan's face had gone blank with shock when he saw the cut. He reached in slowly, with shaking hands, and held it up for everyone to see. It was indeed the cut of a fully patched-in SDMC member, with his name embroidered on the front. He slipped his arms through the holes and the whole house erupted in applause.

"I don't have a fuckin' road name for ya." Reaper waved his hand in front of him. "Nor an official job title for you yet, but everyone here knows you deserve this patch. You've saved our asses back at the Sandia outpost, and kept my old lady safe in Blakeworth. You're a Demon, Lark. You always have been, even before today. This is just sealin' the deal. Thanks for having our backs, brother."

"Thank you, Reaper," Larkan said so softly, it was almost a whisper.

My husband jumped down from the table and the two men clapped arms around each other in a rough hug. They clung to each other while everyone cheered, whistled, and applauded. When Larkan pulled away, he immediately turned to the stairs where Noelle beamed at him proudly.

"Baby, can you come here?" He extended a hand out to her.

A soft murmur of, *"Awww"* rose up from the onlookers as Noelle came down to join him.

"You better not embarrass me, you—"

Her words cut off abruptly when he dropped to one knee.

The *"Aww"*'s turned to gasps and hushed exclamations. Even I sucked in a breath and brought a hand to my chest.

"Marry me, Noelle." Larkan's eyes were only on her, his hands wrapped around her fingers. "Ever since you and Mari pulled me out of that wreck, I've only wanted two things in life. This cut, and for you to be my old lady."

"Are you…are you serious?" She stared at him, wide-eyed with disbelief.

"I've never been more serious in my life." He brought her fingers to his lips. "I don't have a ring yet, 'cause I wasn't exactly expecting this." He looked back at Reaper with a soft laugh. "But I told you, woman, I'd make you officially mine the moment I got a patch."

"I didn't think you'd do it so…literally," Noelle laughed nervously.

Everyone, Larkan included, seemed to hold their

breath as they waited for an answer.

"I love you," he said, kissing her fingers again. "I want to spend the rest of my life taking care of you and whatever family we make."

"Too much information," Reaper muttered, earning a punch on the arm from Gunner.

"So what do you say, baby?" Larkan asked, his nerves starting to show.

Noelle grinned, wrapping her arms around his neck as she leaned over and kissed him, much like the way he did on the stairs.

"Of course I'll marry you, dummy."

The house erupted into cheers so loud, my ears started to ring. That still didn't stop me from joining in the noise as Larkan rose to his feet and picked up Noelle to kiss her again. Her palms against his cheeks, she broke the kiss and said loud enough for everyone to hear, "But pull this embarrassing shit again and I'll divorce your ass."

"We need a toast!" Reaper shouted over everyone's raucous laughter, trying not to bump into people as he headed into the kitchen.

The energy turned up several notches after the proposal. More drinks were flowing and everyone was excitedly congratulating the new couple. Even Tessa was smiling and hugging them both. I was glad and relieved she could feel at least some happiness tonight.

"Hey, Lark!" someone shouted across the room. Imagine my surprise to see that it was Shadow.

"What's up, dude?" the newest Demon grinned after releasing someone from a hug.

Shadow smiled back. "When do you want that tattoo?"

It only took a moment for Larkan to decide. "You good to do it right now?" He lifted up his T-shirt, revealing sculpted pecs and rows of abs. "Give it to me right here, man." He slapped his chest.

Shadow's grin grew wider. "Let me finish my drink and get set up."

"Wooo!" Larkan slid off his new cut and removed his shirt completely.

Much to Noelle's dismay, he whipped the shirt around his head a few times before tossing it in a random direction. He nearly fell over laughing when it landed on Governor Vance's head. Noelle placed a hand on her forehead and turned away, but I saw her shoulders shaking with laughter too.

"Have fun holding that wiggly one down," I said to Shadow as he headed toward his bedroom.

He paused to draw me in for a kiss, gently squeezing my waist. "I know a few tricks of the trade. He won't be nearly as solid as you, though."

His voice was low and warm, husky from just enough alcohol for a light buzz. I would have swooned if he hadn't been holding on to me. I stole a few more kisses before he released me, watching his wide shoulders swing through the door of his bedroom.

I was tipsy enough to consider following him, closing the door, and finally having our first moment alone since he got back. Preferably several moments. Even more preferably, all night long. I wanted him on top of me, inside me, all over my skin. Every taste of him leading up to now felt like meager scraps. Nothing was enough until we had consumed each other whole.

The tattoo would take a few hours, which felt like an eternity right then. I had already waited days, months really, to make this man truly mine. I was at the point where I didn't care who saw. If Shadow wanted to take me bent over the couch, I'd get into position before he finished the sentence.

Despite his growing comfort in social situations, I knew he wouldn't go that far. So I had to keep being a good hostess for the next few hours at least.

Considering people were still using our kitchen table to eat, Shadow decided to set Larkan up on the coffee table. People gathered around to watch, and the newest Demon turned out to be not as wiggly as I thought.

"Can you put Noelle's name on the skull's forehead?" he asked at one point.

"You better not!" Noelle cried from across the room.

"No," Shadow answered in his more serious tone. "The Demon can't be altered in any way. I can put her name somewhere else, though."

"My ass, then." Larkan nodded determinedly.

"We're divorced!" Noelle bellowed, unable to contain her laughter. "Shortest marriage ever!"

"Love you too, babe!" Larkan laced his hands behind his head as Shadow worked.

People started filtering out of the house as the darkest areas of the tattoo were getting filled in. Governor Vance, Finn, and Lis were among the first to leave, making cracks about being too old to party with us as they said their goodbyes.

The house had finally quieted down, with only a few guests remaining as Shadow made the finishing touches on Larkan. Most of them talked quietly with my other men across the house in the sunroom, which they were using as a smoking lounge.

My fourth man twisted and stretched, rolling his neck around on his shoulders once he finally put the tattoo gun down. Larkan thanked him and rolled off the coffee table, looking pretty exhausted himself.

"Had enough of socializing yet?" I asked Shadow, coming up behind him to rub his shoulders.

"Just about hit my limit, yeah." He turned to look at me. "That never includes you, though."

"Smart thing to say," I smirked, circling around him until I landed in his lap.

He snapped his gloves off and pulled me higher up his thigh, kissing me like a starving man. My pulse shot up, heat throbbing between my legs. He was just as responsive and giving as ever, but his kisses seemed far more eager than ever before.

Our lips parted slowly on a breath, his eyes meeting mine before flicking down slightly. I couldn't help myself from leaning in, tracing that scar tissue through his brow and eyelid with my lips.

"Come to my room with me?" he asked so softly, like he was afraid of what the answer might be.

I slid a hand up his chest, the organ inside pounding like a drum under my palm. That steady, firm beat contrasted with the buzzing in my body, the anticipation of finally being with him like a beehive in my chest.

"I'd love that, Shadow."

MARIPOSA

Following Shadow into his room, I turned and locked the door behind me with a soft click. He stood in the center of the room when I turned back to face him, his face a mix of curiosity and apprehension.

"You okay?" I approached him, taking both of his hands.

His fingers squeezed around mine. "I'm just not sure what I'm supposed to do."

"That's okay." I offered him a smile. "We'll learn together. Do you want to sit down?"

He backed up slowly, lowering to sit at the edge of his bed. I placed a knee on either side of his thighs, lowering into his lap as my palms skimmed up his massive shoulders. In the familiar position, some tension drained out of him already, his gaze softening as his hands came around my back.

"You know how to kiss me," I told him, nudging my nose against his. "So why don't we start there?"

Shadow needed no further instruction, his lips

finding mine with a soft press. I closed my eyes to return the pressure, seeking nothing but the taste of him. We had all the time in the world now. No dangerous mission to take him away tomorrow. None of our people with gunshots or stab wounds calling me away to the hospital. We were still on the brink of war with all the worries that came with that. But right now, it was just us.

He sighed when my fingers came up to stroke his neck and face, pushing his hair back and dragging my touch along his scalp. One day, he'd figure out how much I just loved touching him.

Kissing him left me breathless. He never rushed or tried to dominate my mouth, but savored each taste along with me. A strong hand left a trail of heat up my back, while the other encircled my waist and pulled me closer. Only after several minutes of kissing, when he'd utterly relaxed into a puddle in my arms, did I prompt him to escalate things further.

My lips trailed across his cheek to his ear. "Touch me anywhere you want to," I whispered, darting my tongue out against his earlobe. "I mean it. Anywhere."

He let out a shuddering groan as my tongue trailed down the side of his neck, sucking lightly at the rapid pulse. His fingers curled at my hip but didn't move for the longest time. I brought a kiss back to his mouth and then, his hand inched under my shirt to graze against my bare skin.

"Can I—"

I grabbed the hem of my top and flung it over my head before he could finish asking the question.

"Yes, Shadow." I palmed the sides of his neck,

pulling another deep kiss from him. "Anything you ask me tonight, the answer is going to be yes."

He smiled, beautiful and unrestrained as his fingers now made tentative, exploratory trails of heat on my bare skin. Bolder now, he dragged kisses down the front of my throat. I tilted my head back to give him access, leaning into his hands still caressing me in relatively tame areas. One finger skimmed up my arm, over the tattoo he gave me, then hooked under the bra strap on my shoulder.

He dropped a kiss on my collarbone while slowly pulling the strap down over my arm. I knew he was giving me ample opportunity to stop him, to take back my enthusiastic *yes, anything*. But that was never going to happen.

I pulled my arm out when the strap reached my elbow and removed the other one myself. His gaze flicked back up to mine, our mouths finding each other in another sensual kiss as his hands slid around my ribcage to unhook my bra. He slid the garment out from between us and it fell discarded on the floor.

Hands and forearms covered my naked back as he crushed me to his chest, his kisses growing hungrier with each ragged breath. Just as he did with me, I grazed my fingertips along his waist and dipped them under the hem of his shirt.

"Can I?"

He froze for a moment, then leaned away from me to pull his shirt off his massive body.

For a few seconds, I could only stare and marvel. So, *so* many cuts that had healed and been reopened, overlapping on more that had healed and been reopened, with a few burns thrown in. So many of them were old and had stretched as his body grew. Scar tissue layered on itself again and again on top of muscle, like a type of armor. And probably to him, a kind of cage.

Shadow held his T-shirt in his fists like a barrier between us, his shoulders going rigid again. "I'll put this back on—"

"No." I grabbed the shirt from him and flung it away to the same dark corner where mine now resided. "Whatever you're thinking now, stop."

His brows lifted, eyes blinking as I tapped a finger to his forehead. "Stay out of there and just *be* with me." I placed that same hand on his chest, dragging it over the planes of muscles and scar tissue unabashedly. "I want you, Shadow." My other hand ran along the back of his shoulders, pulling him close to me again. "I want *all* of you."

My next kiss was forceful, shoving my tongue into his mouth while grinding on his erection to drive the point home. The next moan rumbling through him had my core clenching with need. He palmed my ass, squeezing and pulling me forward to increase the friction on him. Finally, *finally*, his touch slid up my ribs to fill his palms with my breasts.

I leaned into the scarred, calloused hands gently kneading and massaging, his breaths quieted as he watched for my response.

"What feels good here?" Shadow's teeth grazed along my shoulder, skimming back up to kiss my neck.

I had to bite back my whimper just at how sexy and

low his voice was, never mind what his hands and mouth were already doing.

"That," I gasped when his thumb and forefinger closed around my nipple, the peak already aching. "Anything, really. You can kiss me there too."

He let out a soft hum as his lips trailed lower, kissing the swells of my breasts as his hands continued to explore different touches and my reactions. I was halfway convinced I was soaking through my pants *and* his by the time he pulled a nipple into his mouth.

"Yes!" My fingers curled into his hair at the light drag of teeth on the sensitive point, his tongue quick to soothe the light sting of pain away. "That feels so good…" I was downright drunk on him, this man treating me with such care when he'd gotten so little of it in his lifetime.

I ran my hands down his back when he moved on to my other nipple, resting my cheek on his forehead while I praised and touched him with abandon. At the first chance I got, I'd be kissing every one of those scars. He deserved to feel every bit as good as he was making me feel.

His lips returned to mine when both breasts were marked red from his mouth, nipples and clit thoroughly stimulated and buzzing with need.

"Do you want to lie down?" I asked between kisses.

"Okay," he grunted, already leaning us to the side.

Our kisses never stopped on the way down to the bed. Shadow landed on his side, arms still wrapped around me as I began my scar-kissing journey at the top of his chest.

"Mari?" His mouth rested against my hair, fingers gliding along my sides.

"Mm-hm?" I kissed a deep line cutting across his sternum, tongue flicking out to give it a little extra love.

A hand came under my chin, bringing my gaze up.

"Will you show me how to please you?" The question was asked shyly, his warm gaze resting on my lips with a flush in his cheeks.

I brought his hand to my lips, pressing kisses to the scars on his knuckles until his eyes met mine.

"You already please me *immensely*, just by being you." I kissed his mouth, letting my lips hover over his. "But I can show you how to make me come."

"Yes," he rasped, warm breath fanning over my lips as his eyes heated. "Show me how."

I laced my fingers through his, dragging our joined hands between my breasts and down my belly.

"What most men don't realize," I paused over my jeans, unlinking our hands to get my clothes off easier, "is how important foreplay is to getting us off."

"Is that so?" Shadow mused, flicking open the button and dragging my zipper down. Together we shimmied my pants and underwear down my hips and peeled them off my legs.

"Everything we just did." I touched his face, bringing his attention back upward. "The way you touch me, kiss me, all of that is at *least* half the battle. Making a woman come starts long before her pants come off."

"I'll remember that," he murmured, nuzzling his forehead to mine as he skimmed fingertips across my ribs. "I could do nothing but kiss you for days," he added with a sigh.

Like magnets, our lips connected again. Warm contentment passed through our kisses and it tasted nothing short of delicious on him. I guided his hand on my belly lower, inching toward the heat between my legs that ached for some attention from him. His breath hitched as I led him over my mound and bypassed my clit, despite craving the heaviness of that hand on it, preferably with my legs clamped around him. Instead I guided his fingers through my folds, letting him spread and caress the sensitive flesh.

"Fuck," he bit out, his breath choked. "You're so wet already."

Leaving his hand in place to explore, I returned my palm to his cheek. "Because you turn me on so fucking much."

His smile was shy, face turned down in the pillow next to mine, but those fingers between my legs stroked and caressed with confidence.

"What do you like here?" He gazed along the length of my body, taking in my reactions from my eyes to my toes.

"Exactly what you're doing," I breathed over his lips, an agonizing two inches away. "Don't stop."

He kissed me again, answering my silent plea. His tongue and fingers mirrored each other, stroking and licking, his touch becoming more refined as my body gave him more information. Shadow was incredible at reading me—I learned that from our first kiss. When a finger dipped inside me, I released a gasp, my hips bucking up against his hand.

"Are you okay?" A flash of worry crossed his face and I clamped my thighs around his hand before he could pull it away.

"Yes, yes." I wrapped an arm around the back of his head, pulling him back down to me. "More, Shadow. That feels so good."

With his mouth returned to mine, I directed his hand a bit more, sweeping his thumb over my clit in a motion that had me writhing. "Right there, that's the key to making me come." He hummed thoughtfully in response, his kisses moving to my neck as my instructions came out in breathy pants. "You can curl your fingers inside me—oh, fuck! Yes, Shadow. Just like that..."

Thank all the gods for Shadow being so keenly observant. He tried different angles, varying speeds, depths, and pressures—all of which drove me wild and left me trembling at the mercy of how he played my body.

"You're so beautiful to watch," he murmured, lips dragging a hot trail to my nipple.

I whimpered as he pulled the aching peak into his mouth, fingers gliding steadily in and out of me while his thumb teased my clit. My hips raised off the bed, pressing up into his hand to chase the feeling that crackled over me like electricity.

"Don't stop," I begged, clutching his arm like it would get me there faster. "Shadow, I'm so close."

"Holy fuck..." was the last thing I heard him utter

before the blood pounding in my ears became a roar.

My release sent me shaking, pleasure exploding from my core outward like fireworks. Shadow thankfully didn't remove his hand from me until after my pleasure crested, the convulsions around his thick fingers so incredibly satisfying.

"Goddamn." Shadow caressed his hand up my thigh, watching in awe as the shivers wracked through me and my chest became heavy with ragged breaths. "How did that feel?"

"How does it feel when you come?" I grinned breathlessly.

"Pretty fuckin' good, but nothing that looks like that." He palmed my hip and my waist, my wetness on his fingers leaving glossy marks on my skin. "You can do that again, can't you?"

"You're just as bad as Reaper," I laughed, skimming both hands up his chest to wind around his neck. "Give me a minute to catch my breath."

"Fine." I felt his smile in his kiss and pulled him over me until his chest rested on mine with a comforting weight. "I'm not crushing you?" His hands slid under my back, holding me to him.

"No, I love how you feel." My lips found his forehead and eyelids, placing soft, lingering kisses there while I relished in his gentle sighs.

"I love how you feel." His forehead rested against my neck, placing small kisses on my collarbones. "I've never felt so...*good.*"

I laughed lightly, scratching over his neck and upper back. "I haven't even done anything to you yet."

"You don't need to." He lifted up from me slightly, returning that mouth to my neck with just enough suction and bite to bring back my shivers. "Pleasing you is just…everything."

I spread my palms on Shadow's back, trying to pull him back down, but he resisted, grinning wickedly as his hand returned to the slick, sensitive flesh between my legs.

"Have you rested enough?"

I answered him with a groan and a deep, tongue-fucking kiss. I wanted his cock, not his hand, but he made no move to even adjust that bulge pressing against the front of his jeans. My leg hooked around his hip, seeing if he would go along with the friction of his pants sliding down, but he remained steadfast and focused on me.

"Can I kiss you here?" he whispered with a swipe of his thumb over my clit.

"Yes," I panted, hips lifting again as I grew dizzy with the realization that he really was going to make tonight all about me. It was both immensely touching and incredibly frustrating. *Shadow, you deserve to get your cock sucked, god damn it.*

He began his journey down my body slowly, rolling my breasts in his hands and savoring my nipples in his mouth like he never wanted to release them. The roughness of his beard awakened the sensitivity of my skin, large hands tracing over my ribs as his kisses moved lower. My eyes closed as I just sunk into the care and gentleness of his touch, fingers running over his scalp and neck.

"What's this from?"

My eyes flew open and I lifted my head. Shadow's black hair spilled like ink over my belly, his face level with the small scar next to my right hip.

"Oh, I got my appendix removed years ago. In high school, I think."

I had honestly forgotten about the scar. It had been a part of me for so long and had faded over the years. If the other guys had noticed it, they made no mention of it to me. They had all probably kissed it at some point and moved on to more interesting parts of me. But Shadow was fixated, inspecting it so closely that his nose pressed against my skin. He traced it with a fingertip and pressed a long kiss to the mark.

"It's beautiful," he murmured, eyes flicking up to mine. "Because it's part of you."

"Shadow, oh—!"

My words were stolen as his mouth fell to my pussy, devouring me with a long, pulling kiss. Hands gripped the outside of my thighs, spreading me open like he was seeking more of me to taste. His tongue dragged from my clit to my opening, lips sucking, kissing, tasting every part of me he could find.

"Shadow…" My thigh pulled against his grip, wanting to clamp around his head and already shaking from the building of another orgasm. It wasn't even from what he was *doing* specifically, just that he couldn't seem to get enough of me.

"Fuck, your taste," he groaned between kisses, nips, and sucks of my flesh. "I want you as a meal every day."

My laughter died on a moan as he slid those well-practiced fingers inside me, his tongue swirling a storm of pleasure around my clit before topping the aching point with a light kiss.

"More, please," I panted, my hips already rolling and fucking his hand as he stilled, amusement dancing in his eyes. "Fuck, I need to come. Shadow, please."

"Mm, I think I want to drag this one out." He kissed my appendectomy scar again, his hand inside me passive while my heels dug into the mattress, desperate for leverage.

"Don't be mean," I whined.

"If you're really not enjoying this, I'll stop." He turned his head and sucked a kiss along my inner thigh, smiling wickedly at my resulting trembles. "But I think you do like it."

"It's too good," I growled, my chest heavy. "You have no business being such a generous lover." I lifted my head to grin at him, to show I was kidding.

"You had no business being so good to me." He kissed my other thigh, lips making a trail to my hip crease. "To make me crave you, want you like I've never wanted anyone." His head rested on my leg for a brief moment, lips shining in my arousal as he looked up at me. "The least I can do is try to be worth the effort."

"Shadow." I sat up as far as I could, reaching for his face. He kissed my palms and that just amplified the yearning in my chest. "You were always worth the effort. I'm still stunned to be the first person to tell you that."

He hugged an arm around my leg, leaning his head against my knee as he stared at me with such pure adoration.

"Maybe it was supposed to be you," he whispered, lips gliding down toward my pussy again. "I can't imagine anyone else making me feel like you do."

My head dipped back as the warmth of his mouth hovered over my clit, his fingers stroking and pressing inside me again.

"Please…"

Finally, his lips sealed over my clit with a groan, the suction so hard and jolting that I cried out. His tongue slid over the hard spot with delicious pressure, aided by his fingers curling inside me and beckoning my orgasm.

"Yes, yes! Like that, don't stop."

He made wet, sucking sounds crashing his hand into me again and again. The moment my walls contracted around him, his moan against my flesh set me off like a stick of dynamite.

I thrashed and shivered, biting the pillow to keep from alerting the whole house as Shadow's mouth and hand rode out my orgasm. Even as I floated down from my finish, he licked my flesh and placed soft kisses on me before withdrawing his hand.

Looking down at him, his grin even looked a bit smug as he leaned against my thigh again. "Well, how was that?"

"Fucking shut up and come here," I laughed breathlessly, holding my arms out to him.

He only managed a few kisses on his way up my body before I tugged impatiently at his hair, laughing huskily as I drew his mouth up to mine and wrapped my arms around his back.

SHADOW

I wasn't a complete stranger to sex. But I'd never had this before—a woman flushed and panting underneath me. Breathless and smiling *because* of me.

From how she kept pulling me down, Mari seemed to like my weight on top of her. Her legs hugged around my waist, arms banded around my back, clinging to me with every kiss. As much as I was dying to sink into her, I was still worried about crushing her, with how fragile she felt underneath me.

"Again?" I mumbled through a kiss on her shoulder, my hand drifting down her body.

"No!" she laughed, nipping the side of my neck with that pain and pleasure mix that made my cock jolt. "You'll spoil me and make me selfish."

"I'm not sure that's possible." I rolled her breast in my hand, watching to see if she'd relent and let me make her come again.

And again.

And again, just for good measure.

Instead she glared at me playfully, tapping my arm. "Roll us over. I want to be on top."

I scooped my hands under her back, taking her with me as I rolled to my side and then my back. She straddled my legs, running her hands over me while sitting straight up. That touch and the view of her gave me a jarring sense of *deja vu*.

"What are you thinking?" Mari seemed to notice right away, fingers stroking over my abdomen before gliding back up to my chest.

"That we've been here before," I admitted.

"We have," she agreed. "Under very different circumstances."

I skimmed my hands up her thighs, taking my grip across her hips and behind to feel the curves of her ass before continuing on to her waist.

"I wanted to touch you like this so badly back then." Her small ribcage felt so fragile, like a bird's, against my palms. My touch reached her breasts, her nipples already tightening from the contact. "I was terrified of scaring you. I already felt guilty enough for—"

"I would've let you." She drew one of my hands up her chest, to her neck and face, turning to kiss my palm. "I thought about kissing you, wondered how you'd react to it."

"Probably not well. Just because I never let anyone get close to my face." I watched her bring my thumb to her lips, biting lightly over the tip. The pressure and light tinge of pain from her teeth made me swell underneath her.

"I like your face, Shadow. I have since I first saw it."

She released my thumb, leaning over me with her hands braced on my chest. Her hair tickled my skin before her lips made contact on my sternum. "I like all of you, what's inside and outside." She sucked at the edge of my ribcage, no doubt leaving another dark hickey on me as the sweet tingles of pain expanded from the spot. "You're mine, and I'm happy to keep reminding you of the fact."

"Yours," I groaned, my breaths coming shorter as her kisses moved downward.

My cock was positively aching since she'd first planted herself in my lap, but I expected nothing from tonight except to learn from her. I was painfully aware of being behind the curve when it came to a woman's body, and would've been content to spend the night studying every square inch of Mari. But after only making her come twice, and now that her lips were trailing below my navel, it seemed she had other plans.

"What are you—mm!"

She rubbed the front of my jeans, my length jumping at the pressure of her touch, as if seeking her out.

"Making tonight a little less one-sided." I heard the smile in her voice as she pulled my zipper down.

"It's not one-si—mm, fuck. Mari, you don't have to."

"I know." Her finger dipped into the waistband of my boxer briefs, planting a kiss low on my hip. "But I'd like to, if you'd enjoy it."

My fists curled around the sheets as I sat up to get a better view. Her cheeks were still flushed, her long back stretched out between my legs and her cute ass in the air. She returned my gaze, smiling wider as I slid a pillow behind my back to stay propped up.

"I'll take that as a yes." She began shimmying my pants down, still watching me for a response.

"Oh. Yes, yes." I raised my hips to assist her. "I'd enjoy anything from you."

Her eyes fell to my length as she revealed me, those swollen, well-kissed lips pulling between her teeth. My apprehension returned while she finished stripping me bare. The size of my cock was just another reason on the long list of why women looked at me in fear.

But she stroked me from base to tip, the soft pressure from her palm so sweet I clutched the sheets with a groan.

"Has anyone ever touched you here?" Her fingers glided up and down my shaft, tongue wetting her lips as she stared at it.

"Once or twice," I admitted, my breath tight in my chest. It was only ever to get me hard, or to guide me inside.

For the first time in my life, I was at a woman's mercy and completely unafraid. I was eager for her touch, fighting the urge to jerk my hips through the grip of her hand.

"With their mouth?" she asked, bringing her smile closer to me.

"Uh, n-no," I stammered. "Never that."

Mari's eyes stayed locked on mine as her lips parted, tongue peeking out. Time seemed to move impossibly slow as she neared and I was certain I didn't breathe.

Not until her tongue actually met the underside of my head, lips sliding over my crown.

"Ohh, Mar—fuck!"

The softest heat enveloped me, light suction pulling at my head and making me forget how to talk. Mari's tongue circled, licking the tip of me like an ice cream cone while my fists curled and twisted in the sheets.

"This good?" She asked the question tentatively, but her face was anything but. She liked watching me, I realized. She enjoyed putting her mouth on me just to see my reaction.

She *wanted* to please me too.

"So good," I said in a choked whisper, mesmerized at the sight of her. "Please don't stop."

That pink tongue traveled down my stiff length, swirling and licking with the heat of her mouth. She took her time, gliding those soft lips all over my cock like there was nothing else she'd rather do. Mari tasted me indulgently, like I was something *meant* to be enjoyed. She used both hands to stroke me, spreading the wetness from her mouth from base to tip.

I could only groan and curse under my breath, sometimes tipping my head back for a few seconds before I was desperate to watch her again. I had no instructions for her, none. While she so patiently led me through pleasing her, my words disappeared the moment she touched me. There were simply no words that existed for how this woman made me feel.

Mari's palms started twisting in opposite directions, working my length as her sweet mouth returned to my head. She hummed over me, sucking me in like a deep kiss, the vibration of her voice shivering up my back and down to my toes.

So, so good. Holy fuck, I didn't know it could be this good.

I ached to touch her, still a bit stunned that I could do so now without a stab of anxiety in my chest. Her hair spilled like a dark waterfall over my stomach and thigh, and I gathered up the silky strands to hold them out of her face.

Mari released me with a pop of her mouth, flushed and grinning with my dick resting on her lips as she panted for breath.

"Fuck, you're beautiful," I blurted out, my only coherent thought over the last five minutes.

She actually looked shy for a moment, eyes cast down while taking more sensual licks of me, hands still gliding up and down my shaft with sweet pressure.

"You're, um," her teeth came down over her lip, "a bit bigger than I'm used to."

"I'm sorry."

She laughed, leaning her head against my thigh. "Men everywhere would be jealous of you if they knew you had *this*."

"I don't care. I just don't want to hurt you."

"You won't, Shadow." Her mouth returned to me, hands resting on my thighs as she licked every stiff inch of me. "I know you won't. Because I know *you*."

Those lips sealed over my head again and I was fucking done for. She gripped my base, jerking upward as her mouth moved down, that tongue feeling like fucking heaven pressing on the underside.

"Oh fuck, Mari...fuck, yes..." Every word came out strangled, ripping out from my chest with a tight breath.

My hands sought out her shoulders, her back, her face, just desperate to feel more of her. I wanted her touch like a brand on me, as if it could erase my decades of scars. My greedy, frenzied touch found a breast and rolled her nipple between my fingers, palm kneading her soft flesh.

She moaned over me, taking me deeper in her mouth. I tapped the back of her throat and a growl dragged out of me. That couldn't have felt good for her, but her throat squeezed around my dick like—

"Oh God, Mari! Fuckkk..."

She sucked me down again, and—oh fuck—again. Her whole mouth slid over me, taking greedy gulps as she reached further down my shaft. My hips started bucking towards her face before I was aware of doing it, tapping the back of her throat eagerly for that tight feeling that made me see stars.

Stop, don't hurt her. Don't you dare fucking hurt her.

But every time I pulled back, she descended on me for more. Lips and hands now met each other on my shaft, her mouth so hot and wet and soft. Her cheeks hollowed out, sexy moans and whimpers floating up as she sucked me greedily.

"Mari, I'm so fucking close," I rasped. "Where do you want me to—ungh, God..."

She just stroked me faster, brows pinching with effort as she took me deeper, harder down her throat. Her breaths quickened too and she moaned even louder. No, she wouldn't really want me to finish in her mouth...would she?

"Mari," I tried again, keeping my grip on her shoulder as light as I could muster. "I'm about to come."

"Mm-hm," was the only reply I got before the sweet ache became overwhelming.

Sensation left my fingers and toes, the digits numb as pleasure concentrated in the base of my spine, licking out like flames of heat as Mari drew it out of me with her hands and mouth.

And then, sweet explosive release.

I was at her mercy, boneless as the sensitivity crashed over me, so intense it was almost painful. Her mouth never left me until I was utterly drained. Even as I began to soften, she licked me through the shivers and aftershocks.

My heart pounded like a drum, my whole body spent and rubbery like I'd just completed a workout. Mari crawled up the mattress, licking her lips and grinning as she slid down to nestle into my side, her cheek over my drumming heart.

"Again?" she joked, fingertips trailing over my chest.

I huffed out a breathless laugh, placing a kiss in her sweet-smelling hair. "I don't recover anywhere near as quickly as you do."

"In the morning, then." She lifted her head, brushing kisses over the scars that touched the edges of my tattoo.

"Not if I get you off first." My arm slid along her back, cupping her hip before I realized what she said. "Wait, morning?"

"Or in the middle of the night. Whenever someone wakes up first." She slid down a few inches, placing a kiss on one of my ribs before looking up, eyes brightening. "If you want to turn this into a race, it's on, Shadow."

"So, you're..." I hoped to every god listening that I wasn't misinterpreting this. "...spending the night with me?"

She looked bewildered before bringing a playful bite down on my nipple.

"Ow."

"Of course I am! You're not a booty call." Her hand slid across my abdomen, hugging around my waist. "That is, if you want me here."

"I do, yes." I wrapped both arms around her, drawing her mouth up toward mine with a hand under her jaw. "Stay with me."

"Happily," she murmured, fingertips grazing the scar on my cheek as our mouths connected.

Her kisses tasted softer now, if that was even possible. Our lips and tongues collided with a lazy satisfaction that I just wanted to sink into, to drown in. She sighed and hummed content little noises that I couldn't get enough of, hands stroking over me so gently. We kissed until the need for air forced us to separate, and even then I never wanted to stop tasting her skin.

"Mari?" I whispered against her forehead.

"Hm?"

"What's a booty call?"

She laughed into my neck, shoulders shaking before peppering more kisses on me.

"It's if I were to come see you to get laid and nothing else." Her fingertips danced over my chest. "I'd get what I want and then leave."

"Oh." I ran my fingers down her spine, feeling each of the bumps on her back. "You don't do that to anyone."

"No." She grinned up at me and tapped a finger to my nose. "You're stuck with me."

I pulled her closer until she was flush to me with a leg over mine. "I can think of far worse places to be stuck." *I was in one for over twenty years.*

No, I wouldn't let my mind go there tonight. At some point I would tell her, but not now. That long, miserable part of my life almost didn't seem real compared to this. In a single lifetime I'd somehow felt the deepest despair, and also the greatest joy I'd ever known—which was right now, and every moment with her.

It felt impossible for this woman, nestled in my arms and kissing me, to exist in the same universe as the ones who had carved into me like an animal. My brain still had to process that lips and hands were running tenderly over the same places I had bled for simply being born male. Mari was kissing my shoulder now, lips tracing years-old scars with the occasional soft lick from her tongue.

"I'm going to kiss all of these." Her smile was warm on my skin. "Just so you're aware."

"Huh," I mused. "You'll be here a long time."

She settled against my side, cheek resting over my heart. "That's the plan, Shadow."

I caressed a hand over her cheek, just taking in the face of this beautiful woman who saw something in me that she was determined to care for. "You really want me to be yours?"

"You *are* mine," she corrected. "If I have to suck your dick again to prove it, so be it."

"I thought you were going to do that anyway."

"I'll leave a hickey on your dick. There, double proving it."

I laughed, nudging my nose against hers. "I do like it when you mark me up with hickeys. It feels like you're claiming me."

"Then I'll keep doing it." Her eyelids blinked slowly, heavy with sleepiness as her palm settled over my chest. "I like seeing you happy, Shadow."

Stretching one arm over to the nightstand, I turned off the bedside lamp before returning my arm to wrap around her protectively.

"I'm happy because of you," I whispered, now that we were bathed in darkness. "I never thought it was possible but it feels like…you're healing me."

Mari curled into me, releasing a sigh as she settled against my body for sleep. "You deserve it."

As her breathing deepened and my own eyelids fell shut with fatigue, I wanted so badly to believe her.

TRIGGER WARNING

Triggering content begins here. Skip to Chapter 25 if you are sensitive to incidents of assault and injury.

TWENTY-THREE

MARIPOSA

A loud noise jolted me awake.

I had been so deeply asleep, I was only vaguely aware of the noises in the room until the bed lifted and I was suddenly rolling toward the opposite side. The whole world spun like I was in a hamster wheel until coming to a sudden, hard stop.

"What the—fuck, ow!"

Well, *now* I was awake. And, once I got my bearings, realized I was on the floor between the wall and the upturned bed.

Huh?

I knew *where* I was, but still couldn't make sense of anything. The room was completely dark. It had to be the middle of the night or very early morning. Was it an earthquake?

It wasn't until I heard the heavy footsteps pacing around the room, the pained groans, and the fists thumping at walls and whatever furniture was in the way, that started to clue me in.

Oh no.

"Shadow?" I called, my voice weak and timid.

No answer came except for more pacing, more thumps and bangs with the occasional whimper mixed in. I scooted along the floor, daring to peek around the upturned bedframe and mattress to look. What I saw broke my heart.

Shadow paced back and forth in the center of the room, no bigger than a six-by-six foot square, scratching at his arms as he whimpered and muttered to himself. He stopped abruptly to clutch at his head and release a pained cry into his hands. Then he swung his arms, catching the nearby chair and flinging it at the wall with a moan of pain I felt split my heart wide open.

My panicked gaze swept across the floor littered with his things. It was so dark, I could only make out rough shapes, but one bright object gave me all the answers—the bottle of his sleeping pills.

Oh no. Oh, Shadow!

The orange container had fallen off of the night-stand—which now lay in pieces on the other side of the room. His pills scattered along the floor, the bottle on its side against the baseboard. He must have forgotten to take one last night. It was the only explanation for this.

My sweet, brave man was in the grips of a nightmare.

"Fucking *stop*!" he bellowed, falling to his knees with his hands over his face. "I didn't *do* anything!" His chest wracked with a sob, a sound that made my heart shatter and want to run over and hold him, to love and soothe him. I went so far as to take three steps, my hand outstretched, before stopping myself and shrinking back against the wall.

Fifteen minutes. I remembered what Jandro told me when I first heard Shadow having a nightmare. These episodes only lasted for about fifteen minutes. Getting close to him during that time was dangerous, as Jandro had learned. I had to stay quiet and let the night terrors run their course. Then I'd have *my* Shadow back.

But it killed me to do nothing, to just watch him suffer instead of shaking him into awakeness. Every part of me yearned to touch him, to remind him that I was here and that he was safe. It went against every one of my instincts to do nothing, even if the suffering he endured was in his mind and no longer his body.

Shadow stayed on his knees, hands covering his face for a few long minutes before I started scooting out from my hiding place. He seemed calmer now that a bit of time passed since his last outburst. Maybe it was over.

My eyes drifted to his cut, now discarded on the floor. I reached for the soft leather, feeling around until I found one of the daggers he always kept hidden, just to protect myself if necessary. I hated that it was the same type of weapon that triggered him, but it was all I had.

I approached him slowly, the weapon low and slightly behind me so as not to alarm him with the sight of it.

"Shadow?" I called tentatively from several feet away.

His gaze snapped up to me, but there was no recognition in his eyes. He scowled cruelly, an expression I'd never once seen him wear. On his face, the same one I couldn't get enough of kissing, such a scowl looked downright terrifying.

"What do you want from me, bitch?" he ground out, the bitterness in his voice making him sound like a completely different person. "Haven't you taken enough already?"

"Shadow," I gasped, my heart now withering at how harshly he spoke to me. "It's me, Mari. I don't want to hurt you."

"I'm not falling for that again. Just leave me alone." He curled up into himself, arms wrapping around his knees like a child would.

I have to get out of this room, I realized.

He hadn't lashed out physically yet, but now I understood why Jandro locked him in his room back in Sheol. Shadow was wildly unpredictable in this state, his body curled up and muscles coiled so tight, like the smallest thing could set him off.

I pressed myself against the wall, following its path as I took slow steps heading for the door. He looked so sad but I couldn't help him, not while he was like this. When I reached the far corner of the room where my clothes had been discarded the night before, I hurriedly stepped into my underwear and jeans, keeping my eyes locked on him until I reached for my shirt. I had to set the blade down and did so without a sound, but the reflection of silver metal must have caught his eye.

Shadow's head snapped over to me, and he moved before I could blink. My mind could barely register his hand around my throat, the force with which he swung his arm and took me with him. The pain, the squeezing.

The sudden lack of air making my lungs cry out. None of it could be real, not from him.

Shadow would never hurt me. The thought screamed in my head as I crashed to the floor, my forehead pounding as I tried to orient myself, tried to get away. *This isn't him.* Cruel fingers closed in my hair and yanked my head up as I screamed.

"Shadow, stop!" I cried, clawing desperately at his arm and fist. "Wake up!"

He pulled my head back by my hair, his grip callous and the angle of my neck so painful I thought it might break. Then he shoved me down as he released me, my forehead and nose slamming on the floor with pain that rattled my skull. Wetness coated my face, getting into my mouth and clogging my sinuses as I coughed and struggled to breath.

The weight of his grip came down on my head again and I fought desperately to scramble away across the floor, but he pulled me back, hair yanking painfully from my scalp.

"No, no, please! Help!"

Shadow pulled my head to the side, forcefully turning my whole body over onto my back. I let out a choked cry at the sight of him above me, pain stabbing through my head and whole body from his abuse. My heart felt just as abused, tearing, pulling, and screaming over this heartless man I didn't recognize.

The same eyes that watched me so carefully for any discomfort now radiated pure hatred. The same hands that pleased me so thoroughly were now instruments in hurting me as much as possible. Nothing hurt as much knowing the same person was capable of two such extremes.

"How does it feel?" he asked cruelly, lifting my head once again to let it thump back on the floor. "To be trapped and bleeding? To feel small and helpless?"

"Shadow, please…" I wheezed, coughing on the blood that trickled into my mouth from my nose, only to feel his other hand clasp around my throat.

"I've always wanted to do this," he continued, fingers pressing into my flesh. "To make you suffer as I have."

"HELLLP!" I screeched at the top of my lungs, knowing I wouldn't have a voice for much longer. "Somebody help me!"

"Mari!"

I heard thumping at the door, and saw the wood buckle as its hinges groaned to keep it in place.

"Reaper!" I called. "Help me! Hel—"

My cry choked off as Shadow's hand tightened, black dots swarming my vision as I struggled to breathe. Trapped in his nightmare, he didn't pay any attention to the door or how I pleaded and fought for my life. I kicked my legs out and clawed at his hand, but my strength was nothing compared to his.

Still I lashed out at him, fighting with everything I had left, even as my limbs grew heavier, his cruel scowl above me fading to blackness. Sensation started to leave my body, leaving me to sink into the worst heartbreak I'd ever felt. This loving, gentle man was literally killing me because of the abuse *he* had endured.

I'm so sorry, Shadow…

I knew the sleeping pills were only a band-aid solution to the nightmares. He pushed back when I broached the idea of getting more help, but I should have insisted. Maybe then we would have a normal night together, waking each other up with soft words, more kisses and exploring touches.

As the darkness began to swallow me up, I only wished that I hadn't been too late to save him.

REAPER

"Wake up."

"Huh?"

I blinked slowly to see Daren standing at the foot of the bed.

"Wake up, Rory. She needs you."

"Why, what's—"

Something cracked over the side of my face like a hand slapping me, and then I really did wake up.

"What the fuck?" I grumbled, rubbing my eyes.

Hades growled at my bedside, teeth glinting white in the dark room.

"What's gotten into you?" I peered at him.

A thumping sound came from somewhere in the house, making me pause and listen. It was only our third night in the new house, and Vance's builders insulated it like a fortress. I still couldn't tell exactly where noises were coming from.

I heard another thump, and then a scream. A woman's scream.

"Fuck, Mari!"

I shot out of bed, Hades already running down the hallway. Wearing nothing but my boxers, I somehow found the coordination in my panicked state to race down the stairs to Shadow's room. I jiggled the knob. Locked, of course. I jammed my shoulder hard into the door and it didn't budge. Fucking Vance just had to make every door in the house from solid oak.

"Shadow!" I yelled through the wood, slamming my fist against it. "Open the door!"

"No, no, please! Help!"

Mari's fear-stricken cry from inside spurred me into desperate, frantic action. My mind was blank except for the burning *need* to get her out. I tried my shoulder again, then a kick to the door, to no avail.

Fuck, fuck, fuck I had no time! What could I do?

"Helllp! Somebody help me!"

"Mari!" I slammed and clawed at the wood like I could tear through it. "Shadow, let her go! I'll fucking kill you if you don't!"

Her screams cut off with strangled coughs and wheezes. Crazed, desperate fear consumed me as I unleashed every ounce of my strength into that door. No, I could *not* lose her, but she was going to die if I didn't get in that room.

You'll have to break down the door, Reaper. She'll die if you don't.

I stopped assaulting the door and looked around behind me, eyes landing on the bronze sculpture next to the stairs just as Jandro, Gunner, and Hades came flying down from the second level.

"What's going on?" Jandro demanded.

"Bring that over," I said, pointing. "Fucking now!"

It took both of them to carry the heavy thing to me. Once in front of the door, the three of us held it like a battering ram, flat base toward the door, and started swinging.

"On three," I instructed, my chest already collapsing like a black hole at the silence in the room. "One, two, *three!*"

We used momentum and all of our strength to drive the bronze into the door. The wood splintered and buckled at the first hit, but didn't open. On the second try, it caved in and with a kick from Jandro, the damn door finally crashed open.

None of us stopped to assess, we just acted. We saw Shadow kneeling on the floor with his hand around Mari's throat, her face covered in blood and her body too fucking still. All three of us went straight for Shadow, but Jandro and Gunner were faster. While they pulled him off of her, tackling him to the ground, I feared the worst as I went to check on my wife.

"M-Mari..." I shook so fucking hard, my teeth chattered as I leaned over her to listen for breathing. But Jandro and Gunner were whaling on Shadow and I couldn't hear shit over the pounds of fists on flesh.

My trembling fingers felt along the side of her neck, and I wanted to scream at the feel of tacky blood on her skin. How the fuck could this have happened? How could we *let* this happen?

Her pulse was weak but steady under my fingers,

and a shaky sigh of relief escaped me, my head dropping heavily.

"She's alive…she's alive." Coherency was flowing back to my brain now that I knew we still had her, at least for now. "We have to get her to the hospital."

"What do we do with him?" Gunner shook out his fist, his face full of disdain for Shadow, now lying passed out between him and Gunner. Jandro on the other hand, appeared torn, his face a grimace of pain as he looked between Mari and the friend we'd all wrongly trusted with her.

I didn't give a shit how he felt.

Once we got Mari stable, Shadow's life was mine to take.

"Throw him in the governor's jail at City Hall," I ordered, scooping Mari up carefully. "I'll deal with him later."

DAWN WAS PEEKING over the sky once Dr. Brooks came to update me, his sneakers squeaking over the tiled hospital floor. I rose up from the waiting room chair, Hades and I walking up to meet him.

"How is she?" I demanded before he could get a word out.

The doctor gave me an odd look, his brows knitting over the frames of his glasses, almost as if he was suspicious of me.

"She's doing okay, resting now. Some ligaments in her neck have torn, so she'll need to be in a neck brace for a few weeks and will be sore for a while. But she'll make a full recovery."

I will kill him. Then I'll bring him back to life so I can kill him again. He'll wish for the filthy cage he was born in when I'm done with him.

"Thank fuck." My head tipped backward, eyes closed in relief despite the rage roaring in my ears. "Can I see her?"

"Not tonight." The doctor was tight-lipped and firm. "She is sedated and the most important thing she needs right now is rest. And," he lifted his chin at me, "before you speak with her, we'll need to hear from her what happened."

I blinked at him. "I told you what happened."

"Yes, but," he sucked in a breath, "should your wife tell us a different version of events, we'll need to take her account into consideration. Everyone at this hospital has gotten to know Mariposa and cares deeply about her. We'll keep her safe."

The implication of his words sent my blood boiling. My fingers itched at my sides to swing into his judg-mental face, but I knew that wouldn't help me.

"She is *my wife.*" My teeth felt like boulders grinding against each other.

"Yes, well, she wouldn't be the first woman on earth abused by a spouse."

"How dare you fucking—" I forced myself to stop, spinning away from the doctor before I crashed a fist through his jaw.

My breaths sawed in and out of my chest as I fought to keep myself from losing my shit. I had barely saved her in time, and now this overeducated prick was talking to me like I'd done this to her myself.

I fucking might as well have, I realized with despair. How could I not have seen this happening? Jandro had gotten dozens of black eyes and split lips from trying to subdue Shadow during his nightmares. We all should have known Mari wouldn't have been able to tame him completely. He was too much of a loose cannon, but Mari seemed to be doing so well with him that we got careless.

Now he hurt what was most precious to me. And I fucking let it happen.

"You're right about one thing, Dr. Brooks," I said, turning back to face him. He was still there, arms crossed and eyebrows raised at my concession. "I didn't lay a hand on her, but I also didn't protect her from the man that did this. And for that, I'm a shitty husband."

Dr. Brooks dipped his chin in a small nod of acknowledgment, the wrinkles smoothing out in his forehead.

"But I can promise you one thing, doctor." My hand drifted down to skim my fingertips along Hades' back. "I'm never allowing this to happen again."

MARIPOSA

Ow.

Oh fucking *ow*. Everything hurt. And I was so thirsty.

My eyelids weighed down like bricks as I tried to force them open. The first peek of light hurt too, sending a stabbing pain that ricocheted through my whole skull.

"Ah, Sleeping Beauty's waking up." Rhonda's voice was like a hug to my ears. "Take it easy, sweetheart. I know it hurts, I'm giving you a little something."

"Uh, wha…" I could barely get a whisper out, my throat was so dry.

"I got it for you, hon. Give me a sec."

I tried to look down at my hand, but the movement was stopped by something hard underneath my chin. Attempting to look to either side was also stopped. My sore fingertips flew up to my neck, touching the stiff piece of plastic holding me still. A dull ache ran from my fingertips down my arm, and I raised my hands to find bruised fingers and broken, jagged nails. A jolting reminder of what happened.

"How…" My whispery voice shook, as did my hands. "How did I…?"

"Survive? By a miracle. Drink up, sweetheart. I know you're parched."

Rhonda held the glass out in front of me, which thankfully had a straw. The sweet ache of cool water running down my throat awoke new pains, memories of being unable to breathe and feeling certain I would die.

Rhonda watched me shrewdly as I drank, her eyes like a hawk's. "I know you're in shock and in pain, but is there anything I need to know, Mariposa?"

"I..I…" *can't believe Shadow wouldn't recognize me, that he wouldn't stop.*

His face hovered with startling clarity in my mind, the mismatched eyes so full of hatred they were unrecognizable. Fresh pain sliced through my chest at the memories from earlier in the evening, when he made me feel so good, contrasted with when he hurt me so badly.

"Here's an easier question." Rhonda gripped the foot of my bed. "Do your injuries have anything to do with the biker president that won't leave the waiting room?"

Reaper! Reaper was here, which meant he had managed to get me out.

"No." I tried to clear my throat, wincing at how much it hurt to talk. "No, h-he didn't do this."

Rhonda nodded, accepting that answer. "He's been wanting to see you. Are you up for visitors?"

I tried to pull my head down in a nod, before

remembering the neck brace holding me immobile. "Y-yes. You can let him in."

"Ten minutes, max," she told me sternly as she turned to leave. "You need to rest."

The moment I saw Reaper, all my frozen shock melted away. Fat tears rolled down my cheeks as he entered my room. By the time he reached my bedside and put his arms around me, I was full-on sobbing.

"Mari," he choked, his breaths ragged and green eyes filled with unspilled tears. "Fuck, baby, I—"

"You saved me," I rasped, cupping his face. "Thank all the gods you were there."

"I almost wasn't." He pressed his hand over mine, blinking and making a single tear track down his cheek. "If I had been even a minute late, he could've—"

"It's okay." I wiped his tear away and pulled him forward to kiss his forehead. "I'm okay, and I love you."

"You shouldn't be the one comforting me," he huffed, holding my hands and squeezing them like he'd never let go. "It's never happening again, sugar. I promise you. I never should have let it happen in the first place, but I'll spend every last breath I have protecting you. I swear."

His eyes hardened as he spoke, the ruthless scowl growing deeper on his face. I knew he was trying to make me feel safe, but the knot in my gut just twisted and contorted even tighter.

"What are you saying?" I asked.

Reaper's hands lowered to my lap. "Shadow is going to answer for what he did to you, of course."

"But he..." My brain spun, trying to reconcile all

the conflicting feelings in my body, my heart, and my gut. Terror still gripped me, my brain flashing images of my last moments of consciousness in an attempt to process the trauma. My heart raced, the panic still running high. And right alongside those images and sensations, I saw the Shadow I knew. The one I loved and trusted just as much as any of my men. I may have felt all kinds of contradictory ways, but I knew one thing for certain—the truth.

"It was an accident, Reaper."

My husband's eyes were venomous as he straightened up, all tears gone in the wake of his hard set jaw. "Don't, Mari. Don't you dare defend him, not on this."

"He forgot to take a pill," I insisted. "I was so scared, more than I've been in my life, but he wasn't in his right mind—"

"Stop. Just stop." Reaper raised a hand, squeezing his eyes shut. "Are you listening to yourself?" he demanded, his pulse throbbing in his neck as he fought to keep his voice at a normal level. "He almost ki—fuck, I can't even say it, Mari."

"But he didn't," I argued. "Because you were there. This was what Daren was telling you about."

Rhonda pushed in before he could argue, which was excellent timing on her part. My husband's shoulders shook with rage and I knew this battle wasn't over.

"Alright, up and at 'em," the nurse held the door open. "Mari needs to rest."

Steeling himself with a deep breath, Reaper leaned in and planted a fast kiss on my lips. "I'll be back tomorrow. I love you."

"Love you…" My voice had already faded away, weariness sinking into my limbs.

———

I FELT like a different person before even opening my eyes the next morning. Everything still hurt, but with more of a dull ache than the stabbing, blinding pain of the night before. Cracking my eyes open was easier, and it didn't even hurt to smile at the black cat lounging on my hospital bed.

"Hey, Freyja." My voice felt stronger too as I held my fingers out to her. She butted my hand with a loud purr, coming closer to rest in my lap. "I was about to thank the gods for strong drugs," I whispered, petting down her back. "But it's you healing me, isn't it? Healing us all."

I didn't get an answer besides an intense stare from those sharp green eyes. In the wake of what happened, I was hoping she'd have more to say. This cat had loved on Shadow since she first appeared to me. My connection to him had been guided by this goddess' presence, and now that connection was wounded, if not severed completely.

"Did you know this would happen?" I asked, stroking lightly over the cat's head. "Did you know he would…" My fingers began to shake, heart speeding up too fast in my chest. Accelerated physical healing apparently did nothing for my emotional state. At least *I* didn't have any nightmares yet. That, I could thank the drugs for.

His mind is still deeply wounded and has not healed. The warm, omniscient voice rolled over me moments later. *Regressions are to be expected with someone as fragile as him.* Freyja looked directly at me. *I would not have taken you, daughter. You still have much to do.*

"So, I wouldn't have died?"

The limits of the human body can be extended by the strength of the spirit, but even that is not infallible. The cat's ears flicked back and forth. *I would have held onto you for as long I could have managed. But there was no need.*

"Because Reaper was there, thanks to Daren." My fingers nervously curled and extended over the sheets. "He's not going to let Shadow get away with this. I'm worried, Freyja."

It felt wrong to feel worried. Shadow *did* attack me. I'd never felt so scared in my life and the roiling, sickening feeling in my gut was as strong as ever. If it were any other man who hurt me after spending the night together, there would be no questions. I'd let my men dole out whatever grueling punishment they saw fit. I'd happily never see the man again.

But this was Shadow. I felt guilty for feeling so afraid of him, and then gut-wrenching confusion about the guilt.

It was a simple mistake. One with terrible, painful consequences, but I'd bet my life he never would have raised a finger to harm me in his right mind. Wrapped up in each other that night, his sleeping pills were the furthest thing from my mind, and most likely his as well.

I turned over every moment of our evening in my mind. His touches had been so hesitant before they were confident, and even then, he made sure to be careful with me. None of that lined up with the cold, aggressive man who assaulted me.

"I still want to help him heal," I said to Freyja. "It'll have to be different, but we *can* make it happen. I know we can."

A soft knock rapped at my room door, and I looked up to see Reaper and Gunner shouldering their way in.

"There she is," Reaper said softly. "Looking a lot better already."

"Brought you these." Gunner produced the bouquet of flowers from behind his back with a lopsided smile. Red and golden sunflowers immediately brightened up the drab hospital room.

"Thank you, Gun." I beamed up at them. "I'll have Rhonda find a vase for them."

"You sound so much stronger too." Reaper leaned over the bed to kiss me, scratching Freyja as he pulled back. "Guess that's thanks to you, huh?"

The cat closed her eyes with a proud purr as Reaper moved aside so Gunner could kiss me.

"How are you, baby girl?" Gunner pulled a chair up next to my bed, blue eyes wide and searching my face, and I knew he didn't mean just physically.

"I'm...okay. Still kind of shaken, I guess."

He nodded, taking one of my hands to kiss. "We're never letting this happen to you again."

I swallowed, not wanting to argue with my men when they were only concerned and eager to take care of me.

"Where's Jandro?"

Gunner let out a disdainful scoff, dropping my hand. "With *him*."

Reaper focused his gaze on me, not missing a single breath or twitch of my face. So much for not arguing. It seemed we'd be continuing our conversation where we left off.

"Where—" I swallowed, clearing my still-sore throat. "Where are you keeping him?"

"Contained," Reaper said flatly.

"And what will you do?"

Gunner took both of my hands, moving to sit next to me on my bed since I still couldn't turn my head to face him. "Mari…you have to understand, there's only one option, right?"

"What, kill him?" My eyes darted between his and Reaper's. I knew in my gut that was their answer to this, but I needed to hear it from them.

"It's not up for discussion." Reaper's voice was flat and emotionless. "I'll take no pleasure in doing it, but it has to be done."

"Reaper, you can't!" I pulled away from Gunner's hands to reach for his. "Love, please listen to me. He needs help."

"I don't give a fuck what *he* needs," he growled between his teeth. "Shadow had his chance to be with you and fucked it up beyond all repair. He already doesn't deserve the privilege of breathing right now."

"It was an *accident*!" I cried.

"Baby girl." Gunner stared at me, his voice low in an attempt to be calming. "It sucks what he's been through, yes. But there has to be consequences for what he did to you."

"Okay, I agree with that, but killing him is *not* the answer!" I grabbed for his arm. "Please listen to me, Gun. You know Shadow wouldn't hurt anyone, you both know that."

"He *did!*" Reaper yelled, so loud that he made the windows rattle in their panes. He turned away for a moment, scrubbing his hands down his face. Then he mumbled, "Gun, can we have a minute?"

Gunner frowned, but then nodded sharply. He bent down to kiss my forehead before turning and swiftly exiting the room. A long, uncomfortable silence stretched between me and Reaper, and I knew his temper was close to snapping. Not even Freyja could soothe the tension in the room.

"Do you still want to be with him?" The question came out of him so quietly, I nearly missed it.

"I'm not sure," I admitted. "I…I don't know about that, but I do want to keep helping him after…we have some time to move on from this."

"*Move on from this?*" Reaper repeated, incredulous.

"Sorry, I'm still tired and shaken up. I might not use the best words to fit the situation, okay?"

"*Situation?*" he went on. "For fuck's sake, Mari. Why do you keep downplaying this?"

"Because he didn't *mean* to do it!" I cried out, exasperated. "Yes, I was scared. Yes, it was awful, and my feelings are all confused but I'm sure of *that*, Reaper. And you know it, too. If he had only taken a pill   "

"Do I have to tell you what I saw?" Reaper's voice

cracked. "Because I'll paint that picture. I broke the door to find him on top of you, his hands around your neck, your face covered in blood—"

"I know. I was there," I cut in, sounding more snippy than I intended. "I felt everything. I couldn't breathe and thought for sure I was going to die. I *know* how bad it was."

My husband's face crumpled with despair. "Then how can you excuse any of it?"

"I'm not," I sighed. "Something does need to happen. I'm not spending the night with him again until—"

"You are *never* seeing him again," Reaper snarled. "He is not worthy to be yours and never will be."

"That's *my* decision, Reaper."

"God damn, fuck everything." He lowered his head into his hands, fingers tearing through his hair. "I was really hoping you'd come to your senses after you got some rest."

"I have," I insisted. "I'm feeling a lot more certain about this now than yesterday."

"Mari, please…"

His voice softened to a whisper, a plea of desperation tugging at my heart. He dragged a chair next to my bed and sat down, tears filling his eyes as he took my hand. "Please try to understand where I'm coming from. I *love* you—"

"I love you too," I said.

"No, listen." He drew in a shaky breath, fingertip rubbing over the stone on my ring. "You are my *wife*. My whole world." One hand stretched out to caress my waist and lower abdomen. "I want to put my babies inside you and watch them grow." He huffed out a humorless laugh. "If I break a hip in forty years, I want it to be because I was chasing your fine ass. If he—" Reaper's breath stuttered as his grip tightened on my hand. "If he had taken all of that away from me...I don't know what I'd do, Mari. I'd have *nothing*. Do you understand?"

I turned toward him, sliding my hands up to his shoulders, caressing his neck and scalp. His arms came around my waist to hold me, his face in my chest.

"I love you so much," I whispered, brushing kisses across his forehead. "You're my husband in body and spirit, the father of my future children." My whole body felt heavy, like a pile of bricks, as I brought my lips to his ear. "But if you kill him—" My breath halted, stuck in my chest for a moment before I pushed through. "I'm sorry my love, but if you do this, I can't ever forgive you."

TWENTY-SIX

SHADOW

y head pounded like the worst fucking hangover. Which was odd, considering I made sure to keep my drinking under control at the party. I rubbed my temples with a groan, confused to find sticky, flaky blood stuck to my skin.

"What..." My eyes fluttered open with the quick realization that I was not in my bedroom. I was in a jail cell, the bars reminiscent of the cage I grew up in. And Mari was nowhere to be found.

"What the fuck?" I demanded of the barren, cold room as I scrambled to my feet. "What happened?"

No one was around to answer me. I inspected my hands and arms, cold dread seeping in at the state of myself. Dried blood and scratches covered my hands and forearms. Bruises and splinters were embedded in my skin. A throbbing in my head. I touched my face gingerly, feeling the swelling around my eye and jaw.

"Mari..."

I fell asleep next to her with no clothes on. Now I

was alone, in a dark, dingy jail cell, dressed haphazardly in a pair of pants. A shirt had been crumpled and tossed onto the cot in my cell.

Panic gripped my chest, the sensation as unwelcome as it was familiar. I hadn't felt like this in weeks and now it was back with a vengeance.

Oh fuck, no. Fuck, what did I do?

I walked up to the iron bars, wrapping my hands around them as I took in my surroundings. The room had other jail cells, but mine was the only one occupied. There were no windows, so I had no idea what time of day it was or how long I'd been out. Nothing good came from me waking up in strange places and feeling like roadkill, I knew that much.

Did I take a sleeping pill?

The thought cut through me, anxiety slashing from my abdomen to my throat as I replayed the details of that night. My bottle of pills had been on the nightstand, like always. Then Mari came to my room with me and...I forgot about everything outside of being with her. She finished pleasing me and we talked, held each other. She started falling asleep and then I...

No...

No.

Oh please fucking God, no.

I slammed my forehead on a cross bar, wishing I could feel the pain rattling through my skull. I deserved it a hundred times over if I really...

Maybe I didn't. I could never, not to her.

But waking up alone in a cage never boded well for me.

Did I… Fuck, what if I…

I couldn't bring myself to complete the thought, a wave of nausea surging through me until bile coated my throat.

I'd never killed anyone by accident. Every life I took had been intentional and with purpose. But Mari… fucking sweet, beautiful Mari…

I was a dead man if I did. And also if I didn't, most likely. I didn't care. If I had a weapon nearby, I'd end my own life so Reaper wouldn't have to burden himself with the task. He could keep Mari safe—if she was still alive—while the vultures picked at me until I was forgotten. That would be better for everyone.

A door at the far end of the room opened, light pouring in from a hallway. I instantly recognized the silhouette of the man walking through and my heart dared to leap with a tiny spark of hope.

"Jandro!"

"Shadow," he greeted gruffly.

There was no humor in his voice—no easygoing, lighthearted demeanor as he came in and leaned against the bars of my neighboring cell to stare at me. His jaw was tense, muscles jumping in his arms like he was dying to take a swing at me.

No, the tension radiating off his body was more intense than that. He looked like he wanted to kill me.

"Jandro," I breathed, fists tightening around my bars. "What did I do?"

"You don't remember?"

"No." I rocked my forehead from side to side against

the bars. "Mari and I…we fell asleep together and… then I woke up here."

He nodded without an ounce of sympathy. "One of your usual episodes then."

"Jandro…" I looked down at my bare feet, unable to meet his eye. "…did I hurt her?"

It felt like an eternity passed before he answered. "She's at the hospital, in stable condition. Reap and Gun are with her."

My stomach felt like it dropped out of my body. I'd never felt anything remotely like that sensation, like I was falling and also collapsing in on myself. Distantly, I was aware that I'd sunk to my knees against the cell bars, but my mind and thought process felt completely *out* of my body.

I hurt her.

Badly enough to put her in the hospital.

It felt like a boot was stomping down on my chest, impairing my breathing, and I wished for the feeling to kill me. To crush my ribcage and magically allow me to feel the pain of every bone breaking. I had hurt the person I cared about most.

"How…how bad is she?" Talking felt impossible but I forced the words out. I had to know.

"She's in a neck brace, pretty banged up. But she'll be okay."

A fucking neck brace. God, what kind of fucking monster am I?

"Fuck, Jandro…" I ground my teeth, banged my forehead on the metal bars, drew ragged anxicty-filled breaths, and none of it was enough. My stupid fucking body couldn't sense the pain I deserved for hurting her, couldn't keep the nightmares away for the one fucking night I forgot to take a pill.

"Reaper wants you executed." Jandro said, ignoring my outburst.

"Good. I'm ready any time."

"Yeah?"

"Yes." I pulled my face away from the bars, nothing but a throbbing sensation in my head. "Fuck, I'll do it myself so Reaper doesn't have to."

"So that's how it's gonna be, huh?" His voice betrayed some emotion for the first time since walking in. "You just gonna give up? Not make a case for yourself?"

"What case is there to make?" I cried. "She's his wife. *Your* wife! You all trusted me with her and I..." I couldn't bring myself to say or even imagine what I'd done to her.

"Did you take your meds?"

"No," I shook my head. "I forgot. I'm so fucking stupid. She'd be fine if I had just remembered to take a fucking pill."

Jandro let out an exhausted sigh, rubbing both hands down his face. "I don't know if it'll make a difference, but Reaper should know that."

"It doesn't make a difference to me," I said. "I don't deserve to walk out of here alive."

"Man, pissed as I am, fucking terrified as I was," Jandro spread his hands "you've whaled on me a number of times before Mari put you on those pills. And with me, it wasn't a big thing. I know you in your right mind wouldn't attack me for no reason." He paused, taking a long look at me. "And I know the real you wouldn't hurt Mari like that."

"But I *did*," I protested. "At least you could defend yourself against me. She's so…fuck, a fucking *neck brace*, Jandro!"

"I know. This whole situation is fucked." He rubbed the back of his neck. "But she is stronger than she looks. She'll be okay."

"Good, I hope so. But she shouldn't be forced to see me every day."

"Yeah, we'll have to do something about that." He leaned his head back against the bars. "And hear what she has to say when she wakes up."

"She can't…" I pressed my throat against a bar, wishing it was a sharp blade so it could decapitate me. "You can't let her have any sympathy toward me."

"Shadow—"

"I mean it, Jandro. If she doesn't want me executed, you can't take that into account."

"Don't you think *her* opinion is what counts most in this situation?"

"It does, but…" My head throbbed, but still with no pain. "I'm afraid she'll want to help me, not punish me. I don't deserve her help." *I don't deserve a single ounce of her kindness.*

"Maybe it doesn't have to be either or." Jandro's boot scuffled against the wall. "We can figure out a punishment that's also a form of rehabilitation."

"Ugh." I hated every minute of this, internally raging at my body for still being alive and drawing air. I needed to just stop existing so Mari could move on and live without fear. "Where's your gun? I just need to be fucking gone already."

"I purposely came unarmed because I know how much of a sneaky fucker you are." Jandro opened the sides of his cut to show me that his holsters were empty. "And there's one thing you're forgetting, my man."

"What?"

He paused to rub his jaw, seemingly struggling to get the words out. "If you do die, how's that gonna affect her?"

I unwrapped my hands from the bars to shrug. "She'll be relieved. She'll never have to see me and be afraid for her life again."

"Nah." My once-friend shook his head. "She would never celebrate your death. And for the record, neither would I."

"You and her," I scoffed. "Both of you. Too fucking good to me, and the ones I treated the worst."

"It's not that simple, man," he sighed. "Everyone fucks up. You know that."

"Right." I turned away, heading for the small cot now that I knew he wouldn't help end my life. "And her biggest fuck-up was me."

REAPER

I sat on the edge of my bed, turning my knife over in my hands. He hated blades. It would be especially cruel to kill him with one.

Did I *want* him to suffer? That was the question that kept turning over in my mind as I looked at my guns, knives, brass knuckles, and various other weapons spread out on the bed.

A quick death by a gunshot seemed almost too merciful after what he did to Mari. Some part of me felt gleeful at the expression he'd wear if I took my time cutting him up—to embroil him in the same horrors that gave him all those scars. I didn't know the full story, but I got the gist. Shadow couldn't feel pain, so using a knife to kill him would be more psychological torture than anything.

Mari deserved justice. She *would* forgive me for what I had to do. She had to. There were plenty of things about MC life she didn't care for, but accepted. She knew Python's death, and the manner in which he died, was necessary.

This one would be too, even if Shadow was nothing like Python.

"Fuck, man." I slid the knife into its sheath and tossed it away, picking up my handgun.

Shadow had been loyal, obedient, and efficient. His artistry created the symbol of the Steel Demons and he inked it onto every one of us. He followed me every-where, and I knew he would continue to do so. He took things so literally, living and breathing by our code, including to never harm another Steel Demon outside of Fight Night, unless it was in self-defense.

Until he took my wife to bed with him and put her in a neck brace.

I'd never wanted to kill anyone so badly, while at the same time wished there was another way.

Mari begged me not to, and fuck me, I *wanted* to give in. I yearned to tell her yes, I would spare him and we'd find another way to handle this. But then I'd see that thing around her neck, the cuts and bruising on her nose and forehead, her fingernails broken and splintered from how she scratched at him, and the white-hot rage would consume me.

Fuck that it was an accident. Fuck him being unmedicated. She nearly lost her life for no fucking reason.

And then there was the club I had to consider. What kind of leader would I be if I let my old lady's attacker get off with no consequence? While proving myself to them was the least of my worries, it still factored into my decision.

I slammed my clip into the gun, holstered my weapon and left the bedroom, Hades following dutifully at my side. He'd been silent since the day Eduardo stabbed me, and I wasn't sure what to make of it. Not that it mattered. I didn't need a god to tell me Shadow's life was mine to take.

Gunner supported me in this. Jandro probably didn't, but he would fall in line. Mari…

Forgive me, beautiful, I thought as I sat on my bike and turned the ignition. *I have to do this. For you.*

The ride to the jail felt both torturously long and far too short, my gun heavy and hot on my hip. Pulling up in front of the low brick building, I still couldn't decide if I wanted to drag this out or get it over with quickly.

Word might have spread at this point, but I wasn't about to make this a public display. I made the decision never to humiliate a man again like I did with Python. This would be taken care of quietly, a president avenging his old lady and handling business.

My boots felt like lead as I walked inside, the click of Hades' nails echoing over the concrete floor. Shadow didn't move at my approach. He sat like a statue on the edge of a cot in the far-right cell, forearms on his thighs and his head hanging low.

I paused in front of his cell door, waiting to see if he'd react to my presence at all. After a long silence, he spoke in a weak whisper, "I can do it myself, if you'd rather not carry that burden, Reaper."

"You'll address me as president," I said. "And it will

be my pleasure to take your life with my own hands." A lie for him just as much as for me.

His head moved in the slightest nod. "Then I will accept your judgment, president."

My hand drifted to my holster, thumb flicking off the safety. "Any last words?"

"Just…I'm sorry." His white eye caught the sliver of light from the single bulb in the room as he looked up. "I wish I'd never hurt her. And…I hope she heals. And spends the rest of her life happy."

Shadow looked more broken down and beaten in that cell than when Jandro first brought him home. Like a caged animal waiting to die. I hesitated, fingers hovering over the pistol. Mari was the probably the best thing to walk into his life, aside from the club. Hell, she was the best thing in all of our lives. But Shadow never had family, friends, or the freedom of being a human until he came to live with us.

He had been dealt a shit hand in life and that was unfortunate. Ending his story here was sad from every angle, but a shitty upbringing didn't excuse him from abusing a defenseless woman. I brought the heartbreaking image of Mari in her hospital bed to mind, drawing on it for strength as my fingers wrapped around the pistol grip.

"I'll tell her you were remorseful," I said, pulling the gun from my holster. "And that you wish her well."

Shadow lowered his head. "Thank you, president." He said nothing else—no begging or pleading for his life. He truly believed this was what he deserved. That made this a little easier.

And yet, so much fucking harder.

I raised the gun, aiming it at his head. This close, one shot would be enough. But I'd take three just to be sure. With a deep breath, I squeezed around the trigger.

You will not reap.

My breath froze in my chest. I looked down at Hades, meeting those dark eyes looking straight through me.

His life is not yours to take. Do not reap.

"How can you tell me that?" I demanded. "How can I *not* take his life?"

He has not yet reached his end. Stay your hand.

I lowered the gun, turning to face the god at my side who was asking the impossible of me.

"You promised to protect her," I said. "And *he* almost took her life! Where were you then, huh?"

She was *protected. Her life was salvaged. The human Shadow's life must continue alongside hers.*

I crouched down, lowering my face to the dog's level. "I don't care. I will *not* obey. His life *is* mine to take." I returned to standing, spinning with my shooting arm outstretched toward Shadow's jail cell, to find a man blocking my shot.

He was a flash before my eyes, barely even an image, more of a hazy outline. I caught no details, just a murky silhouette before my gun was wrenched from my hand and tossed toward the door.

I pulled my hand back to my chest with a shout, the cramping painful and immediate. I was decently strong and always carried a good grip on my gun, but this thing broke my hold like I was a newborn.

This is my command, Hades bellowed, his voice like scraping metal in my head and clanging over every bar in the room. *You will* not *reap. His life. Is Not. Yours. To take.*

"Fuck you!" I yelled in the dog's face. He was completely impassive. Not even his ears went back. "I have fucking obeyed you, let me have this *one!*"

I went for the jail doors, deciding I'd strangle Shadow if I couldn't shoot him. Something hit me from the side with the force of a linebacker, and I went sprawling across the concrete floor.

Your human body will wear out if you continue this, Reaper. But I rule the dead and I am eternal. My word is law. Shadow's life will not be reaped until it is time.

"What about Mari's?" I hissed. "The next time he attacks her, will we get there in time? Huh? Or are you just gonna keep playing fast and loose with our lives?"

As long as Freyja, Horus, and I walk alongside you, those nearest to you will only die when their time comes.

"Swear to me," I said. "Promise me no one I love will have another brush with death. Especially not her. Swear it, fucking god!"

I owe you nothing beyond what I've said, human. You know the protection I offer. And you will *carry out this command, and every one after, until our time together is finished.*

The dog walked up to where I still sat on the floor, his presence almost unbearably heavy. More than a dog, more than a man, but an odd feeling like the whole pressure of the atmosphere sat on my chest.

Swear to me *now, my reaper.* His teeth bared, a low warning growl pulling from his throat. *You* will *obey. Shadow's life is not yours to take.*

"I…I will." The suffocating pressure on my chest eased just a little. "And…I will spare Shadow's life."

Hades backed away, his presence no longer closing in on me. *Return to Mariposa now. She is feeling much better.*

I climbed to my feet, shakily picking up my gun and returning it to my holster. Not bothering to look back at Shadow, I felt dazed as I left the building. Sweaty, feverish, and nauseous. *Did that just fucking happen? A god intervening on me taking a life?*

Hades was all dopey and smiling at my side again. He licked at my hand but I yanked it away, the thought of touching him just too fucking weird in that moment. I mounted my bike slowly, turning it on and guiding it back out to the road when I started to feel more normal.

Once I was a good distance away from the jail, the hospital looming into view, the wheels started turning in my head again.

I couldn't kill Shadow.

Which meant I had to do something else.

TWENTY-EIGHT

SHADOW

Disappointment didn't cover a fraction of what I felt.

Hades wouldn't allow me to die, and if I ventured a guess, that included by my own hand. So I'd be forced to live, and for what?

They could keep me here in this jail cell and that would work for me. Mariposa would never see me, and I'd reacquaint myself with a lifeless existence in a cage. That seemed like a fitting punishment.

I couldn't tell how much time had passed. I was brought six meals by people I didn't recognize, and barely touched the food. I was offered books to read, but refused them all. I passed the time by pacing my cage like I always used to. By staring at the walls—none of which had cracks that lead to glimpses of an outside sky. When I was feeling particularly masochistic, I thought back to all my moments with Mariposa.

I held on to every detail, sometimes wishing I had a

pencil and sketchpad so I could draw my memories into something real. That one sketch I made of her was still in my room, and I yearned to fold and unfold the paper in my hands for one last look at her, stretched out and unafraid of me.

I often had to remind myself that I didn't deserve anything of hers, not even her likeness on a piece of paper. She had almost convinced me otherwise, but that truth would never change.

When the jailhouse door opened and booted foot-steps approached my cell, I didn't react, thinking it was just my food for the day. But the footsteps stopped, my visitor motionless at my cell door, until I looked up.

Reaper stood there with something in his hand. He said nothing for several long moments and I wondered if he was going to make another attempt at killing me. If so, I couldn't blame him for trying.

"Have you decided what to do with me?" I asked after he continued to stand there and do nothing.

"Yes," he said, holding out the first item in his hand. "We have."

It was my cut, complete with my name and patches still affixed to it. So they had been in my room, and had probably searched through my things for all I knew. I just hoped my drawing of Mari hadn't been destroyed.

Reaper opened his hand and dropped the garment on the floor, the worn-out leather making a soft swishing sound as it hit the concrete. His eyes never left mine as he unscrewed the cap on the other item he held—a can of lighter fluid.

He bathed my cut in a generous amount of gasoline, the stench quickly filling the stale air of the jail. I watched as he emptied the can of flammable liquid all over the vest I designed and proudly wore for years. Even now, I'd pick that thing up from the floor and put it on if he asked me to.

Reaper tossed the empty can away, letting it clatter against the wall, before he took out a matchbox from his cut pocket. He removed a match, struck it against the side of the box, and dropped it onto my cut.

The leather caught fire in a deep *whoof* sound, fire consuming the cut in a sudden rush of heat. Flames licked the air almost to chest level between us, illuminating Reaper's face as we stared at each other across the blaze.

For a moment it reminded me of bonfires out on our rides, my brothers' faces lit up, glowing orange as they laughed, drank, and talked shit. But this wasn't any kind of unifying event. This fire was the opposite, a clear severing of me from him. Me from the club, and from everything that made me see how good life could be.

The one part of my life that had been worth living, burned away before my eyes.

Reaper stood there until my cut became nothing but ashes on the ground, the flames dying down slowly until there was nothing left to consume. Then he produced a set of keys from his pocket and proceeded to unlock my cell door.

"You have one hour to gather your belongings from your room," Reaper said. "And then you will ride. You'll ride as far as you can the fuck away from here. If I even hear whispers of you being near the Four Corners territory, I *will* end your life. And this time, no god will be able to stop me."

"Yes, president," I said numbly.

He opened my cage and headed for the door. "Two escorts are waiting for you outside."

———

I WAS every bit as numb on the way to the house—their *house, not yours anymore*—as when I watched my cut burn. My escorts were two soldiers from General Bray's army. Other than us, the place was empty. No one was around, not even for me to say good-bye to.

I stood in the doorway of my bedroom for a while, eyes just flicking around to the few things I owned. Aside from a few changes of clothes, weapons, and my tattooing equipment, I had nothing worth taking.

Where would I even go? What would I do?

The first thing I reached for though, was not any of my essentials. I went for the drawer in my nightstand, pulling it open to reveal the folded piece of paper in the bottom. I stuffed it in my pants pocket without looking at it. With my limited time, I just needed to know it was on me and safe.

My necessities were packed within minutes, all of it stuffed robotically into my saddlebags under the watchful eyes of my escorts. What to do with the rest of my time? I could just take off and not look back, be gone from the Steel Demons without a trace. That didn't feel right, but it wasn't like I could go around saying goodbyes either. Not face-to-face anyway.

A thought hit me as I eyed my guards. They were posted just inside of my door, still and solemn as statues. I couldn't do anything about them hovering over me, as much as I would have preferred privacy. I had limited time and a few things I wanted to say, so I had to make it count.

I pulled out my sketchbook and a pen, ripped out a blank page, sat down at the desk, and proceeded to write.

———

IT WAS dusk as I went out to my motorcycle, everything I owned fitting on the vehicle that carried me, even saved me. My guards relieved themselves of their duty the moment my machine roared to life and I started on the road heading out of town. I switched my headlight on, deliberately turning down a side street in one of the smaller neighborhoods in search of someone, anyone who could do the one final thing I needed.

I almost gave up hope and started weighing the risks of doubling back to the house to leave the letter there. I'd be shot at, for sure. And even with Hades determined to make me live out my life until its natural end, I had my doubts about how far his protection would go.

My headlight caught a flash of reflective paint and my heart jumped. A horned skull grinned at me, shining in my light against the night falling. I accelerated to catch up and see who it was—Slick. Fuck, maybe the gods were looking out for me in some twisted way. I could not have run into anyone better.

"Slick!" I called out, slowing my bike alongside him. "I need a quick favor."

"Look Shadow, man." He shook his head, quickening his pace. "I'm sorry about everything, but I can't be seen talking to you. You're supposed to be gone and Reaper will—"

"I know. I'm on my way out now," I said, keeping pace with his hurried walking. "I just need you to give something to Jandro for me."

"Naw man, I can't—"

"Just this. Here." I pulled the letter out of my pocket and shoved it at him.

"Dude, I really—"

"Please, Slick!" Desperation bled into my voice. "Please just do this one thing for me. Jandro needs to get this and no one else."

The kid sighed heavily, finally stopping and whipping around to face me. "That's it?"

"Yes, I swear. Just give this to Jandro. He'll know what to do with it."

Looking both ways down the street first, Slick snatched the letter from my hand and stuffed it in his cut pocket. He barely looked at it, but I knew he caught the glimpse of Mari's name written on the front.

"I won't read it," he muttered. "Swear."

"I know you won't. You're..." I sighed, revving up my engine. This was the worst fucking time to get sentimental. "You're a good kid, Slick. I've always liked you."

"Thanks, Shadow." His head bobbed up and down

in a nod, still looking from side to side. "Sorry to hear about…everything. Good luck out there."

"You too."

With nothing left to say, I picked my feet up from the ground, drove the bike forward, and never looked back.

MARIPOSA

I couldn't stop rolling my neck around on my shoulders. Having the brace off was both freeing and strange. Rhonda and Dr. Brooks couldn't believe that I requested to have it taken off after just three days, but they relented after much pestering. I had to act just as surprised as them, while my men and the animals stood by trying to hold back their grins.

With my arms wrapped around Reaper's waist, the chilly wind in my hair, and the rumble of the bike underneath us, it was such a relief to be heading home after my hospital stay.

Being laid up in that room, only allowed to go on short walks, gave me too much time to think, to circle back on what happened with Shadow again and again.

Ultimately, I knew I wanted to try things again with him, after some time. But I kept that between myself and Freyja. Reaper and Gunner would blow a gasket if they knew. Although I was pretty certain Jandro wouldn't.

My sweet VP had been the only one to visit Shadow, although he didn't share much about how he was or what the club's plans were. Jandro, usually full of smiles and warmth, was the most sullen and quiet I'd ever seen him. I knew he could see Reaper's point of view, but he was also Shadow's longest and closest friend. He had to feel some of the same conflicting feelings as I did.

Reaper avoided all talk of Shadow since I told him how I felt. He was not a man of inaction, so I hoped he would have some answers by the time I got home.

As far as I was concerned, Shadow was still mine. He'd be among the men at my side once he had time to work through his trauma. I knew in my heart he was remorseful and that was all that mattered to me. I didn't need to hear an apology right away. My chest ached at the thought of how much he surely blamed himself, how guilt-ridden he must have felt. He might never want to touch me again out of fear, and that thought hurt almost as much as the torn ligaments in my neck.

I wasn't ready to see him yet, but maybe soon. And eventually we'd be able to put this behind us.

Reaper pulled slowly up to our house, the lights in the windows warm and inviting. My fingers tightened for a moment around the edge of his cut.

"Is he…?"

"No, sugar." He brought my fingers to his lips and quickly kissed them before dismounting.

"Where is he?" I asked.

He looked at me, lips setting in a hard line before holding his arms out. "Let me help you off. I think Jandro's got dinner ready."

Avoiding the subject again. But I *was* tired and hungry, and let him lift me off the bike. After settling back in at home, I'd press him for information. But not right now.

Reaper led me inside, mumbling some excuse as he took off down the hall to his study.

"Baby girl!" Shirtless and barefoot, Gunner slid off the couch and came to greet me with an embrace and a smile. "Welcome home." He pulled me into his chest and I could have dozed off right then, perfectly content against his warm skin.

"It's good to be home," I sighed, squeezing around his waist.

He brought his hands to my face, tilting it up for kisses. I melted under the soft presses of his lips, always like gentle rain.

"What do you need? Food? A drink? Sleep?" He pecked kisses on my mouth between each question, making a smile pull across my lips.

"Hm, all of the above. In that order, please."

"Coming right up," he murmured, pulling away to holler toward the kitchen. "Jandrooo, make her a plate."

"What d'you think I'm doing, asshole?"

Gunner and I both flinched at the sound of his voice, full of malice and not a hint of Jandro's usual playfulness.

"He's in a shitty fuckin' mood," Gunner whispered.

"Let me go see him." I squeezed his hand before sliding past him into the kitchen. "Hey *guapito*," I said tentatively to the man hunched over the kitchen counter.

"Mariposita," Jandro muttered, rounding the counter toward me.

He wrapped me in a bear hug, pulling me tightly into his chest with his face buried in my neck. The hug was warm, affectionate with missing me, but I picked up on a deep sadness from him too.

"Jandro." I held tightly around his broad shoulders, one hand scratching over his scalp. "What's wrong, *mi amor?*"

He loosened his hold on me, pulling away to search my face intently, then looked to Gunner in the living room. "Did you fuckers *not* tell her?"

Cold dread filled me. "Tell me what? What's happened?"

"Reaper was going to," Gunner answered defensively.

"Fucking *when?*" Jandro roared.

"After she got settled back in and rested." Reaper re-emerged from his study, the harsh scowl he usually reserved for his club on his face.

"Tell me what?" I demanded, pulling away from Jandro. "What have you done?"

"Sugar—"

"Do not fucking *sugar* me. What did you *do*, Reaper?"

My husband's throat worked in a hard swallow but he didn't answer, which was telling enough. He did something that I wouldn't approve of, and my mind immediately jumped to the worst possible scenario.

No...

Oh no, no. How could he? I told him. I told him I wouldn't forgive him. Does he value our love so little?

"Check Shadow's room," Jandro said softly from behind me.

I headed that way immediately, snapping my arm away as Gunner tried to reach out and stop me.

"Mari, please—"

"Stop, Gunner," I growled. "Just fucking don't."

My feet carried me to the threshold of Shadow's room, the door wide open, which was unusual in itself. I felt along the inside wall for the light switch, my pulse accelerating with the realization that this was where everything went wrong.

The light flicked on, and I found myself staring at an empty room.

Completely barren, with none of Shadow's personal touches, as minimal as they were. No tattoo supplies scattered out on the desk. No sketchbook and pen on the nightstand. No black long-sleeved shirts hanging in the closet. Even the bed was stripped of all the sheets, with only a mattress remaining.

"What did you do?" I whispered to the empty room, then turning around slowly to face the two guilty men behind me. "What the *fuck* did you do?"

"I didn't kill him, if that's where your mind's going." Reaper's voice was laced with bitterness.

"Then where is he?" It took all of my resolve not to scream. "I'm getting sick of repeating myself. What did you do, Reaper?"

"I burned his cut," he snapped back. "The act of

which eliminates him permanently from the Steel Demons. And told him to get the fuck out of here."

Blood rushed to my ears, filling my head with a dull, angry pulse. No, this could *not* be happening.

"What? Where?"

"Anywhere. Just told him to get as far away from you and us as possible." Reaper crossed his arms, looking defiant, if even proud. "Not that there's enough space in the world between us and him that would make me satisfied."

Gunner said nothing, but copied Reaper's stance, clearly aligned with his president. Only Jandro was sullen, fists at his sides as he looked blankly into the empty room.

"You…you sent him away?" My voice shook in a disbelieving whisper. "Just…cut him off and sent him out into the world?"

"Yes." Reaper lifted his chin. "I would have preferred something else but that didn't seem favorable to you."

My fear and disbelief shifted to an all-consuming anger. I stared at Reaper, standing there so proudly, wondering in that moment what I ever saw in this bloodthirsty, deceitful man.

"How could you?"

He narrowed his eyes. "Excuse me? I did this *for you.*"

"Right, even though you never told me this was your plan?"

Reaper sighed, scrubbing a hand down his face. "I

knew you wouldn't want this, yes. But I did what you asked, and this was the best solution for everyone."

"The best solution?!" I screeched. "This club was everything to him, and you *burned* his cut?"

"He was no longer a Steel Demon the moment he put hands on you," Reaper growled. "That fact is not up for debate—only worthy men wear the patch. The only reason I didn't burn the tattoo off his body was because he wouldn't have felt it."

Something inside me snapped. Sending Shadow away was one thing, but knowing Reaper would have subjected him to torture, after everything he'd been through, changed everything. I didn't know this man standing in front of me. And I sure as hell did *not* love him.

"You fucking barbarian," I hissed. "I told you it was an accident and he needs help! And now you've cast him out into the world where he has no one and nothing?"

"I don't fucking care about him!" Reaper leaned toward me to yell, far enough that Jandro and Gunner had to pull back on his shoulders. "I care about *you*. You told me not to kill him and I respected that. Beyond that, it's *my* decision what happens to him, and I want him far away from *my* wife, my family."

"I wish he did kill me," I said, enjoying the look of shock on Reaper's face as I wrenched his ring off my finger. "Then I wouldn't have to live with a husband who's a heartless piece of shit!"

The ring clattered noisily to the floor, the sound echoing deafeningly throughout the whole house as my men stared at me in stunned silence. Desperate to get away, I slid past them and up the stairs to the master bedroom. I slammed the door behind me and sank to the floor, too weary to even collapse on the bed.

I sobbed noisily, releasing all my heartbreak through painful wracks of my chest and not caring who heard. Not even Freyja was here to comfort me. Maybe she could sense that I didn't want to be comforted. In that moment, I just wanted to wallow in the hurt.

It happened just like Noelle said—my heart had been broken by two men.

Shadow, at first for hurting me, then the fact that he was gone without a trace. And now Reaper, trying to act like a savior when he just hurt me worse.

Shadow…Oh, poor Shadow.

Where would he go? A fresh sob escaped me at the thought of him alone, trying to navigate a world filled with strangers. It would be lonely and isolating even for the most well-adjusted person. My chest ached so badly, like my very soul was splitting in half.

I cried until I had no strength left to sob with. My head ached and my whole body felt encased in cement. Tired of sitting against the door, I slid down to the floor on my side. If Shadow was out there all alone, with no friends or support, what right did I have to a comfortable bed?

My mind wouldn't shut off to sleep. The exhaustion would take me eventually, but all of their faces played on a reel through my mind, each one another prick of a needle through my heart.

Shadow kissing the scar on my belly, the warmth in his eyes when he asked me to stay. Then in contrast, his face full of hatred, eyes cold and unflinching as I begged for my life. Reaper with tears in his eyes. Reaper with no remorse. Gunner siding with him, which felt like another betrayal to me. And Jandro, my poor Jandro. The only one besides me with enough heart to care.

My head against the floor, I heard footsteps slowly ascend the stairs. A fresh bolt of anger struck through me. If any of them thought they could convince me this was the right thing to do, I wouldn't just discard their jewelry. I'd kick and punch my way out of here until I had some peace. I was sick of these men, even hated them in the moment.

The floorboards creaked under the weight of the footsteps. They approached the bedroom door slowly, as though unsure if they really wanted to see me or not. The footsteps paused just on the other side while I waited, listening while curled up on the ground.

"Mari? It's me."

Jandro.

Something in my chest lurched, and I pressed up from the floor. The sadness in his voice called to mine, and now I was desperate to not be alone.

I opened the door to let him in. He didn't say a word but pulled me into another embrace. And somehow, I found the strength to cry again.

Jandro let me sob on his shoulder, running his hands up and down my back. His body occasionally jerked with a rough breath and I knew he was fighting tears too.

"He's...he's gone..." It seemed to hit me hardest right then, that I would never see Shadow again.

"I know." Jandro's breath rattled shakily out of his chest. "I know. I'm so sorry."

"You couldn't have stopped him." I leaned my forehead into his neck, cradling my arms between his chest and mine. "Reaper would never let anyone get in his way."

Jandro stroked my back without saying any more, his breaths growing deeper and steadier. "He left something for you."

I lifted my head. "Shadow did?"

He nodded, reaching into his cut pocket and producing a folded piece of paper which read *Mariposa* in blocky handwriting. "I didn't read it. Promise."

I took the letter with both hands, unable to do anything but stare at my name on the front. So clearly, I could picture Shadow's hand moving across it as he wrote, the same way his hands moved over me as he tattooed me, pleased me.

"Do you want me to leave?" Jandro asked.

"No." I reached for his hand, walking us both toward the bed. "Stay with me?"

"*Siempre,*" he whispered. *Always.*

We sank down on the mattress together, his touch drifting over my arms and waist. Always near, always supportive, even when I felt almost too afraid to open a letter. I took a few steadying breaths while he just held me, lips resting on the back of my head. Then with shaking hands, I unfolded the letter and began to read.

MARIPOSA,

I will never ask you to forgive me. I don't deserve it.

I'm sorry beyond what words can express for hurting you. You're one of the bravest, strongest people I've ever met, so I know you will recover, especially with the love of your men surrounding you. But I will carry this for the rest of my days. It's the least I can do after what I put you through.

You're always thinking of others before yourself, so please be assured that I will never allow this to happen again to another person. I'm not sure where I'll end up, but I'm making that promise to you now. No one will get hurt because of me.

Thank you for everything you've shown me. I'll always be grateful for your kindness and care, for taking a chance on me when no one else did. I hope what I did doesn't dampen your willingness to help others. There are people who need you, Mariposa. People more worthy of your kindness than me.

If I can make one request—heal from the pain I've caused you. Heal completely, like I was never in your life to begin with. Forget about me. Let me become nothing more than a faded scar from your past. I don't deserve the space in your mind. Live a long, happy life with your men who will always do right by you. I will never forget you, but please forget me.

Don't miss me. Don't be sad for me. It's better this way.

Shadow

MY EYES STARTED BLURRING with tears before I finished reading the first paragraph. By the time I reached the end, I was sobbing again.

Jandro wrapped tightly around me, pressing kisses

into my hair and stroking me as he gently pulled me down on the bed. Finally, the exhaustion overtook me.

————

MY FACE WAS HOT. My head pounded. I'd been crying so hard, my eyes felt practically swollen shut as I started to rouse.

The heat on my face came from the late-morning sun streaming through the window. A bright, sunny day, as if the nightmarish last few days hadn't happened at all.

I stretched my sore, aching body, cracking my swollen eyes open to find toast and eggs on a plate on the nightstand, a mug of tea still steaming. Looking behind me, the sheets were rumpled on the bed but Jandro was missing. I allowed myself a smile, a small touch of warmth to soothe the deep ache in my chest as I scooted over to the food he left.

The eggs and toast were still warm, and I finished off the plate with the realization that I skipped dinner last night.

Fuck, last night.

A wave of regret hit me, clamping around the food in my stomach. I stretched out the fingers of my left hand, looking at the tan line left behind where my ring used to be.

I said awful things to Reaper, the man I promised to love forever. My hand closed into a fist, dropping down onto my thigh. I meant what I said in the moment, although my explosive anger had now given way to exhaustion and a deep, painful ache. He hurt me, so I wanted to hurt him back.

Guilt now consumed the regret, my sore eyes threatening to spill more tears if I wallowed in it. I'd never wanted to hurt someone I loved but he…

No. This is on you.

Reaper thought he was protecting me by sending Shadow away. He knew I'd be upset, but saw it as a fair trade-off for keeping me safe in the long term. I'd always known he was a man of absolution. He took no half-measures. His decisions were final, permanent. This was just another example of that.

I shook my head with a groan and rubbed my temples. He deserved an apology for what I said, for taking the ring off, but I wasn't ready to forgive him. I wasn't sure when or if that day would ever come.

A tapping sound brought my gaze up, and I spotted Horus peering at me through the window. As much as I didn't want to leave bed, I slipped out and went to slide the pane open. Chilly air rushed into the room, and I rubbed my arms against the cold.

Fresh air and sunlight will do you good, daughter.

Like Hades, Horus's voice sounded ancient. Powerful enough to rattle through my sore head, but right then he spoke with a gentleness, like a parent would to soothe a child. And he was right. I could already breathe easier, the cool air feeling like it revitalized my lungs and calmed the puffiness of my face.

"Do you know where he went?" I asked the falcon.

I see him, the bird answered. *I always do.*

"Is he okay?"

No. But he is alive.

I pulled in a deep breath, looking out over the landscape below my window.

"Will he come back?"

Not without a reason.

My gaze returned to the small, fearsome bird perched on my windowsill. He'd never come to me on his own, not without Gunner nearby, and had certainly never spoken to me before. But here he was now, like he'd been waiting for this moment to speak to me.

"I have to go find him." The words flew out of my mouth without a thought. "I have to give him a reason to come back."

Yes, Horus said, as though it were obvious. *But not yet, daughter.*

"When?"

I will tell you when the time is right. The bird fluffed up his feathers before smoothing them down again. *Shadow must learn to fly and he has only just opened his wings.*

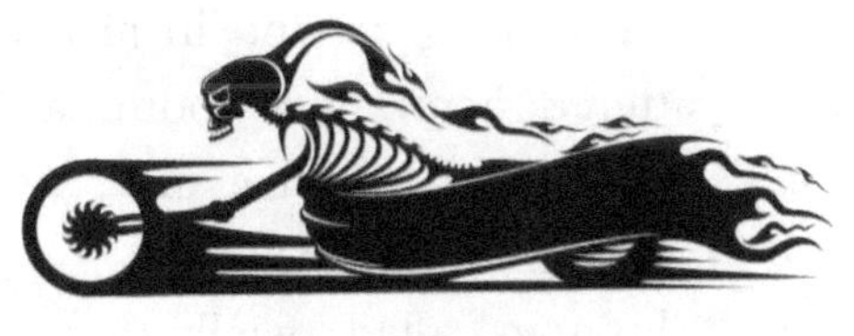

Epilogue

SHADOW

ONE WEEK LATER

I finally hit my breaking point where I needed to stop. Everything ached when I pulled up to the service center, another hotel from before the Collapse that had been converted into something between a hostel and brothel. I'd crashed in a few of them throughout my long, aimless journey, but never for more than a night. This time, I needed to stay in one place for a bit. A week or so to figure out what I would do next.

This particular service center also had a bar, from what the blinking neon lights in the windows claimed. Now that I could no longer be properly medicated, it was back to booze to chase away the nightmares.

Parking out front, I noticed a few motorcycles and muscle cars out in a side yard that had seen better days. They were cobwebbed and filthy, but some had to be in driving condition.

I pulled the front door open to a dark, smoke-filled

bar. A middle-aged man with glasses wiped down the bar, while a much younger woman in ripped stockings, a miniskirt, and a cropped T-shirt stood on a stepladder to put away bottles. Lounging around in arm chairs and low couches scattered across the room, a few other women drank and talked. Service girls, naturally. A couple of whom looked pregnant.

"Welcome," the man called jovially to me. "What're you lookin' for? A drink? A room? A good time? All three?"

"Uh, just a drink and a room," I said, approaching the bar. "For a few nights, if that's available."

The woman next to him jumped down from her stepladder, whirling around to face me. She had dark makeup on and several piercings through her nose, lips, and eyebrows. "How're you payin'?"

"Well, I saw your junkyard out front. I know basic vehicle maintenance if you're looking to sell or get those running again."

The woman elbowed the older man, who shot her an annoyed look.

I cleared my throat. "I'm, uh, also a tattoo artist. I'll be happy to trade ink for room and board if that sounds fair."

"Ooh, tattoos?" The woman's eyebrows shot up, dark lips pulling into a smile. "Can you do any style?"

"Just about. I can show you flash art if you'd like."

"Oh, yes! Doc, let him stay." She put her elbows on the bar, cradling her face as she looked at the man. "You know I've been wanting to get some pretty sleeves."

"Uh huh." The guy pushed his glasses up his nose,

taking another look at me. "You been in some fights, huh?" He gestured at my face.

Fuck. I'd forgotten to cover my scar with my hair. After Mariposa and I got closer, I fell out of the habit. She'd always push my hair aside to kiss me there anyway.

Don't think about that. It's over now. That chapter of your life is closed.

"None that I've started," was how I chose to answer. "I'm not a violent person. I won't bring any trouble to your establishment."

It felt like a lie, considering the reason I was at this center in the first place. But this place looked well-stocked with alcohol, so chances were high I could drink myself into oblivion, where I wasn't a danger to anyone.

The barman nodded at me, peering at me with more curiosity than the average person. "I believe you, son. Thing is, trouble tends to find us."

"Oh, yeah?" The woman had poured a drink and slid it across the bar to me. I raised it to my lips without bothering to ask what it was. "Thank you."

She winked at me. "Sure thing, handsome."

The gesture and affectionate name felt odd. No one talked to me like that except Mari.

"'Bout ten miles from here is one of those girls' camps," the man explained. "Where they train young females, children even, into being obedient and shit. Personally, I like my women with bite." He reached over to slap the barwoman's ass and she snarled, whirling around on him.

"Fuck off, dirty old man."

"Anyway," he continued. "We get a lot of runaways. Some of them stay and work. Most of them move on. And others," he paused with a sigh, "their captors come lookin' for 'em, dragging them back kicking and screaming. It's awful what they do to those girls and if they didn't come in here all guns blazing, I'd tell 'em to fuck off—"

"You're asking me for protection," I ventured.

"Well." He shrugged. "You look like a guy that can handle yourself."

I downed my drink, which turned out to be a cheap whiskey, mulling it over as I swallowed.

"I can handle traffickers trying to take women away," I conceded. "But my stay will be temporary. What I can do is teach some weapons skills, show the women how to defend themselves."

"So you're running from something." The barman's stare was probing, unabashedly trying to figure me out.

No thanks, guy. I almost killed the last person who tried to understand me.

"That's my offer." I chose to ignore his remark. "In exchange for one week's room and board."

"You got yourself a deal." Thankfully he didn't push the psychoanalysis and stuck his hand out. "Name's Bill Harman, but everyone around here calls me Doc."

I accepted his handshake, settling on giving him the name I decided on a couple hundred miles ago.

"Ivan."

"Ivan what?"

"Just Ivan," I repeated. "I'll grab my things and get settled in my room, if that'll be all."

"Ah, sure." Doc seemed a lot more hesitant about making a deal with me now, but he didn't argue. "Jen, get him a key, will ya?"

I turned and left the counter, heading back to my bike. Without my cut, my patches, and now not even my name, I felt like a stranger to myself. Like a new person had possessed my scarred-up husk and was trying to navigate the world without a past, and now with a completely uncertain future.

Because Shadow, the Steel Demons MC assassin, was dead.

TO BE CONTINUED IN SENSELESS - STEEL DEMONS MC BOOK 7

PRE-ORDER SENSELESS HERE

Acknowledgments

Oh man, this book was a tough one to write. So many highs and such deep lows. Thank you, reader, for trusting me so far on this journey. There are more hurdles for the Steel Demons to overcome, but I promise you the ending will be worth it. We've got three more books before the end of the road. I hope you'll hang in there with me!

For regular updates, exclusive teasers, and excerpts, join my reader group, Crystal's Coven. We're a friendly bunch, and I'm always posting in the Coven first before anywhere else online.

I was so nervous about this arc of Mari's relationships with Shadow and Reaper. Thank you to my pack mamis, Kathryn and Aleera, for hearing out my worries and encouraging me to write these characters truthfully, with no sugarcoating.

Telisha, Janet, and Izzy, thank you for being such amazing cheerleaders, friends, and confidants throughout the evolution of this series. You all help me write the best books I possibly can!

See you all in the next book!

-Crystal

Glossary of Spanish terms

Mija/mijita: My daughter, a term of endearment that combines the words *mi* and *hija*

Reposado: A type of tequila that has been aged for two to twelve months

Añejo: A type of tequila which has been aged for a minimum of one year, and tends to be the smoothest for drinking

Viejito: Little old man, meant in an affectionate or teasing way

Esposa/Esposo: Wife/Husband

Guapito: Handsome

Bonita: Pretty

Mariposita: Little butterfly

Siempre: Always (can also mean forever)

Te amo: I love you (romantic intention, said to a partner)

Te quiero: I love you (more general intention which can be said to a partner, friends, blood family members, etc.)

About the Author

Crystal Ash is a USA Today Bestselling Author from California. She loves writing steamy, heart-wrenching romance with tortured heroes, especially if they're in a reverse harem. Crystal's other loves include animals, mythology, and well-crafted alcohol, most of which can also be found in her stories.

When she's not writing, she's probably drinking craft beer with her husband or trying to coax her feral cat into accepting affection.

crystalashbooks.com

facebook.com/Crystal.Ash.Romance

instagram.com/crystalashbooks

amazon.com/author/crystalash

bookbub.com/profile/crystal-ash